A Novel By

Daniel P. Coughlin

A HellBound Books Publishing LLC Book
Houston TX

Daniel P. Coughlin

A HellBound Books LLC
Publication

www.hellboundbookspublishing.com

Printed in the United States of America

Part 1: The Holiday Season

Prologue

1

Trevor Caffey stumbled out of The Quarter. A local Wisconsin University tavern with brick wall that was hidden at the corner of Seventh Street and University Drive in the city of Oshkosh, a town north of Appleton on the way to Green Bay.

Barely lifting his left foot, he tripped on the lip of the sidewalk, slid sideways, and landed on his ass in a pile of accumulated slush.

The bouncer, Ricky Mack, whose massive body was stuffed beneath an aged, black leather coat, grabbed Trevor beneath the arm, yanked him from the ground, and escorted him to the alleyway that separated the bar from the University bookstore. On his way up, Trevor watched Ricky's chest heave as he expelled a frosty breath, which resembled a plume of smoke in the frigid night air.

Planting his feet—to the best of his drunken ability—Trevor turned to face Ricky, but again slipped on the ice. The fall was abrupt. He landed on a jagged clump of ice. A sharp pain shot along his spine and rung behind his ear. He yelped, tilted his head toward Ricky and stated: "Second time is a sobering charm."

"That looked like it hurt. You okay, Trev?" Ricky replied with a cynical grin.

Trevor couldn't differentiate whether Ricky was ribbing him or genuinely concerned. "Give a drunkard a helping hand?" He extended his hand.

Ricky's massive, swollen and callused hand enveloped Trevor's and he lifted him to his feet. "Here to serve."

The muscles and ligaments in Trevor's shoulder strained when Ricky ripped him from the ground. Feet planted on the slick cement, Trevor shook the chalky snow from his jacket. "You got a hell of a grip. You still on the football team?"

"Tore my MCL and ACL least season." Ricky responded. He seemed to lighten up and his cheeks reddened with shame.

"That hit on Mike Addelberg from Whitewater? I remember that. You making a comeback?" Trevor asked, curious. Having been at the game, Trevor recalled Ricky's highlight tackle on a player that was now a third string NFL running back. He also remembered Ricky being carted off the field on a stretcher. Acknowledging Ricky's humiliation, he witnessed hurt generate in Ricky's expression.

"Well, to add insult to injury, I got cut from the team. Asshole coaching staff could have cared less about my health or wellbeing. The school yanked my scholarship and now I'm a bouncer. Saving up some coin until I figure out my next move."

"That's pretty…" Trevor started, but slipped again. This time Ricky grabbed his shirt and steadied him, preventing another fall. "Don't you still get free schooling?"

"Fuck no. These assholes probably think I owe the athletic department for getting hurt. Athletes are just variables to the *cash-equation* that is college football."

"I'll never root for the team again." Trevor felt Ricky's hurt and reacted.

"You gonna be alright?" Ricky seemed genuinely concerned.

"I'd feel better if you let me back in the bar. That brunette with the straight hair, wearing that light blue halter-top… she liked me."

"She absolutely *did not* like you. In fact, you repulsed her. Next time, don't drink so much, and if you like a girl… try talking to her first. Chicks don't like to be grabbed. And when they throw a drink in your face, that means they think you're a dipshit."

Trevor nodded. It all made sense—what the bouncer said. Trevor liked Ricky, even though he was kicking him out of the bar. He could sympathize with the tall, muscle bound giant sporting a military haircut below a round, ruddy face. Just a few years earlier, Trevor had been a high school athlete. He'd been a defensive lineman for Watertown High School—a small Wisconsin town fifty miles south of Oshkosh.

Trevor was still fit. He lifted weights six days a week, ran, and played intermural football in the fall. When he was in middle school he'd earned a black belt in Tai Kwon Do. Since then, he hadn't been active in martial arts except during bar fights. The mental toughness and some of the skillset still remained. *At least he liked to think so.*

Exhaling a deep breath, Trevor held his fist out to Ricky who returned the fist-bump.

Ricky added, "You sure you're good?"

Wobbling foot to foot, Trevor answered, "I'll get home."

"Cover your ears, frostbite'll sneak up on you quick." Ricky turned toward the open door of The Quarter, raised his hand, extended his index finger and shook it. "Later, dude."

Neither Ricky nor Trevor saw the black van with no windows glide over the snow-covered street, turn left, and follow Trevor toward the north end of town.

2

Tingling numbness spread from Trevor's lips to his tongue. The warmth of his jacket dwindled as the bitter wind stalked, snuck into, and penetrated his sleeves and chilled his body temperature to a startling degree. In twenty-five minutes he'd certainly fall prey to hypothermia. His jacket wasn't doing the trick and when his armpits began to freeze, a twinge of panic struck. The wetness of his eyes froze and his vision went hazy. His tears had frozen and draped from his eyelashes. He knew he was in trouble when blinking became a problem. Even the corners of his eyes froze and the stiff flesh chapped badly. Sure, walking too long in the cold had happened before, but the symptoms hadn't been *this* bad. The falling snow dampened and soaked his jeans. The cold had bitten the skin beneath the denim.

When he rounded the corner of Main Street and shuffled onto Ninth Street he tilted his shaky head upward and saw the decrepit, three story house that he and four other boys were renting, which inspired hope.

The snowfall had thickened. Flurries had become a substance, heavy, with low visibility. The darkness didn't help and the streetlights were caked and barely shed light. Then he realized that he couldn't walk. His legs wouldn't move. Desperation encompassed Trevor. If he couldn't move he'd freeze to death in front of his own house, not thirty yards from the front door.

How humiliating would it be to die drunk and stupid in front of your own house?

It was one thing to die tragically, but if this happened his family would be slapped with insult.

His pulse slowed. He tried to speak, but his vocal cords were frozen-taut and he couldn't translate his thoughts into words.

Then a beam of brightness appeared and grew stronger as did the sound of a revving engine.

A glimmer of hope struck. His shaky arms flailed for help.

Maybe the headlights belonged to someone he knew? Who would let someone freeze to death?

It just wasn't right.

If they saw him, they'd have to stop. He assumed.

Long shadows stretched as the headlights elongated from the trees that lined the street. The vehicle approached. The intensity of the headlight warmed his frozen eyelids.

Turning in the direction of the vehicle, he attempted a smile, but his mouth and lips cracked. The closeness of the van—*it had to be a van*—startled him. Pulling beside him he saw that it was a black van.

The window rolled down and a face appeared from within. Then the sliding door creaked, twisted and eventually opened. The passenger door opened. His alertness heightened. He'd hardly noticed that his fist was frozen in place. But he could still move his fingers, barely, which was good.

"Trevor!" A voice called out. "Eeeehaaa!" Trevor attempted to say "yes," but his mouth, tongue, and vocal cords still didn't permit. Truth told, he didn't know if he was drunk anymore or if his brain had frozen.

He was complacent. Even though his house was close, he *needed* warmth. And he needed it right now. He hoped these people in the van would actualize his emergency state, drag him into the warm van, maybe drive him to the hospital, and rid him of the accumulating panic. His entire body rattled as if convulsing while he shook at the possibility of warmth. He didn't even care who was calling his name, even though it would be nice to know who these people were.

Finally, the question rose from the acid pit of his stomach. But, again, his voice locked as he called out. He swallowed, straining his throat muscles. He gagged, tried again, and this time wetness coated his throat. It was difficult, but he spoke. Each word felt like sandpaper ripping apart his esophagus. "Ide? I's eeed a wide."

Close enough.

"…ssssmeeee." The returning voice was muffled by the howling wind and sounded like a snake's hiss. Then it spoke louder. "It's me!"

Trevor didn't care who it was. His frozen legs felt like a thousand pounds. But he moved them forward, one at a time. The wind blustered hard and nearly knocked him down. Frostbite had certainly set in at this point. His right ear was frozen through. Another gust of this bitter wind could blow it right off. Not knowing where the strength to move had come from, he stepped to the sidewalk. Fear struck when he saw the people in the van.

Huddled together in thick black winter coats with their hoods camouflaging their heads he saw rubber masks.

Maybe ski masks?

Two of them hung out of the sliding door. One was a boy that leaned outward and extended his hand.

"Get in here!" He called above the wind. His voce was barely audible through the strange mask—*such an odd mask.* Maybe he'd drifted into hypothermia and he was hallucinating?

He was in trouble.

Now he saw things that were questionable in terms of reality. The boy hanging out of the van was wearing a yellow smiley-face mask. His shoulder rose and then swung forward.

The fist-sized rock that struck the side of Trevor's face didn't hurt. The stream of blood that pulsated from the jagged tear near his right temple felt good because it was warm and ran the length of his face.

Before consciousness left him, he felt hands and arms yank him into the van. A cold stream of fluid soaked his face. Tingling, burning sensations fluttered across his skin.

Although he couldn't breathe, it felt good to lie on the carpeted floor of this heated van. Dread seized him when the cruelty of laughter belted into his ears.

The sinister laughs of these masked figures sent doom into the marrow of his bones. Raw fear. Falling into blackness, he felt the boys remove his clothes with knives. Fists crashed into his face allowing blackness to take him.

The van rumbled and skidded forward.

Trevor rode with Death on this icy night.

3

At first his breathing was quick and shallow. Then, sudden panic took command. Trevor's breath continued in bursts, hard to catch. Cold liquid spread along the contour between his nose and high cheekbones. He couldn't decipher what substance this was—blood or water. Either was bad. Complete sobriety sharpened his consciousness and he understood that it was water running into his mouth and nose.

A callused hand cupped his forehead and applied pressure. Unable to connect his brain to his limbs, he lay paralyzed to his attackers. His face slid beneath the surface of the water. Finally, his right eye shot open—his left eye was swollen shut. Sharp needling pain flared like flashes of thunder and sunk deep into his facial bones.

Forcing his eyelid open was hellish, like tearing a surgical scab. Even beneath the surface of the water, he could feel blood seep into and baste his eye. The sting was intense. He screamed, but only bubbles emerged. Lungs burning, his body begged for air. Finally, he was able to focus. Concentration found the strange faces that stared down at him—at least three of them. They stood around the aluminum basin he was being drowned in. All held smiles. Their faces contorted, wickedly. There was something animated about them.

Trevor grew up catholic. He'd gone to church and spent first grade through sixth in catholic school. He hated his teachers—nuns who were mean as snakes. Their joy was to punish. Cruelty was there divine pleasure. Trevor was certain of this immaterial fact.

In the sixth grade, Trevor had pleaded with his mother to allow him entrance into public school. The transfer was like a breath of fresh air after being drowned in a basin of cold water, like what was happening now.

He liked public school, made lifelong friends, and was able to focus on his studies. Not worrying about the nuns even allowed him to retain his schoolwork without bias.

Now, staring upward at the snarling faces that humiliated him, he thought of the nuns.

The final image was that horrid gown. The gown of black robes that bled upward to the white hoods. The nuns would forever bid his hell. Imprisoned, he didn't want to see the nuns. But here they were, in this other place.

The final, cruel vision he saw was a second hand. It dipped beneath the surface of the water and covered his mouth and nose.

There was a shower curtain. And for a brief moment he saw the source of this night in the form of a blood-red pentagram that was neatly scrawled in blood on the aged, peeling, off-white wall of this bathroom. He'd been made a sacrifice and now he only wondered if it was real—heaven and hell. Then he thought about the past few moments of raw fear and terror and was renewed. Baptized a believer.

Before death stole his inner being he pondered whose bathtub this was and if a child had ever been bathed here.

The laughter and cruelty ended only to begin on the other side.

Chapter 1

February 3, 2019

1

Obnoxious red and blue lights swirled and reflected off the fast falling snowflakes and illuminated the gray Buick Century parked along the roadside on this icy Wisconsin night. Inside the car, plump bulbs of sweat erupted and then ran down Lance Barryman's young face. While it was bitter cold outside, inside the car was sweltering. The heater had broken last winter. It blasted on high at all times and felt like a hair dryer blowing in his face.

In all of Lance's twenty-one years he'd never been pulled over by law enforcement. He was well behaved and respected the law. He was the voice of reason among his circle of life-long family friends. Other than immediate family, this group consisted of Brock Hills and Brianna Zastrow. Mediator and logician were the roles Lance assumed until recent weeks. Now, he was in great trouble. Being pulled over wasn't good, given his situation.

Why was he being pulled over?
How was he going to get out of this mess?
Maybe it wasn't as bad as he thought?

These questions spun his train of thought into a sensation of vertigo. Still, he had to focus. Right now. Fleeing law enforcement wasn't going to do him any good. Well, what he'd done a few hours prior warranted this brand of escape. Maybe fleeing was the only answer. He'd have to focus on this interaction like his life and/or freedom depended on it. His narrative needed solid lineage that did not stray from the story he'd concocted.

He placed the car in park, but didn't kill the engine. He tried to turn the heat down, temporarily forgetting that it was broken. The dry air disrupted his already frayed nerves.

Maybe he could slam the car into reverse, plow into the cop cruiser, send it into the ditch and then peel out while the officer scrambled to get control of the situation. But this was only an entertaining thought. The possibility that he *wasn't* in trouble was likely, *he hoped*. But he couldn't deny that he'd caused a great deal of criminal activity, involved himself in illegal acts that would haunt him for life. The actions he'd participated in would damn him into the afterlife. Maybe he should drive away, run out of town, and keep going until no one could find him and there was nothing. Maybe he could stumble into some small town someplace, and start a new life. God knew his life here was over. If he were discovered, which was likely.

God.

He felt guilty saying *God*. God was disappointed—had to be—after what had taken place since November.

The officer's LED flashlight brightened in the reflection of the side mirror, which refocused Lance's thoughts on his current situation. Lance's freedom and his quality of life depended on the next few minutes.

Technology. It was amazing how much brightness was shed from these new LED lights. The intensity was blinding. Then came the tap, tap of metal on glass. He turned left and saw the cold officer tapping his Maglite against the window. The window would break if he hit it any harder.

Taking a deep breath, he placed his index finger on the small button that would lower the side window. Then he looked to the stick shift. His fingers twitched, wanting to yank the shifter into first gear.

Nerves.

He wondered if the officer had seen his finger twitch.

This was it—his last chance to escape. He either needed to peel out or prepare to reap hell. A mental block had prevented him from stepping on the gas.

He lowered the window. Icy wind drifted into the car and spread like cancer, overpowering the heat. The icy wind chapped his lungs, caused him to choke.

"License and registration, please." The officer demanded. He made no eye contact. He looked comfortable, bored even.

Lance leaned across the passenger seat, opened the glove box, retrieved the registration, and handed it to the officer.

He'd not given his license to the officer. The error caused him to squint upon realization. He was so nervous that he couldn't remember quick order. Now his right eyelid twitched repeatedly and he knew that the cop had noticed. Surely, he knew something was wrong.

"License, sir. Have you been drinking?" the officer repeated, then asked.

Lance dug into his pocket and retrieved his wallet. With a shaky hand, he removed the driver's license from the plastic sheath and handed it to the officer. "I haven't been drinking, sir, no."

"Turn the engine off," the officer ordered while shining his flashlight onto Lance's driver's license and registration. With his index finger, the officer flicked the plastic ID. Then he focused on the papers that crinkled in the strong wind.

"It's a bit cold tonight," Lance offered with an accompanying awkward fake-laugh.

The officer darted a wide-eyed glance at Lance.

Lance understood this look as *kill the engine, you stupid fucking college asshole.*

Lance killed the engine.

"Sit tight." The officer returned to his cruiser. The blackness of the dark evening melded with the distribution of headlights and suddenly Lance couldn't see the officer. But he heard the crinkle of cold metal as the cruiser door opened and closed. The officer would take his time. Drag this situation to the point that Lance's nerves would be shot. He would lose his mind. He would inspect Lance's credentials in the comfort of his heated cruiser while deciding how long he wanted to torment the dumbass college boy.

Why had the officer told Lance to kill his engine?

He wanted him to freeze a little. Keep him uncomfortable.

Typical cop.

The temperature was negative twenty degrees, with wind chill. Just watching the heavy gusts of snow blow across the desolate country road caused Lance to shiver.

From the rear view mirror, Lance watched the officer. He didn't appear concerned. In fact, he was yawning. Lance eased up. There was no way the cop knew about what had happened earlier in the evening, or over the past few months. This opinion was developed from the lack of excitement in the officer's mulled expression. Not that the cop was lazy. He was simply not privy to the information pummeling Lance's current path of thought.

God, Lance would give anything to have the last two months of his life back.

Stop it.

Now, he was just being paranoid.

But why wouldn't he feel paranoid?

Given what had happened, he should be paranoid.

Lance glanced at his watch. Only a minute had passed, but it felt like an hour. The wait pried at his sanity. More sweat spilled from his forehead. Realizing that moisture was spilling down his forehead heightened his paranoia. The officer would wonder why he was sweating when it was so cold. Clearly, the officer would think he was hiding something. The wetness wasn't perspiration. It was fast running sweat. If the officer interpreted Lance's nervousness he would surely become suspicious and continue the inquiry.

Again, Lance thought, *why did he pull me over?* He'd done nothing wrong in regard to potential traffic violation. He certainly hadn't been speeding. Not in this weather. He'd been driving *under* the speed limit, if anything.

Maybe that was why he'd been pulled over?

This didn't make any sense.

Maybe the officer was involved?

This thought caused his hands to shake.

There was no way he'd been pulled over for driving too slow.

Well, maybe?

Nothing about tonight was right.

Startled, Lance sat up too quick and whacked his head on the low roof when the officer returned. He tapped on the driver's side window, which juggled Lance's focus.

Lance rolled the window down. Immediately, the officer blasted his face with the flashlight and stated: "Sir, please exit the car."

Lance's mouth dried. He hoped that he'd be released. Immediately, his tongue felt like it weighed a hundred pounds and his throat closed off. For a moment, he thought he was going to choke. "What's this all about, officer?"

"Step out of the vehicle," the officer repeated.

With a shaky hand and quaking legs, Lance opened the door and stepped out. A gust of cold air encompassed him. His open throat caught the bitter bite of this subzero weather. His feet felt like cinderblocks. Foot after foot, he shuffled toward the rear of the vehicle where the officer stood.

Never, had he felt the need for prayer. This was different. He prayed that this officer would become cold or get another call or simply write him a ticket for having a broken taillight and then leave.

Bundling his coat, Lance looked to the officer. He motioned Lance forward with a flat, gloved hand.

Lance followed directions.

"Do you know why I pulled you over?" the officer asked.

"I don't," Lance responded. Probably best to answer with simple responses. That way he wouldn't nervously reveal any information he'd prefer to keep secret.

"Your taillight," the officer stated, shining the LED in Lance's face again. The brightness was unsettling. His eyes watered from the intensity of the light. He raised a hand to cover his eyes, and the cop scowled. Clearly, he didn't like that Lance had moved.

"Hey," the officer said with authority.

"Sorry, it's bright." Lance had to say something. Irritating the officer was the last thing he wanted, but the light was bright and he was on edge and doing his best not to lose control. If the officer saw what was in the trunk Lance's life would become interrupted. He'd succumb to the officer's orders for now and hope to be freed quickly, especially if the officer planned to let him go.

"What do you want me to do?" Lance stuttered. He wanted to ask if he could go, but the officer didn't seem worried about time. In fact, it was beginning to feel like he'd pulled Lance over just to pass a little. Also, he probably wanted to make Lance as nervous as possible. A sadistic cop playing games wasn't uncommon.

Or was it?

"Take a look at your taillight," the officer ordered while taking a few steps backward. He repeatedly turned his gaze toward the taillight.

Lance acted as directed and followed the officer. When he reached the back of the vehicle his eyes went to the LED beam as it lowered to the passenger side taillight.

Terrified by what he saw, Lance sucked in a hard breath. The coldness burned his lungs. Snot ran from both nostrils. He wiped the clear slime away from his face with the back of his freezing hand. To Lance's surprise the taillight wasn't broken. In fact it was perfectly intact and in working order.

"I don't understand," Lance remarked.

"You don't?"

"No."

"Look at the taillight." The officer tilted the LED. The red plastic that covered the taillight twinkled.

Lance focused on the contours of the taillight. After a moment, he acknowledged the smeared blood. It was undeniable as it dripped onto the snow and painted the falling flakes red.

"You want to tell me something?" the officer asked.

"I don't know what that is. I thought you stopped me for a broken taillight?" Lance didn't know what to say. His vision was spinning.

"Looks like blood. You hit a deer?" The officer questioned.

The wind howled and Lance couldn't hear the officer. The blizzard was striking. But the next order was clear, concise, and unavoidable. "Open the trunk."

Lance pretended not to hear the request. He hollered above the gusting wind, "What?"

"Pop the trunk! Now!" The officer hammered his fist onto the hood of the trunk, and shined his light on the lock.

Lance thought about running away. He even thought about attacking the officer. "You need a warrant," Lance returned. There was nothing else to say. This was where his situation was going to get bad and he knew it.

The officer marched forward, stood in front of Lance, lifted the light and said, "Sure, we'll wait right here for the warrant."

Lance looked toward the acres of field to his right and left. He thought about making a run for it. The officer, probably in his forties, looked fit. He had broad shoulders with large arms. Even his blocky jaw was strong.

Looking to the sky, Lance closed his eyes, mouthed a short prayer and then walked to the driver's side. He popped the trunk, and waited for the officer's discovery.

The trunk lid slowly creaked open, seemingly in slow motion.

A miracle needed to take place. Divine intervention.

Instead, thick blood drained from the woman he loved—Brianna Zastrow—and spilled onto the icy road.

The officer drew his gun and shouted, "On your knees! Interlock your fingers!"

Lance did as he was told. Once cuffed, he looked into the trunk. The girl he'd loved since the beginning of time was dead and staring up at him from the trunk of this shitty Buick with Brock Hills' hunting knife erected from her torn throat.

The last fourteen weeks had destroyed his life.

This murderous night had stemmed from lust. The sex was supposed to have been an experiment with no feelings involved. No one was supposed to have been hurt.

Lance Barryman, Brock Hills, and Brianna Zastrow had been friends since birth. Their parents were best friends from high school. They'd planned their futures together, even agreed on Wisconsin University Oshkosh for college.

Brock Hills—his other best friend—brother, really—wasn't here but his hunting knife protruded from Brianna's once perfect neck, which was now split wide open. The gaping wound appeared surreal. The cold had frozen the ripped skin and gore from her neck. The love of his life looked like a sick wax sculpture at a horror museum. He knew they shouldn't have opened Pandora's box. While their plan had been perfect at the time—and perfectly understood—they hadn't calculated human flaw, ignorance or stupidity into the equation.

Before the knife had nearly severed Brianna's head, she'd been perfect. Lance wouldn't have changed a thing about her. Not the way she looked, acted, thought—she was heaven in human form.

Dropping to his knees on the icy road, he remembered kissing her neck. The sweet perfume she wore would never leave his nostrils. He remembered making love to her. He remembered he and Brock both making love to her simultaneously. They shared love and they shared each other. But Brianna only loved Brock and Lance only loved Brianna and Brock only loved Brock. And neither Lance nor Brock was her boyfriend. Grady, the California boy, was her boyfriend and he was a different story all together.

The only comforting thought that Lance could summon was that he didn't kill her.

Time was cruel. Time didn't extend a helping hand and it didn't reverse on request. If able, he would have said no to the affair.

He would have used common sense—a three way sexual relationship never worked and he was an idiot to think that it would.

Part 2: Thanksgiving, 2018

Chapter 2

Trinity

1

Intense beams of early sunlight sliced through Brianna Zastrow's parted dorm room curtains and rose until agitating her consciousness. Her eyes focused on her iPhone. She sighed at the sound of the alarm and the digital faceplate revealed the time to be just after seven o'clock. The chilly draft penetrating through the windowpane admitted the cold November morning. Thanksgiving was soon.

Rolling over in bed, she recalled the night before and the many drinks she'd sipped at that stupid frat party. All those drunken morons, many grabbing their Viagra induced erections as they attempted to seduce her, poorly. Thinking about their foul breath churned her stomach. Sitting upward, she was fairly pleased. The nausea she'd anticipated to swim in her stomach wasn't present. Still, her stomach growled and her head ached, but not badly.

The party at Delta house was average, but was a decent way to pass time on a boring Monday night.

She'd pissed off her boyfriend, Grady Riggins, by denying him sex in the upstairs bathroom. The aura of frat-douche-baggery had crept into Grady's drunken head, allowing him to dismiss the fact that she wasn't the transparently stupid cum dumpster that most of the girls inhabiting the party were. He'd tried to bend her over a badly scratched ceramic sink that held rust circles around the drain where at least half an inch of dried-up used toothpaste had caked. The door was locked with a crappy metal hook that was secured into a screwed-in loop, also rusted. Brianna liked to have fun, but a girl had standards. She laughed out loud, rolled out of bed, and walked to the full-length mirror set at the south end of her room. She hadn't decorated the place, and the mirror was gaudy, but convenient. She picked up a violet hairbrush with matted long blonde hair clung to the bristles and ran it through the tangled mess on top of her head. Tilting her neck, she straightened her posture and studied her appearance. Her face was a bit swollen from the alcohol, but not noticeable. Twisting to the left, she checked out the nicely toned backside that waved downward into long athletic legs.

Not bad.

Playing college volleyball was a great way to keep in shape, even though the season had ended poorly. Brianna used to love the game, but playing at the college level dismissed her passion for it. Talent wasn't the issue. The overwhelming intensity of college level competition ruined the connection. Still, she'd been awarded a scholarship, which motivated her to play at a high level, not her highest. The University also paid for housing. After adding tuition, books, spending allowance and a meal plan, playing volleyball for the university came out to over six figures over four years. Her parents, especially her father, would have been more than happy to pay for her education, but she knew that they'd secretly worried about how they were going to meet the payments. Their debt would never end. The scholarship worked out nicely. Her parents saved a literal fortune and she received the education she desired. She only took the spending cash that her father secretly slid to her because she knew that it made him feel good to give. That, and she'd saved him so much money with the scholarship.

She stared out the window of her high-rise dorm room. Everything appeared so small from above. The people and cars were only ants scurrying through the human farm. Growing up in a small town she'd learned about community and connectedness. Here, at the university, nothing was woven together—just a wide variety of strangers searching for new connections with new people. In the end, most would never find the enlightenment they sought. Winter added something depressing to the view, something instinctually cruel.

Although the season had concluded, she'd managed to keep a fairly vigorous workout routine, which allowed her to look and feel the way she liked. To Brianna's thinking, there was no way to argue that exercise made people feel better. While there was so much more that she wanted people to know about her, she allowed herself to love the tight ass she'd worked so hard to tone. Secretly, she enjoyed being the object of desire and lust.

After a quick shower, she pulled on a pair of light colored jeans and a fresh sweater, grabbed her History book, and scurried out of her dorm room.

Laughter echoed down the hallway. A group of fellow classmates scoured the hallway, shouting and laughing and sneering and trading thoughts and philosophies. Most headed to class. Some were hung over, returning home from a bedroom mistake the night prior. Shelly Riley had the look of utter shame as she strolled along the cream colored wall and disappeared into her room. Her mascara was running and her red lipstick smeared diagonally across her cheek. Brianna wasn't entirely sure, but it looked like tears had welled up in Shelly's eyes. Brianna could relate. In a not so distant past, Brianna had fallen into a similar mistake. Not often. In fact, she hadn't lost her virginity until the summer after high school graduation. And the sex had been on her terms, the way she wanted it. It was her father, not her mother that taught her to respect herself and her body. Her few late night conquests had appeased her curiosities and the men—boys, really—had treated her with respect both before and after. Well, maybe respect wasn't the right word. They'd been nice and had manners. That was a better way to describe *those* suitors.

The sliding glass doors of Bratman Hall—the female sports dorm—slid open allowing icy air to intrude into the lobby. A chill rattled her bones from feet to head. She shivered. The strands of her damp hair hardened. Digging into her bag, she retrieved a Navy blue beanie. She'd purchased the wool cap at the outlet mall a few weeks earlier and it'd proven to be a wise purchase. The warmth soothed as she pulled it over her head while a fuzzy sensation spread from her noggin to her ears. When her ears finally heated, she thought about Brock Hills kissing them. This new sensation tingled downward along the center of her neck.

Again, she shivered.

Admitting that she thought about Brock as a lover would remain her secret. Every girl on campus fantasized about Brock like *that—that* meaning erotic. Brianna was different. Brianna had grown up with Brock. She knew him and loved him before looks had formed him into physical perfection. She'd cared for him that day in the woods when he cried after falling off of his bike and scraping his knee, when they were six. She could remember the taste of his tears after his father struck him one Sunday afternoon for misbehaving in church. She remembered the knock at her door, she lived three houses down—on Amber Lane—a small residential street. She'd answered the door, saw his raw eyes, and kissed his tears.

Afterward, they stole two Root Beers from her father's junk drawer in the garage refrigerator, the one she wasn't allowed to explore. They'd gone to the laundry room in the basement to drink them. After he explained how much he hated his father, she held him. She'd felt motherly. Sitting on the ratty, oil and grease stained rug was the first time she'd taken the role of a nurturer. And after he cried in her arms she'd asked him, "Can I taste them?"

"Can you taste what?" He separated from her, sniffled, tilted his head to meet her eyes, and blinked.

"Your tears. Can I taste them?" She'd traced his lower eyelashes with her thumb, gathering a plump tear between her small finger and the nail. The wetness evaporated onto her thumb.

"I guess." He sniffled again.

She leaned in until she could feel his hot breath on her face. She kissed the wetness away from his eye and tasted his tears. They were warm and salty, but not too salty like she'd imagined. She visualized the tear soaking into the pores of her tongue. A silly thought, she felt that she'd taken part of his soul when she absorbed his tears, his sadness. Part of him belonged to her. In that moment—and ever since—she felt protective of him. In a sense, they'd become family—spiritually connected through tears.

Shaking away these distant memories, Brianna lunged down the remaining stairs of Bratman hall, turned left onto the sidewalk, and scurried toward the group of students headed to the main campus.

Building 714 appeared. Brianna hoped she would remember the Western Civilization material she'd studied two nights prior. She'd studied hard and she studied often. A good pattern, she held a knack for studying early, not cramming. But she would forget theories. The dates sometimes melded together and historic events cluttered and weaved into similarity. Grades weren't a problem for her and never had been, but she liked A's and preferred not to fall below ninety percent on quizzes. Her Western Civilization professor was notorious for pop quizzes.

Warmth encompassed her when she entered the building, shivering away the blustering cold. Carefully, she removed her beanie in the small bathroom to the left of the lecture hall. On her way into the class she shared a chuckle with a few of the stoners she'd passed a joint with at some party, somewhere, sometime last week. Making her way down the right side of the classroom, she took her seat at the end of row two. After retracting the collapsed desk from her seat, she arranged her textbook and notes. She withdrew her pen from the cylinder of wire binding on her notebook, shook it and then tested to see that it worked. She quickly went over her notes from last week.

Good to go.

Professor Lieberman entered the hall through a small door to the left of the podium. Glancing out at the flow of students entering the room, he shook his head, cynically, and made his way toward the Mac computer and projector. A few moments later the lights dimmed. The screen at the front of the hall dropped and expanded. The PowerPoint began.

The professor stood in front of the projector's harsh light that slanted upward and across his thin face. His lips quivered beneath his pointy nose as if a fly had landed on a stray nose hair causing his wire rim glasses to wiggle. Gray hair like a wire-wool brush was plastered to his head. His sideburns, also wool in texture, were too long and frayed. Beard stubble protruded from his ruddy face and gave him the appearance of a Norman Rockwell drunk.

"Everyone ready for a pop quiz?" He raised his eyebrows then held them in place and surveyed his silently gawking class. Audible sighs echoed through the Hall. The shuffling of papers and the electric drum of laptops logging-on ensued.

The obese TA—Fred McInery—wasn't afraid to sweat as he strained to breathe while wobbling up the slow rising stairs passing out stapled papers that made up the quiz. The inner thighs of his worn out tan khaki pants bled perspiration. Long curly, sweaty hair stuck to his reddened cheeks. Even his thick glasses were fogged.

"You'll be given thirty minutes to complete twenty questions. If you went over the material from last week you should be just fine. Remember: go with your first instinct. This is multiple choice, if you think about it for too long, too long will think about you."

Brianna hated this saying of Professor Lieberman's. She couldn't quite grasp the sense of it because it really didn't make sense. She was a girl that liked logic and she couldn't find logic in the expression. Sadly, Professor Lieberman's failure at real academia or non-fiction writing had plateaued prior to the realization of his projected hopes. Well, not really, teaching wasn't a bad gig, but was clearly not the future he'd most likely planned for himself. Otherwise, he wouldn't be so cynical. He sometimes babbled about a book he was writing and had been writing for over a decade. *Whatever*, she thought. She didn't want to think about Professor Lieberman's failed novel any further.

Brianna encouraged logic, but logic didn't explain the rapidity of her heartbeat when it hammered as the door creaked and Brock Hills entered the Hall. Taking a deep breath, she was thankful that the lights had gone down because her cheeks noticeably flushed.

Why had she been so lustful for her best friend as of late? Was it simple science, biology, perhaps natural human lust?

She'd never admit her desires to Lance, her other close friend for as long as she could remember. She, Brock, and

Lance were like family. The small town of Watertown—about seventy miles south of Oshkosh—where they grew-up, had forced their lives to mesh together. Their friendship had kept them entertained throughout their formative years, but small town thinking wasn't enough. They'd banded together to rise above what Watertown's community offered in terms of intellectual capacity. Their imaginations had run wild in the forests and fields of their rural village and they'd been inseparable. Romance and sex hadn't been included during their formative years—at least not for her. To her, Lance and Brock were the brothers she never had. Being an only child, she didn't have sisters or any real form of female influence to relate to. Time had changed her. It had changed her boys too.

Lance was in love with Brianna and she knew it. He'd never admit to it. Except, they'd kissed once at a farm party during their junior year of high school. They'd chalked it up to a drunken mistake. Thankfully, they'd been able to laugh about it the next day, but Brianna knew that it wasn't a drunken mistake. She knew that Lance was in love with her. And the kiss hadn't been bad. In fact, it was enjoyable. Lance's lips were full and he'd kissed her with passion. Unfortunately for Lance, she'd imagined his lips were Brock's. Lance's attraction was something that Brianna felt deeply. And Lance tried to hide his affection. Too hard, even. At the end of the night, he'd apologized and forced laughter. Even made jokes equating the kiss to something incestuous. She knew that he didn't want to lose her—as a friend—and she appreciated his respect. He knew she didn't want him *like that*. Lance was attractive in his own right, but he wasn't oozing sex, like Brock. Brock was unbelievably attractive. Sophomore year of high school had been a period of development for Brock. His looks took shape. He started dating seniors. He always had a girlfriend and three *others* on the side. He was overconfident and over-sexed. His dominant nature played a part too. He'd been into martial arts since a young age—four or five. The self-confidence that carried itself with Brock being feared was something that attracted young girls. Now, it attracted her. She'd never admitted this because the idea that male dominance was somehow attractive was something she feared she believed.

Some of the best bonding moments from high school were of the three of them laughing at Brock's stories of female conquests.

On Sundays, they'd drive to the movies in Delafield, a suburb of Milwaukee just twenty miles east of Watertown. Along the way they would smoke a joint or two and sip on stolen beer, usually something cheap like Pabst or Busch Light. Lance and Brianna would give Brock three dollars each and Brock would pay for entrance into the theater. Then, he'd creep to the far exit, open the door for Brianna and Lance, and they would scurry toward the film of their liking. This was their system. They'd usually stay at the theater and watch two or three movies each Sunday. They spent *some* money on snacks and candy so as to not rip off the theater too badly. A popular theater, there were usually over a hundred people inhabiting the Cineplex on Sunday and therefore Brock, Brianna, and Lance were never really suspected of wrong doing. Also, the theater employees were classmates and didn't care that they'd snuck in, if they'd noticed.

Once inside the theater, they'd huddle in the dark corner rows and watch a new release for the second or third time. This was where Brock would share the tales of his latest female conquests. He'd articulate the steamy, sticky details while Lance and Brianna would laugh and ask questions. Brianna was able to suppress her curiosities by listening to these stories. She secretly fantasized about sex. She hadn't admitted to Brock—never would—but she would get excited when he'd detail the different positions and performances he'd experienced. Lance probably thought these stories were better than porno magazine fodder.

Snapping her attention back to the classroom, Brianna turned in her seat and became startled when her eyes met Brock's intense gaze. Her cheeks flushed again. She was embarrassed, but had to hide it.

Thank God the lights were out.

She nodded with a smile.

Brock took his seat.

"Good morning, Mr. Hills." Professor Lieberman licked his lips. "Welcome to class. Late night?"

"Early morning." Brock smiled while glancing at his fellow classmates.

The girls giggled and the boys tossed cheers. The campus stud had lived fantasies for the boys and articulated them for the female student body. Even Professor Lieberman found him amusing, although he'd made it a point to acknowledge his tardiness.

Brianna secretly hated the girls that stopped and stared, lustfully, at her friend. Watching their gazes was torture. They desired him. Like her, these girls wanted Brock's love and devotion. He was the unattainable man that each and every girl wished they could change. These girls wished they had the special touch—the touch that would magically capture Brock's heart. But Brianna knew the *real* Brock. She knew he'd never settle down. Sure, some day he would get married to a woman, probably have children. She knew that he fancied the idea of a normal small town life, but his appetite would remain unsatisfied. There would be other women, even after he was married. At some point, Brock's magic penis would get him into serious trouble. Not yet, but someday. Someday he would marry some poor girl who, everyday, would have to look in the mirror and lie to herself: "He loves me and only me." And this poor girl would believe this even though in her heart of hearts she'd know that there were random women making love to her husband.

"Shit," Brianna blurted out loud.

Realization struck. Five precious minutes of her time had been wasted thinking about Brock. She hadn't even glanced at her quiz yet. And now half of the class stared at her because she'd blurted an obscenity. She lowered her head, but not before peaking at Brock who silently laughed. He pointed at her, and his eyes were red. Typical, he'd smoked a joint on his way to class.

2

Professor Lieberman concluded class with his signature line, "Stay aware."

Chairs and desks creaked as a sea of uninterested students dashed toward the cramped double doors that led into the hall lobby. At the conclusion of many lectures, students fluttered out the doors excited about the stretching of their minds. Smiles found their faces as they reflected upon the lessons learned that had connected with their own thoughts and processes, but not Professor Lieberman's course, not today. These students were bored and they were tired from forcing their attention to the quiz and the instructor.

Having been seated near the double doors, Brock exited and waited for Brianna by the water fountain, which only worked during warm weather. He blew into his cupped hands for warmth and she found herself doing the same. He was certain they both had covered their mouths to disguise lover's smiles.

"Maybe we should invest in gloves." Brianna's eyes shifted from her left hand to her right.

"I hate Wisconsin winters. I was destined to live someplace warm." Brock pushed off the brick wall with his left foot, smiled seductively at a passing group of freshman girls and only then continued walking with Brianna.

"The snow was a blast when we were kids," Brianna enlightened Brock. A fierce stare darted toward a blonde sorority girl with fantastic tits. She'd locked eyes on Brock.

"You always do that," Brock insisted.

"Always do what?" Brianna refocused her attention on Brock.

"If I say I don't like something, you say something good about what I don't like." Brock engaged her focus.

"No I don't." She shook her head and rolled her eyes.

"Yes, you do," he playfully shoved Brianna.

She slapped at his hand and said, "I guess it's subconscious."

"Well, what's so great about Wisconsin winters?"

"Christmas parties, sledding, hot cocoa, snow days, snowball fights, flannel shirts, winter coats, seeing your own breath. I even like the colored lights that are strung along the trees." She pointed to the campus decorations. "A little early for Christmas, but they're cozy." Brianna blew a plume of icy breath in Brock's face.

"Tiffany Sayers liked getting fucked in the cold. She used to make me bend her over the air conditioner in the backyard while her mom made me dinner."

"You used to have sex with Tiffany? Why didn't you tell me?"

"I knew that you liked her. As a friend."

"What does that have to do with anything? You've had sex with all of my friends."

"You're friendship with her was genuine. Our short-lived affair would have divided your friendship," he stated.

Brianna shrugged, smirked, and then kicked a small clump of ice across the sidewalk. It rolled into a ball and made a frosty explosion against the curb.

"You remember when we were kids ... and we built that snow ramp?" Brock twisted his head toward Brianna and raised his animated hands. This thought had obviously stimulated his ADHD-riddled mind.

Brianna stepped sideways. Whenever Brock became excited, he'd fidget. His hands would recklessly slap her. He didn't know his own strength and sometimes it. Suddenly aware of his actions, he attempted to settle down. His fingers tapped, his smile stretched, and his eyes widened.

"I remember you and Lance building a snow ramp ... and trying to get me to stand up on my sled and jump off. I also remember landing on my ass and it hurting like hell. My left ass cheek was swollen and bruised for a month."

"Nice. I bet that looked sweet." Brock shook his head and dropped his smile. "But remember when Lance went off ... " Brock watched Brianna's face light up with laughter and confusion. She didn't know what to think about what he'd just said, but that was why he'd said it.

" ... and pissed his pants. Because he landed on his head and got a concussion? You're a really shitty friend."

Brock joined Brianna's laughter. Stopping at a slush and snow covered bench, Brock shoved the ice off one side of the bench and sat while Brianna stood in front of him, pacing.

Brianna took a few deep breaths, watching it expel outward and then smiled. Her teeth appeared shiny with spit-polished. Brock knew she'd realized the depth of the joke. They were laughing at the near demise of their good friend, Lance. Concussions weren't funny. Only intimate friends could laugh at each other's injured misfortune.

"We shouldn't laugh about that. He doesn't think it's funny." Brianna's grin was infectious.

Brock stood. The cold had caused his eyes to lubricate and a tear ran down his cheek. He stopped laughing. "I don't know. I don't even know why I thought of that just now."

Brianna knew why he thought the story was funny. Brock was just the tiniest bit sadistic. He enjoyed the mild torment of others on a different scale than what might be considered normal. Granted, Brianna assumed everyone enjoyed the misery of others—just a bit—but Brock enjoyed the misery of others a touch more. And she was aware of his sadism.

The screech of skidding skateboard wheels screeched caused Brianna to cringe.

"What's that look for? You gotta take a dump?" Brock joked.

"You're so gross," she said while shaking her head.

Brianna rolled her eyes and lowered her head, then tilted her attention toward the sound of the incoming skater. "My California guy."

"If you dread seeing him then why are you dating him?" Brock asked sincerely—and Brianna regretted telling Brock that she was annoyed by her boyfriend's presence.

At first, Grady Riggins had been a dream—*a California dream.* He'd moved to Wisconsin from the beach community of Orange County, California. He was the cool surfer dude that all the Midwest girls wanted to date—an exotic animal around these Midwest parts.

Brianna was an equal to the other females that encompassed the university's student body. She desired the attention attached with dating the new guy from somewhere else—somewhere neat and sunny. Sure, this was college and everybody was from somewhere else, but Grady was different. Most of the students at Wisconsin University, Oshkosh were from Wisconsin. There was common ground between everyone, but Grady came from American Paradise.

Who didn't want to move to California after graduation and try their hand at becoming a movie star?

That bright smile exploded from beneath Grady's shaggy blonde hair. His deeply tanned skin allowed his icy blue eyes to accentuate his features. His body was cut, trim, and fit from all those miles of swimming in the Pacific Ocean. He told stories about meeting famous people and partying with them. "They're all normal people just like you and me, bro." He would say. Grady's cool attitude and exciting life experience was what magnetized her attraction to him.

Brianna knew she owned Grady at "hello." That gaudy, puppy-dog expression that boys adopted when they wanted something badly—that was the way he looked at her the first time they'd met. Their eyes had connected between a mist of heavy cigarette and marijuana smoke that fumigated Brock and Lance's living room. It had been September of this year.

Grady, Lance, and Brock shared Advanced Algebra. They thought the new guy was cool and they invited him to their party.

The skateboard popped in the air. The wheels spun before stopping abruptly when Grady stuffed the board beneath his arm. He stood for a moment before setting the board against the bench. He wrapped his arms around Brianna who darted an annoyed glance at Brock and then rolled her eyes.

Brock smiled.

Pouting her bottom lip and slouching her shoulders, Brianna blinked rapidly, "I missed you, sweetie."

"Way cool. Me too. I thought about you in that tight little swim suit you wore to the *School Sucks* party in August." Grady said and winked in Brock's direction.

Brock returned the wink.

Brianna caught the reciprocal winks and smiled sarcastically. Her regard for the male-appreciation-gesture-wink was that of annoyance and it disgusted her.

"Say, you want to grab a drink at the Quarter later?" Grady repeated.

"Sure, what time?" Brianna tucked Grady's long blonde hair behind his small ear.

"Eight?"

"I'll be there."

"You gonna come, Brock?" Grady asked, lifting his fist and bumping Brock's knuckles.

"I never turn down drinks."

"Way cool." Grady finished, kissed Brianna, and then sped off on his board.

Brock and Brianna stood shoulder to shoulder and watched a group of girls dressed in sweats jump to avoid Grady when he swerved along the embankment dangerously close to them. Even though it was December in Wisconsin Grady wore a tee shirt and jeans without a coat.

"He's not afraid of freezing," Brock stated and then chuckled. "Is he cold in bed?"

"Wouldn't you like to know?"

"I certainly would."

She laughed, punching Brock's arm and asked, "You would sleep with me ... totally disregarding our friendship ... wouldn't you?"

"I would experiment. No strings attached." His head tilted up. His eye contact was intense, serious and deep. As deep as the gaze he extended her now. "Look, you're hot. We're comfortable with each other. Why shouldn't we touch fleshy parts and not have it turn into an emotional deal?"

"You're a sociopath. That is *not* how relationships and friendships and sex work." She slowly swiveled her head side-to-side.

"Says who?" Brock asked.

Brianna was caught for a moment and thought he might have had a point.

Why should it matter?

But she knew why it mattered: she was in love with Brock.

If she and Brock experimented, her feelings and attraction for him would intensify. She wouldn't be able to turn those feelings off. It was best to leave fantasies just that, a fantasy.

She responded, "Because we're friends ... because we're practically family ... because you shouldn't think about me like that. You're making me feel uncomfortable."

"Well, excuse me. I thought honesty was our best attribute. We made pacts not to give in to *the bullshit*. We're supposed to be honest with each other. That's our strength." His posture straightened. His smile spilled from full lips. "That ... *and* I'm kidding. We shouldn't sleep with each other. It would ruin our friendship. But don't say you don't think about it."

Brock's head games were awful. He knew what he was doing when he tapped into these topics of discussion. And it wasn't fair. Human beings thought about sex. She knew that just as everyone knew that. Brock enjoyed pushing her into choppy water. He knew everything about her—how to pull her strings, how to toy with her emotions. Most of all, she hated that he was right and she hated exposing her vulnerability to him.

Taking a step forward, away from Brock, she made the mature decision to remain silent. But that wasn't good enough for Brock. He continued prying at her sensitivities, "You can't bow out of this conversation, Brianna."

"I can and I am. Plus, you said you were kidding." She stopped, turned and darted a stiff finger into his chest. Damn, he was strong. His pectorals were rock solid. She stubbed her index finger into the meat of his chest. Hiding the quick pain shuttering through her finger, she was determined not to show weakness. But Brock saw the pain and smiled.

Asshole.

"Admit it," Brock said, not acknowledging the finger still placed between his pectoral muscles.

"Admit what?" She rolled her eyes when he flexed his pecks, first the left then the right. This male machismo act was stupid, childish and, revolting. And yet she was about to start laughing. That stupid, insecure little bitch that lived inside of her mind wanted him to feel impressive. She bit the side of her cheek, hard, and drew blood.

Good.

She should be punished for allowing him to feel impressive for flexing his muscles like a total moron.

Primitive prick.

"Admit that you think about sleeping with me." Slowly, his arms rose, his hands cupped around her shoulders, and he pressed down firmly while squaring off in front of her.

His eyes were beautiful, piercing.

Stop thinking like this, bitch!

Her lungs froze and her heart hammered. For a quick moment, she thought she would hyperventilate.

"I'm not going to admit..." She found it hard to breathe.

"Honesty," Brock insisted.

"I'm not saying anything." She let out a sigh.

"You're better than that." Brock shook his head looking disappointed.

She looked to the sky and shook her head. She wanted to kill him while fresh snowflakes drifted down onto her cheeks and dissolved. "What the hell?"

"Our friendship is stronger than silence. Admit that you've thought about sleeping with me." That teenage boy begging for sex look he seemed so good at had faded.

"I've thought about sleeping with you. Many times. Mostly when I'm in the shower ... if you want to know the truth." Brock's full bottom lip curled and Brianna could feel her cheeks flush.

"You suck." She couldn't contain her adolescent smile.

Brock returned a charming grin. The grin was part of a pattern he displayed before speaking vulgar. "I do suck. On labial folds, and clitorises, and I could suck on yours if you like."

Her discomfort broke with laughter brought on by Brock's disgusting ridiculousness.

"Oh, so now I'm funny?" he asked inching closer to her face. "But you wouldn't sleep with me."

He had to realize how much he was bothering her.

"No, I wouldn't sleep with you," she paused. "But, yes, I have thought about it."

Brock lifted his hands from her shoulders and stepped backward. "That's all I wanted to hear."

"Fine." She punched him in the chest. "You're an asshole."

He winced mockingly grabbing at his chest. "Everyone knows I'm an asshole." He pulled her close.

She was confused by his ability to make her feel so uncomfortable, yet turned on, and then comforted like family the next moment.

Within this thought, she solidified, again, that she loved him more than a friend or brother and she knew they would someday explore each other.

"I don't want to know what you two were talking about, do I?" Lance strolled, cool and collected, down the iced-over sidewalk. He stopped a few feet before them.

"Lance, thank God you're here. Brock is sexually assaulting my sanity." Brianna lunged forward and hugged her other best friend, the sensible one. Lance was real comfort, a friend without threat. She confided in him and didn't feel like he would attempt to seduce her. His body heat and tight grip paralleled a warm Christmas fire.

"Brock, the sanity-rapist. That sounds like a bad horror film." Lance shook his friend's hand while Brock wiggled his fingers around his grip.

"If I told you where that hand was last night ... "

Lance's lips quivered and he asked, "Anal or vaginal?"

"Both, and I've not washed or showered," Brock returned.

Brianna pulled a bottle of anti-bacterial from her coat pocket and squirted a dollop of alcohol-based cleanser into her left palm and then rubbed her hands together.

Brock grinned at Brianna and asked, "You ever do that with cum?"

Brianna stopped rubbing her hands together. "You're a sick bastard, Brock."

Brock turned back to Lance. "Are you coming to the Quarter tonight?"

Brianna chimed in, "You have to come. And I don't mean cum in a sense that sicko here ... " she kicked Brock in the ass. "... means."

"Well, that too, but I'm talking about the party."

She frowned, "What party?"

"The boxed wine and porn party," Brock enlightened.

"We told Grady we'd meet him at The Quarter." Brianna held up a finger.

"You gonna put that finger in my butt?"

She frowned again, "I hate you so, so, so, so much."

"I'm aware that we're supposed to meet Grady. It'll be funny to ditch him," Brock responded.

"You're such a jerk. I'm meeting Grady at The Quarter. If you guys are there we can talk about going to the party," Brianna continued. "Boxed wine and porn. Intriguing. We'll convene at The Quarter."

Part 3: The Transformation

Chapter 3

Boxed Wine and Porn

1

From down a long residential street, the hollow cough of a rusted muffler rattled. The night sky faded into daylight and Brock sat upright from a much-needed nap on his ratty orange couch. All the furniture had come with the house. Each piece was ugly, but comfortable in the most charming way. The cushions were fluffy and coaxed tired minds into relaxation.

Rolling to the side, Brock took a whiff of the armrest and thought that it smelled like nacho cheese. Not good for a living room couch. Standing, he went to the bathroom, grabbed a can of Axe body spray and doused the fabric. A cloud of potent perfume wafted upward until Brock needed to take a step back. Finally, he nodded his approval before going upstairs to pick out his clothes and take a shower. Thoughts of Brianna consumed him. He'd been attracted to her his entire life, but he'd never acted on his desires. Still, he contemplated whether having sex would kill the meaningfulness of their friendship. The sexual tension between he and Brianna was thick and needed to be cut. The fruit of lust needed to be tasted.

Brock zipped his pants, checked out his appearance in the vanity mirror above his dresser drawer and tilted his gaze to a picture of the three of them at a Halloween party when they were only twelve. Back when they were unaware of sex and its complexities. The photo and their joy rang innocent. In the picture they were dressed as soldiers. Through the camouflaged grease paint smeared across their faces they appeared happy.

Somewhere in the subconscious, Brock's oversexed mind maintained the ability to recall innocent memories, times when friendship was everything, life was beautiful and thoughts were pure. The memories of he and Lance chasing Brianna down their street, running through their neighborhood collecting candy, house-by-house, filled him with nostalgic satisfaction. These thoughts angered him, almost as if the innocence of youth was a slap in the face to the harsh realities of now. True happiness fled Brock Hill's life long ago. The sad truth was that sex was his God now. Aware of this fact, he'd never admit it because to do so would be accepting the situation was hopeless. He'd not kill hope, not yet. Hope still lived within his being. He continued to ponder on those early days. Their fun had been so innocent. Sexual corruption hadn't struck until just before his high school years. Brock began to think about Brianna with lust, at thirteen.

What did she look like naked?

Was her nakedness as attractive as clothed?

The heart shaped ass hidden behind her tight clothing had to be perfect. He'd bet an extremity.

Brock couldn't shake these thoughts. Each time he attempted to shed his lustful thoughts he was disappointed to learn that he was unable. For the longest time he believed he was in control of such things. He was wrong.

Suppression was the closest he could manage. He'd been doing this for seven years, but the itch to taste the forbidden fruit was unquenchable now. Even when he was with other girls he would think about Brianna. Her smell, her smile, and the way her perfect blue eyes squinted when she laughed. Even the way she touched him. When they watched scary movies and she became startled she would grab him. She wouldn't squeeze until a full second after she'd placed her hand on his arm. Just the way she touched him as simple as this sent his sexual sensory into overdrive. He knew she could feel it too. She couldn't ignore it, no way. He saw that in the way she stole glances.

There was hope in the idea that Brianna wouldn't be able to suppress her attraction for him forever. And he intended to guide her lustful desires toward his own, and then into bed. These thoughts generated more thoughts. He loved Lance like a brother and wouldn't intentionally do anything to harm him or hurt his feelings. He guessed brotherhood was the label that he would connect to their relationship—there was no other word for it other than *brotherly*.

They'd shared times and experiences, more so than he'd actually experienced with his blood sibling. Sure, he loved his own brother, but not the way he loved Lance. His brother was twelve years older than he. He was more of an uncle than anything. Brock went to Lance with his problems and successes. He confided in Lance. He could open up to him like no one else. He loved women, but did not trust them. And maybe love wasn't the right word. He lusted for women. There was something magical and attractive about each and every female figure. The sight of a woman's hips, breasts, ass, even the soft slant of their facial features and eyes would drive his lust to maniacal heights. His hunger for flesh was unquenchable, always. Almost shamefully, his obsession with Brianna was sexual. That little girl that had once tasted his tears and cared for him like the mother he never knew. But he didn't love Brianna in a romantic way. He loved her like a sister, yet he wanted to have meaningless sex with her.

What the hell did you call that?

"Confused," he said out loud.

Styling his hair, another idea struck; he wanted Brianna, Lance and himself to take that final leap. The three of them had shared so many experiences. They'd not only shared, they'd dissected their life experience with honesty and vulgar regard. Tonight, he would confront Lance and Brianna with his ideas and revelations. What better place to seek counsel than at a party where lustful-images would be broadcast? Sure, his friends would think he was a pervert, they already did. Then again, maybe they wouldn't. They were his closest friends—family, really— and they would try and understand what he was communicating so long as he was upfront about his serious intent. And he *was* serious. To share a sexual experience that slid beneath the surface of physical intimacy would be proving to themselves that they could remain close friends, like family, experience true sexual bliss, and then discuss and digest their experience as adults. This had to happen, Brock thought.

He hadn't realized that he was stabbing his favorite hunting knife into the top portion of his wooden dresser. Oddly, he often carried his knife when he thought about serious issues. It helped him think. Plunging the razor sharp dagger into inanimate objects wasn't the best way to expend nervous energy, but he had to expel it somehow. The twelve-inch stainless steel blade was sharpened daily and maintained. The thing could slice through tin like it was butter. His grandfather had given it to him when he was five. The K-bar had been issued to him in the Marines and held the Corps emblem—eagle, globe and anchor—on the side. Unaware that he was doing so, he slammed the knife through the top surface of his dresser and into his sock drawer. And this was done with only a small amount of applied weight and pressure.

"Whoops," he said out loud and laughed as he opened the drawer and pulled out a shredded pair of black dress socks. He wondered if he'd ever lost his train of thought and stabbed anything other than furniture.

Maybe he'd accidentally killed something before? A cat or dog? Who knew?

He often became lost staring at reflective light along the serrated blade. The solid carbon handle was inviting to squeeze with a tight fist. There was something off about the way he felt the need to stab things while lost in thought. Sometimes, he'd black out. Left the physical space of his mind for a while. Glancing up from the knife's blade to his reflection in the mirror, he flexed his stomach muscles to reveal a tight six-pack. Then he lowered his shirt, smiled, and left his room while shaking his head and confessing, "I m such a narcissist."

2

Lance couldn't place his current feelings. A transformation was taking hold as of late. Maybe it was his brain chemistry, a mental growth spurt. Maybe it was his surroundings or his friends. Both Brianna and Brock were acting odd. Brock normally acted odd, but this was something else entirely. The word *off* was probably a better word. Well, actually, Lance didn't think Brock was *off* so much as he was perverted. He needed a thinking cap for his penis. And his penis didn't think intelligently too often, it could only think hard. He was into sick things, watched a lot of porn, and made crude jokes about women. Always carrying his stupid knife with him to inappropriate places, like class and parties. But he got away with his actions because he was good-looking and good-looking people got away with everything. History was an attestation to this.

Lance ran his hand through his messy brown hair; then used a dollop of regular body lotion to style it. There was a silky quality to his hair, shiny. Plus—in his opinion—there was something silly about perfectly sculpted hair, especially on a male head. Sure, he understood why men attempted to look their best. Hell, they were in college, young, and wanted to get laid. Appearances were everything. That was normal.

Lance's current train of thought broke when he looked to the picture of he, Brianna and Brock at a Halloween party. The corners of the fading photo were stuck in the crook of his vanity mirror, which was badly in need of a good cleaning.

He and Brock shared a house. Their rooms reflected their personalities. Brock's room was scattered with plastic laundry baskets filled with clothes that hadn't been washed in so long that the presence of mold was visible. Girly pictures were tacked to the walls, random DVD's were strewn across the floor and there were puncture marks in all the walls from his knife. The room smelled of old sweat and heavy cologne. Brock was a pig. But again, it didn't matter because he was good looking.

Lance's inspection of this nostalgic photo led his gaze from Brock to Brianna. Lance could look at Brianna until the end of days. Privately, he fantasized about her. In his fantasy, she would realize his greatness. He would treat her well and she'd fall in love with him. Thinking of their imaginary future drew happiness. His heart fluttered. Her wide smile and those icy eyes, not to mention her athletic build and her perfect ... everything. He'd been in love with Brianna since before he could remember.

He knew that she was in love with Brock and had always had been, even before she knew it. Sooner or later she'd act on this attraction. Lance only hoped that she would drop those feelings shortly after she acted on them. Lance hoped and prayed she would then move on to her true destiny—him Lance.

Brock would never change and Brianna carried too much respect for herself. If it came down to commitment, she wouldn't bring herself to hitch onto Brock forever. Eventually, she'd want to settle down with a stable person. A guy she knew and was comfortable with, a guy that was handsome and took care of his appearance, a guy that wasn't a pig.

Gee, was there such a guy out there?

He laughed out loud and hoped that Brock hadn't heard him, but he did. Brock entered the room, lifted his leg, and let one rip.

"Would you fuck Brianna if given the chance?" Brock sat on the corner of Lance's bed.

Lance didn't want to think about Brianna, sexually, while the disgusting brand of Brock's ass filled his room and violated his nasal passages. He grabbed a can of aerosol off of his dresser, aimed it at Brock, and sprayed a cloud of the disinfectant in his direction.

Brock started to move, but then sniffed the air. "What is that, bro?"

"It's disinfectant, you nut," Lance responded.

Brock's bodily functions always amazed Lance. Now, he watched Brock sniff the disinfectant.

"You think that stuff could pass as cologne? And it smells familiar. Is that mine?"

"No, I don't think it could pass as cologne." Lance shook his head. "One of your nightly conquests actually brought an overnight bag last time she came over here to bone you and ended up using my room to prepare for violation. She left a number of products. One of those products was this aerosol and another was an unopened box of condoms."

"Teresa." Brock shouted, held up an index finger and smiled. He didn't even look up. He grabbed the disinfectant and inspected the bottle. His lips mimicked the brand name. "Why would she bring disinfectant?"

"Have you smelled your room?" Lance coughed.

"That bad?"

"You're gonna end up with AIDS, dude." Lance informed his friend.

"That's pretty rude, man. Can we get back to my question?" Brock made eye contact while Lance privately wished that he didn't admire his friend's physical appearance.

"What question?" Lance knew exactly what question.

"If I could talk Brianna into a three way ... with you and me ... would you do it?"

Lance didn't know how to answer the question and he was never very good at being put on the spot. Straight answers like *yes* or *no* didn't come easy either. His lips began to tremble. When he was put on the spot his mouth would always move while his brain strained for an answer. His cheeks burned and his forehead turned red. "I have no idea how to answer that question." His posture slumped.

Brock threw the disinfectant at Lance, barely missing his head. "What the hell do you mean *you don't know how to answer that question?"*

"She's like our sister, dude. We can't just have meaningless sex with her."

"I disagree. She would be the perfect person to have meaningless sex with because she knows us so well that she *can* distinguish the difference. She's matured enough to separate the two."

"If we both *did that* it would ruin our relationship." Lance put forth a half-effort to convince Brock. Plus, while the thought of making love to Brianna was always at the forefront of his thoughts, the jealousy he'd feel if Brock were intimate with her was maddening. That alone might ruin Lance. The thought of them having sex caused his teeth to grind and his jaws to gnash.

"I really don't think it would ruin our relationship. Can you just think about this for a minute."

"She has a boyfriend."

Brock laughed, "That's funny."

"How is that funny?" Lance took an angered step toward Brock.

"Because Grady's kind of a twerp. He's a California turd and he'll be gone by the end of next year. Their relationship is temporary. Don't worry about him. Plus, it is kind of fun to fuck somebody else's girlfriend. It's thrilling, naughty."

Remembering that he'd never get through to Brock, Lance calmed, shook his head and said, "You're unbelievable."

"So, you would? Just entertain the idea for one second. Think about what you would like about it."

Lips twitching, Lance frantically searched his brain for an articulate, concise sentence. The form of an answer trembled and begged to come out, but the damn words wouldn't spill. The answer was too complicated to give on the spot and he wished his lips wouldn't tremble when he was at a loss for words. "We can't, dude. It's Brianna. That's it. Game over."

"What if she's down? Would that ease your mind?" Brock's eyebrows bounced.

"Well, ass-wad, because we're such good friends ... and that we care so much for our friend, we should tell her that it would not be a good idea. And as far as I'm concerned, this conversation is over."

"Dude, just think about it. Like everything else in life, there are pros and cons. No right answer and no wrong answer, only interpretation and instinct. Maybe this is important to me."

"Brock, the philosopher." Lance shook his head. There was something comical about Brock when he exploited his selfishness. "You're the most selfish, self-indulging ... "

"I get it. You're right. I'm a total narcissist, but hear me out. One, all three of us think about what it would be like to sleep with each other. You can't argue that the sex drive is a normal part of humanity. That's science. I mean ... well, I don't think about you and I." Awkwardness stole the moment. Then he waved this thought. "You know what I'm saying." He raised his index and middle finger into a peace sign. "Two, we've known each other our whole lives and done everything together ... bullshit aside, if we all agree on this then we can explore our fantasies with trusted partners. We eliminate risk. I know you like *that*. There's things that I want to do and try and if we have an open understanding of what's going on then we can heighten our friendship."

Lance hated that he understood Brock's philosophy. While he wouldn't admit it, Brock had an arguable point.

But he had to be wrong. He just had to be.

Lance kept his mouth shut.

3

The glass window was cold against Brianna's forehead when she rolled her face to see the world below her dorm room. Eight stories down to be exact. People were visible and she could recognize faces.

Nostalgically, Brianna smiled at her passing thoughts when her friends strolled into view along the sidewalk. Brock was easy to single out. He walked with confidence. He was big, but not bulky-big. He was bigger than life. Avoiding his presence was impossible.

"Are you having sex with one of them?" Her roommate Caroline startled her when she entered the room.

"You scared the hell out of me," Brianna grabbed her chest. She stood from the windowsill, and asked, "Why would you say that?" She fought a smile, but eventually laughter won the battle.

"The only people who look this happy—like you do when those two arrive—are young couples in love. And girl, you got that goo-goo eyed vixen crap going on," Caroline remarked and laughed. "I probably would have slept with them years ago."

"Those guys are like brothers to me. We grew up on the same street, had the same friends in school. All of my memories are with them."

"That don't mean you're not a human being with needs, sexual desires, and a dirty mind. You got memories ... you got a vagina too. Tell you what, I'd do just about anything Brock Hills asked me to ... just for one night. I'd work that cock, girl. And what does growing up with two boys have to do with a steamy night of unadulterated fun? I need to find my dildo just thinking about Brock Hills. And Lance ain't so bad either. Quiet type. He probably cries after sex, but like the good kind of cry, not that mommy-issue kind."

"Never a boring minute with you, Caroline." Brianna bit her thumbnail then stopped when she noticed Caroline watching her.

"Why are you so nervous?" Caroline asked.

Brianna's hand darted to her side and she wiped saliva on her pants. "I'm not nervous, weirdo. I'm uncomfortable because you're talking about my friends like they're meat."

"Let me get this right. You grew up with Lance and Brock? Brock Hills, the biggest stud this side of the Midwest. You've shared all of your experiences with them. Why the hell haven't you been the meat in that sandwich? I would have done awful things with both of them. Times have changed, sister. Get with it and get on it. Girl, you're past due for some kinky, neighbor-boy sex."

They both laughed.

"That would only complicate my feelings for both of them. The last thing I want to do is ruin our friendship." Brianna stood, grabbed her purse, glanced at her reflection in the mirror and ran her fingers through her hair. "Have fun tonight." She opened the door and walked out, leaving Caroline in the living room with her thoughts.

In the lobby, Lance and Brock argued. They always argued like brothers. And like a mother, Brianna stood in the stairwell and watched them adoringly for a moment before announcing her presence.

"You look awful." Brock said, checking out Brianna. "Really ugly."

She knew he was kidding. Conversations with Brock started with light-hearted insults.

"Thanks, you look dumb—really dumb—like, when I look at you I think, now there's a person who wears a football helmet to school." Brianna enjoyed insulting Brock.

Always the observer, Lance laughed at the flying insults.

Brock shook his head. "You know, Brianna, you'd be better off dumb. Being smart will only get you heartache. You're into all this women's rights shit, you're majoring in business, thinking about becoming a lawyer, but you'd actually be much happier if you were an idiot, like a stripper. Just plotting along through life one dick after the next until your looks started to fade and then you could jump onto a sugar daddy."

"How long did it take you to think that one up?" Brianna extended her middle finger. "You look—and have always looked—utterly and completely moronic. I mean, if your IQ were a couple points lower you'd be shitting your pants and rubbing spit all over your face." Brianna smiled, breaking the friendly tension by hugging Brock then

Lance. She couldn't help but to inhale when Brock held her.

"Let's go before you guys draw a crowd and this turns into a comedy insult show." Lance always initiated the breaking up of mindless banter on the brink of an all out roast. "We're meeting Grady at The Quarter?"

"Really?" Brock asked, annoyed.

"Yes, we are really meeting my boyfriend at The Quarter. He probably wouldn't think too highly of me if I ditched him for the porno and wine party."

"Why?" Brock sounded like a two year-old asking his mother questions simply for the sake of asking.

"What the hell do you mean, *why*? He's my boyfriend and I don't do shit like that. It would give him the wrong idea *and* it's not appropriate."

"What idea?"

"That something ... *inappropriate* was going on between me and my two oldest friends." Brianna looked down. She didn't want her boys to see her cheeks flush. She meant what she'd said and hated that she'd felt obligated to say it.

"Well, he knows our past, why would he feel like that?" Brock persisted.

"Leave it alone, dumb ass." Lance dove to Brianna's aid.

"Would you let your girlfriend go to a boxed wine and porno party with two guys that weren't you?"

"That's why I don't date."

"Well ... I do and it's rude. If you don't want to go to The Quarter then don't." Brianna shrugged her shoulders.

"We're going to The Quarter first." Lance shot a grim look at Brock.

"Are you cool with that?" Brianna looked to Brock.

"Are you in love with California-boy?"

"Put me on the spot, why don't you."

"Don't dodge the question."

Brock didn't look like he was kidding anymore.

Was he jealous?

She hated being turned on by Brock, especially when he attempted to make her feel guilty. She didn't tolerate other men that treated her like this, but Brock's persuasion was different from everyone else. His dominance was her weakness. Her father wasn't the dominant male type. Her mother had been the dominant figure in her household. But her father had told her, repeatedly, throughout the duration of her life that she should never let a boy treat her badly or dictate her life. She'd been taught to treat herself with respect. She did. There hadn't been a boy yet that could hold her beneath their thumb. There was no high school sweetheart. No *boy that got away.* She wasn't disrespectful to the men in her life, but she wasn't very respectful either. Respect had to be earned and she gave it when it was due. And thus far, the only respectable men were teachers and her father. Brock was not in that category.

Funny how all that worked.

Brock's control over Brianna was degrading and she was a hypocrite to tolerate and accept it. Hypocrisy was an annoyance of hers. *How could she feel content if she was treating someone else lesser than she was being treated?* That wasn't fair, but she knew that she'd done it. Her relationship with Grady proved her point. Wanting to sexually experiment with her best friend was becoming harder to suppress. Humanity, or God, or the universe, or whatever created *all* was cruel in the construction of humanity. Brianna believed in reason and logic, yet there were aspects of her life that she couldn't control, which were illogical. Her mother was a Born Again Christian and therefore she had impressed upon her the idea of heaven and hell, but this didn't matter. Brianna struggled with her faith. There was no logic to the Immaculate Conception. She refused to believe in it. The idea that a supernatural entity had created *all* ascended from the heavens one night and impregnated a woman without sexual intercourse was absurd. People who believed this were lacking specific knowledge and common sense, she thought. Life and religion didn't work together. Life would be so much easier if Christianity could be proven with logical evidence, but it could not. That said, her attraction to Brock was also illogical in terms of her beliefs and convictions and she believed in the contradictory nature of humanity—an even more flawed ruler of all. Many aspects of her life were illogical these days. Being unable to control her fantasies about Brock, questioning God and her faith, and losing enthusiasm for the sport that had provided her a scholarship were causing her to question everything.

What next?

4

A staggered line of university students, and some townies, waited to get past the security guard and into The Quarter, which had met full capacity as it often did. Music blared, but the crappy kind—billboard top ten dance music. A cloud of cigarette and marijuana smoke lingered over the crowds as they drank their way to mental incapacity.

Lance wasn't particular about The Quarter. He also couldn't understand why the bar was named The Quarter except that at the rear of the establishment, by the pool tables, the wall was papered with a large photo of the New Orleans French Quarter during one of their Mardi Gras, maybe from the nineteen eighties. The owner was of Italian descent and came from Milwaukee. Whatever. In life, sometimes it was best not to think about such things, he thought.

Making their way into the bar was easy. They knew the bouncer, Ricky Mack, a big linebacker for the university football team, or at least he had been. He and Brock were friends, which had been convenient at times. Brock and Ricky often went out drinking and looking for tail.

Once inside the bar, Brock led the way as Lance followed. They weaved through crowds of drunken-horny patrons who whined about finals, coursework or where the next theme party was going to be held. Finally, they reached the bar. Brianna was always the center of attention. Lance hated to watch all these inebriated Neanderthals grabbing at her. It annoyed him that she brushed it off. It wasn't right. She probably enjoyed it. Actually, he couldn't say that. If someone were to touch her—in a private zone—she would stop, get in said Neanderthal's face, and express her mind until the bouncers closed in and diffused the situation.

Finally, all three found an opening and wedged themselves into the bar after a group of flighty freshmen were pulled onto the dance floor. Brock ordered a round of shots while they waited for Grady.

Twenty minutes and two shots later, Grady made an animated entrance by leaping onto Brock's shoulders and shouting, "Brock, you crazy man-slut!"

Brock didn't look thrilled but played the part and spun Grady, bumping into a crowd of drunks who looked annoyed.

Grady's juvenile behavior annoyed Lance, but he played along. He laughed, raised his glass, and downed half of his pint. The alcohol immediately began to take hold of his thoughts. He was buzzed enough that he hadn't realized he'd been staring at Grady and Brianna. He and Brock's relationship with Brianna had to feel somewhat awkward for Grady. His girlfriend spent all her time with the campus stud, and his sensible friend who were both single. There had to be an element of jealousy. Had to.

Brock lowered Grady from his shoulders and nearly dropped him onto his face before ordering another round of shots. They chased the shots—tequila this time—with a couple of light beers. Lance injected himself into the fun.

"How's it going, bro?" Grady addressed Lance with a handshake.

He kissed Brianna. "Hey, babe."

"I'm good, my man. You?" Lance responded. He hated Grady's California accent.

"Funniest thing ... I got invited to a Boxed Wine and Porno party. Never heard of such a thing, but it sounds pretty tight. You wanna go?" He looked to Brianna.

Brock laughed, clasped his hand on Grady's right shoulder and said, "Dude, we were gonna ask you if you wanted to go. Brianna said she wouldn't go without you, bro. You think you could persuade her?"

"For sure, bro." Grady nodded and took down a shot of Jameson that the bartender extended to him on the house. Then he looked to Brianna. "Let's go. It'll be twisted-hella-fun."

"Are you sure this is cool? I wasn't gonna go to a party *like that* with two guys that aren't my boyfriend." Brianna whispered in Grady's ear, but Lance heard her clearly. "I can't get all hot and bothered without my man."

Grady smiled, nibbled on Brianna's ear and finished his beer.

"Sweet." Brock dropped a twenty-dollar bill on the bar.

5

Wisconsin winters had a sharp bite. The holiday season was only a month ahead, but the climate had cooled significantly. The golden, earthy colored leaves had fallen from barren trees. The rustic scenery had been replaced by snow. The group of inebriated youths skipped and hollered down Ninth Street untethered by the icy weather and in good spirits. About a half-mile away from campus, down a residential street they stopped in front of a run-down three-story Victorian house. Ten or fifteen partygoers huddled around the porch smoking cigarettes while a few others puffed on joints. All appeared jolly on this frigid evening.

Brianna shared an embarrassed chuckle with Brock when the audible panting of a woman echoed from within the three-storied Victorian house. A party like this allowed sex to be casual. Being of the college age allowed for an excuse to throw an event like a boxed wine and porn party. The topic of sex positions told in a comedic setting allowed the cluttered youths—attending college and expanding their minds and views—to get worked up, make nervous jokes and ease into each other—if everything went right.

Brock looked to Brianna, Lance, then Grady and announced, "Strap on your boners, ladies. Here we go." Brock shot up the stairs, hugged a few random girls that he probably knew intimately, and shook hands with male acquaintances. A spicy black girl with perfectly set features and icy brown eyes placed a cigarette between Brock's lips and he inhaled. She whispered something in his ear and he smiled. He couldn't quite hear what she'd said, but it had something to do with her lips and his genitals, which only caused him to think of Brianna. Subconscious thought sent his glance toward Brianna as she leapt up the staircase. To his pleasure, she stared back. Quickly, she kissed Grady before he had a chance to become jealous. Brock didn't care that Grady noticed their gaze—one of those gazes where two people know they're entering taboo grounds.

"Come on, you losers!" Brock beckoned.

"Fuck you," Lance blurted out before he dashed up the cheap termite infested staircase and nearly tripped on the first step.

Brianna and Grady followed.

Entering the house, loud panting and moaning echoed in stereo and a thick crowd packed the living room. Glazed eyes and near-drooling mouths gathered, magnetized to the seventy-two inch flat screen that displayed a busty blonde with giant fake breasts being mounted by two beautiful tan boys. The girl begged for sex.

Brock glanced at the slobbering, drunken faces ingesting these animalistic images. All held cheap solo cups and sipped often from them. Smiles—either forced or genuine—were plastered to their geek faces. A few of the males kept *adjusting* themselves then looked up and around to ensure no one had witnessed their displacement of erections.

Brock twisted his attentive gaze toward the girls of Delta House and caught their seduction. Gina Benchley watched him, smiled, licked her lips and then went back to holding Crayton Minten's hand. After Crayton witnessed his girlfriend staring at Brock, he extended a scowl. Probably because he knew that Brock had slept with his girlfriend. Hell, he'd slept with everyone's girlfriend. A few weeks ago, while Crayton stayed with his parents, she had enjoyed Brock's presence. She didn't seem to care about having a boyfriend while she begged for Brock to do awful things.

A random junior sitting with his legs crossed on the floor shouted and laughed. "Is that a wart on that dude's dick?" He raised the remote and paused the image on a genital wart lumped outward from the adult film actor's bulging member.

"Yuck! Ew!" A few random shrieks filled the room. Most chugged alcohol to simmer the awkwardness.

"Hit play, dipshit." A jock kicked the boy sitting on the floor and he pressed play.

Jeff Torrance strolled through the party topping off solo cups with more boxed wine. He stopped in front of Lance and asked, "Where's your box, dude?"

"Right here." Brianna pointed below her belt buckle.

"Ha ha. You're funny," Jeff returned. "Hot chicks are cool, I'm talking about Brock, Lance, and this dude." He pointed to Grady.

"Can I give you some money?" Grady asked.

"I was really clear about everyone bringing boxed wine."

Lance chimed in, "Take it easy, Jeff."

"No, bro. I hate that shit. Get the memo." Jeff frowned, clearly disappointed.

"I totally understand," Lance returned.

"Dudes, you're good for now, but if we start running low you assholes are walking to the store." Jeff shook his head and moved on, continuing to fill drinks.

"What a dick," Brianna whispered.

"Yeah, but I recall that he was pretty intense about the whole *bring boxed wine* thing."

"Fuck him. Half these chicks wouldn't be here if it weren't for me," Brock gloated as he grabbed a solo cup from the counter.

The four walked into the kitchen, which crawled with more horny college kids. One couple obnoxiously groped each other in the corner by the cheap stove while a few uppity drunk boys watched and giggled. Everyone laughed at the couple when her ass knocked the toaster onto the floor.

"Get some!" Brock called out.

The girl parted from the boy, smiled at Brock, grabbed her boyfriend's crotch and shrugged her shoulders. The girl trailed off toward the staircase that led to the upstairs bedrooms. The stoned boys cackled and harassed them as they went.

"Fuck her, everyone else has!"

"Make sure you lick it before you stick it!" A girl called out. She was clearly inebriated and almost fell down after barking.

Throughout the party there were couples kissing or chatting. Their faces close with intent or watching each other with lustful eyes. Brock liked this atmosphere and the consistent tone. This was the perfect place to proposition Brianna.

Now, how was he going to get rid of Grady?

When Jeff Torrance bumped into him a few minutes later on his way to the bathroom, Brock devised a quick plan.

"Jeff!" Brock called out.

It took Jeff a moment to figure out where his name was being called from, but eventually he found Brock's smirk and shook his head. "Fuck do you want?"

"Hey, if you want, Grady will go get you that boxed wine."

"Dude, it's cool, just try and be cool next time. Everyone else brought booze or porn or some other shit. You just showed up," Jeff continued.

"You'd be doing both of us a favor if you got that California dude out of here for a few minutes," Brock influenced.

"You trying to bone his chick or something?"

"Something like that. And you owe me. Half these chicks wouldn't be here if I wasn't."

Jeff pondered this fact before he nodded approvingly.

6

Grady knew that his relationship with Brianna wouldn't last. Still, he enjoyed being with her. She was beautiful, smart, and fun to be around. Brock and Lance were cool, but their relationship with Brianna was odd, Grady thought. He got it, they'd grown up on the same street in some small Wisconsin town and they thought of each other like family. But she spent every waking minute with them. It was a little weird. Everyone on campus believed the rumors that Lance, Brock, and Brianna secretly had three-way sex, but Brianna emphatically denied these rumors and Grady believed her. Still, the idea had entered Grady's mind on occasion. He was certain that Lance was in love with her. That was obvious by the way he looked at her when he didn't know anyone was watching. But Grady had twenty-twenty peripheral vision. The protective nature that Lance provided for her was an indicator too. When she wasn't looking he was always watching her, checking out her body, staring at her with lustful eyes. But Grady accepted this behavior. He was getting what he wanted from her. Beside that, he knew she wasn't into Lance. Maybe Brock, but not Lance. When Grady had sex with Brianna it was fantastic. She wasn't quite willing to experiment the way he wanted her to, but she was spontaneous and knew how to push and pull and excite him to the point that he would have to think cold thoughts in order to simmer down.

And her ass was an American treasure. He could stare at her rump-bump for hours. She worked out all the time. Granted, she was at this university on an athletic scholarship, so that kept her going, but she liked to workout after practice too. He was a lucky guy and he'd treasure this relationship as long as it lasted. He'd never stay in this state forever either and she wasn't necessarily California material. He only wanted to live in the Midwest for a few of his college years. Being from California, he felt the need to escape the endless summer and see how the rest of the country lived. And it was cool, but he wanted to get back to the land of sunshine. He missed surfing and hanging out at the beach. He had a special group of friends. They hadn't grown up on the same block, but they were close and shared many of the same interests.

Grady's thoughts snapped back to the party when he felt a solid grip land on his forearm. Anger seized him for a moment and then he realized that it was Jeff, the owner of the house.

"Hey man, what's up?" Grady smiled.

"Hey dude, we're running low on boxed wine. I've been looking for Lance and Brock, but they're probably blowing each other in the bathroom. I'd ask Brianna, but that seems kind of rude, her being a chick and all."

Grady hated being the gopher that had to make the booze run. Back home he was too cool for this, but he understood. The house was running low on alcohol and he hadn't shown up with the required materials for entrance. "Yeah, is there a liquor store around here?"

"Yeah, bro. Just hang a right at the end of Ninth and you'll see a convenience store next to the Laundromat. Pick up two boxes of something white and we'll be alright."

"No problem," Grady said and felt a tug on his elbow, He turned to find Brianna.

"What was that all about?" she asked.

"Your buddies are MIA and someone needs to pick up more booze. You gonna be alright here for a few minutes if I run out?" Grady asked.

"I think I'll be alright. I might get groped by a drunken dipshit, but Lance and Brock are around to make sure nothing bad happens."

"Good." Grady checked his pockets, ensuring that he had enough scratch to afford a couple boxes of wine.

How much was a box of wine? Ten bucks?

He pulled out a wad of twenties and a ten, nodded, and then left into the chilly night air.

7

From the upstairs bedroom, Brock watched Grady stuff his hands into his pockets, lower his head to block the cold from his neck, and then stroll down the sidewalk toward the liquor store. Brock waited for Grady to round the corner before he pulled out his cell phone and texted Brianna to come upstairs. About three minutes later the bedroom door creaked open and Brianna's confused expression appeared, backlit by the flickering fluorescent hallway light.

"What the hell is this creepiness? Are you guys gonna like come out of the closet or something?"

Brianna was cracking jokes, but still didn't seem to be at ease with this situation. Brock couldn't blame her. He and Lance were tucked away in a small bedroom on the third floor where no one was supposed to be.

"Well, I'm pretty sure Lance is gay. And I get that this is awkward, but I need to talk to you about something." Brock said. He motioned for her to sit on a ratty reclining chair.

With some skepticism she took her seat.

"What's up?" Brianna asked.

"This is gonna be weird. I told him not to, but he's insisting," Lance stated, shaking his head as he turned away from Brianna.

"Insisting on what?" Brianna was starting to look annoyed.

"So, we've known each other all of our lives. We've done everything together."

"Yeah."

"I want to try something. The three of us," Brock continued. He was watching Brianna squirm in her chair. She looked from Lance to Brock and then shook her head.

"Do I want to know where this is headed?" she asked.

"Yes, you know you do." Brock stepped closer. "I want us to experience a three-way together."

Brianna stood, laughed hysterically, and walked toward the door.

Brock grabbed her arm, hard and she stopped. He had her attention. She didn't say anything, not stop, or fuck off. Nothing. She was considering the proposition and he knew it.

"I've wanted this for a long time. We're friends, yes, but we've reached an age where our curiosities are starting to get the best of us. I want us to experience each other."

"Like me being a girlfriend to both of you?" she asked.

"No. Like, we arrange a date to explore all of our fantasies that we've had for one another. I have them. You have them. Lance has them. Why can't we all be mature enough to explore this together?"

Brock watched Brianna's glance dart toward Lance, whose face flushed red.

Brianna took one quick look at Brock and then asked Lance, "This is your idea too?"

"No. It's all Brock."

"But you're not saying no?" Brianna pushed.

"I don't know what to say," Lance stuttered, clearly uncomfortable.

"You could have told Brock 'no' and that this is a very bad idea. That it will ruin our friendship," Brianna persisted.

Brock had become annoyed. He retrieved his knife and spun it in his hand. "Yes, he told me all of that, but luckily for you two I'm pretty good at reading people. I know this is something that's been on all of our minds for a while. At least I have the balls to address it. I want us to do this. If I'm right, we can take our friendship to the next level. We can be best friends, we can be like family, and we can explore our physical fantasies without guilt. We can be everything to each other and I think that we have the strength—as best friends—to do this."

"Can you put your stupid fucking knife away, please? Like this isn't uncomfortable enough." She stared at colored twinkle lights that dressed the window across the street while she waited for Brock to put the knife away before continuing. "Wow, my boyfriend is downstairs."

She turned to leave, but hadn't pulled her arm away from Brock. It remained limp in his hand. Brock knew that she wanted to be convinced. "Lance, do you want to do this?"

Lance's lips moved, but, like always, nothing came out because he was nervous and couldn't find the words.

"Say something!" Brianna shouted. "Do you want to fuck me while he fucks me?"

And then it happened. Brianna grabbed Lance's face. There was no lust in her actions, but she kissed him. Lance's expression was that of horror, but when Brock leaned in and kissed Brianna's ear, she eased up. Her mouth slowed into passion and she kissed Lance with less aggression. She even panted. With a hint of jealousy, Brock moved up behind her and slowly ground into her until she could feel his hardness. She lowered her hand and rubbed the outline of his erection.

"Is this what both of you want? Am I making you har—" Her words turned into pants when Brock slid his hand into her jeans and rubbed. Brock felt the vibration of Lance's trembling hand. He reached for her bosom. "Okay, okay, okay... I was half kidding."

They parted. Brianna's lips were swollen and red.

"I'm so sorry, I don't know what came over me," Lance pleaded and apologized.

Brock smiled and said, "I want more. Is that so bad?"

"What if I say no?" Brianna held a firm stance, her eyes narrowed.

"Then we'll pretend this never happened ... life will go back to the way it was. We'll be friends in the morning ... all honky-dory. Cool?"

Brianna shot her gaze toward Lance.

Lance looked to Brock for affirmation.

"This decision is on you, cowboy," Brock said.

Lance was silent for a long moment while he looked from Brianna to Brock. "Brianna, I'm sorry."

"For what? Be honest," Brianna returned. There was an edge to her voice.

"I want this and I want you, but I will do *anything* not to lose your friendship."

"And that means?" Brianna tapped her foot without noticing that she'd done so.

"That means that I think Brock is right. I think we all want to explore and experience each other. And I think that we're strong enough to do this without getting hurt or jealous or destructive with our friendship."

"Brianna?" Brock asked in a low voice. For the first time in a long time he sounded sincere, genuine.

Brianna stood silent. Then she stepped toward Lance, placed her lips gently against his, and held his kiss. Soon, their tongues twisted into something passionate. Brock stepped forward as if invited, but Brianna stiff-armed his chest to keep him at bay.

After a few more minutes, Brianna parted from Lance, turned and kissed Brock. When he attempted to place his hands on her ass she slid them down. When he tried to place them on her breasts she shoved them away. She parted from him briefly, looked him in the eyes, shook her head, and continued kissing him.

Brock finally understood. He let this be a telling kiss, a kiss that would decide what—if anything—would come next.

"I think that I need to think about this," Brianna stated. "When I kiss each of you I feel different things. With Lance I feel passion and with Brock I feel lust."

"And you can have both ... with both of us," Brock returned.

"I know and I want to, badly, but I also have to think about my soul and what I'm giving in to. Am I being tested? Will this change who I am? Will this change who we are? I love you both and so I have to think about these things before I make a decision."

Lance nodded, "I understand."

Brock remained silent, but nodded in agreement.

They turned toward the staircase when thundering footsteps pounded upstairs.

With a large smile on his face, Grady entered the bedroom. "I thought you dudes left me hanging."

Brock smiled, laughed and said, "Lance and I were trying to get your chick to have a three-way."

"Very funny, asshole. You really shouldn't joke about that kind of shit," Grady said.

"No shit, that was stupid," Brianna chimed in and slapped Brock's arm.

"What are you guys doing up here?" Grady asked, making eye contact with everyone in the room.

Brock quickly reacted by pulling out a freshly rolled joint from his pocket. "Would you care to join us?"

"Absolutely." Grady pulled a lighter from his pocket, kissed Brianna, and then lit the joint hanging from Brock's lips.

Brock looked to Lance and knew that he was wondering whether or not Grady could taste their lips on Brianna's. Brock also knew that Lance was going to feel guilt about turning Grady into a cuckold. Personally, Brock thought it was funny.

After smoking the joint, the four of them went downstairs.

Jeff stood at the base of the staircase stomping his foot. "I told everyone here not to go upstairs. I told everyone here to bring boxed wine. You four assholes are about to get kicked out of my party."

"Bro, we're sorry. I get it, we're batting zero-for-two, but give us one more chance," Brock chilled Jeff.

"Go in the living room, watch people fuck on TV, get laid, just don't go upstairs, cool?" Jeff lightened up.

"Cool," Lance said.

They entered the living room, looked to the flat screen television where a beautiful blonde was blowing a tan, muscle-bound boy that was all of twenty-one years old. Nonchalantly, Brianna leaned close to Brock and whispered, "I want to be that girl ... for you."

Brock knew it.

The pace of the night quickened from that point on. There were secret smiles and light touches of the hand. Even Lance enjoyed his time. He drank at least a box of horrible white wine by himself. Toward the end of the night he was stumbling. His speech was slurred, but he was talking excitedly, which was something that hadn't happened in quite some time. Toward two o'clock in the morning, when the party dwindled, Lance, Brock, Grady and Brianna sat on the couch. While they were all involved in intense conversation, the pornography blaring on the flat screen was a bit of a distraction.

"Is it weird that we're sitting here talking while two, sorry, four people are fucking on the TV in front of us?" Grady asked.

"I don't know. It should be weird, but this is college, which means that this is the time to do these things," Lance chimed in.

"What do you mean, 'do these things?'" Grady asked and for the first time he dropped the whole surfer-chilled-out-I-don't-get-mad-vibe. He looked genuinely perturbed.

"Like, attend parties where there's porn and boxed wine in every room of the house. This is a once in a lifetime experience that we're living, people. We need to enjoy this. Once we graduate there will never be another opportunity like this. You don't go out into the real world, get a job working in some cubicle and then decide to have a boxed wine and porn party. This only happens at college. That's all I meant, man," Lance explained.

"I hear you, man. I think I'm just tired is all." He turned to Brianna. "You want to go back to my apartment and act out some of this stuff?"

Brianna couldn't help but to shoot Brock a shameful glance. Brock was certain that Grady had seen this glance. "Yeah, you're going down on me for like twenty minutes first," Brianna said.

Grady perked and popped-up from the couch, grabbed Brianna's hand, and led her toward the front door.

Brianna stopped to hug Lance and Brock goodbye before she disappeared into the snowy night.

Brock wondered if she would fantasize about him and Lance or if she would stay with Grady in their future moment. Jealousy found its way into Brock's stomach and boiled into anger.

"You alright, man?" Lance asked, nearly falling off the couch.

"Yeah. I'm cool."

"You're thinking about whether or not she's going to imagine that its us while she's fucking that clown tonight, aren't you?"

"I take it you're having the same thoughts."

"I am." He chugged what was left of his cheap wine. "And hey, thank you."

"For what?"

"You were right from the get-go. I've wanted to experience this with the both of you for years." Lance nodded while filling his glass with more cheap wine.

"You're not into me, dude, are you?" Brock hadn't thought about that yet. Could his best guy-friend hold an attraction for him?

"No. I'm not gay. I would like to see you get raped though. Not for any sexual reasons. It would just be fun to watch you cry."

"And you think I'm a heartless prick?"

"Yes. Yes I do."

Two semi-attractive brunettes entered the room. Both clearly held an attraction to Brock. He smiled at them and then patted the cushion on the couch next to him.

The girls sat.

"You ladies want to find a quiet corner?" Brock asked.

The brunette with black-rimmed glasses bit her lip and nodded. "I have a boyfriend, but he's out of town for the weekend. This porn is really working me up."

"As it should. If you like, I can act out some of these positions for you," Brock continued. He turned to Lance who seemed to be doing just fine with the other brunette. Their faces were close, clearly about to kiss.

"Well, lets go find that corner before someone that knows any of our girlfriend or boyfriends finds us."

The four of them scurried through the house and back up to the third floor where they kissed and touched and sweated like vines of perfect flesh.

Chapter 4

Sexting

1

The punk rock band Social Distortion blared '*I Was Wrong*' from the bathroom where Grady sang badly in the shower. Pulling the blankets down, Brianna glanced at the outline of his naked body. She liked what she saw, but at the same time wished the shower door was closed. Letting her negative energy subside, she smiled as she remembered the intense lovemaking they'd shared during the early morning hours. A small amount of guilt interwove with her happiness as she had imagined that it was Brock tasting her. That it had been Lance pushing himself gently into her mouth. The penetration had been more animated than usual and Grady clearly enjoyed himself. He'd sounded like a kicked dog when he climaxed onto her chest. He'd thanked her repeatedly while laughing as he rolled onto his side of the bed.

"You want to jump in here, babe?" Grady called out from the bathroom through the spray of water cleansing his face.

Brianna leaned forward, allowing the blankets to fall from her naked breasts. Her nipples were still tender from the nibbling and pinching. Even though it was painful, she became aroused when she touched them. "Sure, keep the water warm." She slipped out of bed and made her way into the bathroom.

Grady's skin was red, swollen, and slippery from the hot water. She slid the shower door open—*more than it already was*—and stepped beneath the spray. Opening her eyes, she watched Grady morph into Brock. That arrogant smile that shouldn't turn her on glared from his face. He pulled her close and said, "Get in here and fuck me before your boyfriend comes home." She knew it was a fantasy, but felt her lower region generate heat.

Brianna fantasized answering, *Don't you think we'll get caught?*

I don't care, the fantasy Brock demanded.

Grady yanked Brianna fully into the shower and back into the present. He kissed her neck and her shoulders and then leaned down and kissed her breasts. He continued lower, knelt in front of her and kissed her *down there*. She couldn't help but to imagine that it was Brock doing these things to her.

"Oh my God, I'm gonna come," she panted.

He stood and forcefully pushed her toward the corner of the shower where the porcelain jutted out into a shelf. Grady shoved the shampoos and conditioners onto the tile floor for her to prop her leg up and spread her ass cheeks, giving him better access. Again, she imagined that it was Brock entering her. She panted hard. The shampoo bottle resting in front of her became Lance's member and she lightly stroked it. The focused expression on Lance's face popped into her thoughts and then she was into it, being ravaged by Lance and Brock at the same time, or so she imagined. It didn't take long before she was practically screaming.

Judging by the cockeyed grin on Grady's face, Brianna knew that his thoughts were revving high because of her heated behavior. He pulled out and ejaculated onto the top portion of her ass. She enjoyed the feel of water running his semen down the back of her legs. She stood and turned to him and he put his arms around her. Grady smiled wide like a high school sophomore after receiving his first hand job.

"Wow, between last night and this morning ... it's never been this good for me ... ever," Grady breathed deeply.

"Likewise. I like where this is going." Brianna spoke to Grady, but thought of her boys.

"Can we do it again?" Grady begged.

"Maybe tonight."

"Promise." Grady held out his pinky finger and she wrapped hers around his.

"You know how to move your mouth," Brianna laughed, making light of the situation.

"Likewise." He kissed her. "Cheers to talented mouths."

Brianna popped her lips. Both laughed. There was a brief stutter to her laughter when she felt the stab of guilt slide into her stomach. She'd only enjoyed the sex this much because she imagined it was with her boys. Last night, she, Lance, and Brock had opened Pandora's box and now there would be no other way to extinguish this fire, but to act on their desires. That would mean she was going to premeditate an affair, and pull one over on the boyfriend that held her now. The boyfriend that had not done anything wrong and would be crushed if he found out.

2

Brianna and Grady ate breakfast at a small diner just off of campus. She had cottage cheese with a fruit cup while

Grady pounded a garden burger and salad—only a California boy would eat something meat-free in the heart of the Midwest. He paid the tab and left her to sip on her third cup of coffee while he split to his Geology Lab. When she was certain he'd left she went into the bathroom and lowered her pants and thong. She aligned her iPhone centered behind her and took a picture of her ass. After placing the appropriate filter over the photo, she scrolled through her contacts and selected Lance and Brock. She didn't hit send. She went back to her booth and contemplated the *dos* and *don'ts* of sexting. Never had she sexted anyone before. In fact, she thought that it was reckless and stupid to send nude pictures across iPhones. But the thought of what Brock and Lance would do when they saw the photo was driving her. The power of her sex over them was intense and overwhelming. The thought of Brock touching himself while holding his phone out and looking at her naked ass caused tremors. She hated that she'd become *that girl.* She was a good girl. Always had been. But this was college and her sexuality was blooming to fruition at a rapid pace. She would have to act on these desires at some point. *Why not with her best friends?* They wanted this just as bad as she did. And then it made sense.

She clicked *send.*

3

Bored, Brock sat at a small desk in English Composition 104 with his right leg propped up on the empty desk in front of him when his cell phone began to buzz from his front jeans pocket. At first, he disregarded the text. *Maybe it was one of his conquests from last week?* Who knew, but whoever was texting him at noon on a Thursday afternoon could kick rocks. Then he thought better of it. *What if there was a party with limited space?* He'd need to submit his distinguished guest list. Making sure the professor wasn't looking, he pulled his iPhone from his pocket, entered his PIN and waited less than half of a second for the text to pop up. The box was small, but he could see that the picture included a good amount of flesh. Then he saw that the text was from Brianna. *What the hell?* Clicking on the text message caused him to gulp and almost cough. Glancing around the lecture hall, he made sure that no one was watching. His hand trembled when he saw the picture of Brianna's perfectly formed ass. He'd never actually seen her naked. Now, he couldn't un-see it. Her backside was perfect. It was firm and athletic and tan except for the G-String of whiteness. God, he loved it when a woman had that G-string tan line. His erection slowly bulged from within his jeans. His cheeks were reddening.

Brock excused himself from class, went to the restroom, entered the stall at the far end and then pulled *it* out. Fully erect, he snapped a naughty picture and sent it to Brianna.

She quickly texted back, *This is definitely going to happen. Need to talk.*

Brock sent an Emoji of a thumbs-up and included the text, *I'll invite Lance.*

She returned a smiley face emoji.

Chapter 5

Killers Will Kill

1

Soft footsteps lumbered into the small upstairs bedroom. His wet boots compressed the soft gray carpeting. The desk chair rolled back. The Killer sat in front of a laptop computer that was neatly set on a wooden desk. A drawer opened and a gloved hand removed electronic devices that he then plugged into his laptop using USB connectors. The familiar sound of the computer generating life chimed in. Looking out the window and across the street he watched Jeff Torrance stringing Christmas lights—horribly—along the side of his house in preparation for another keg party.

The Killer hadn't found his next victims. These victims had chosen him. These beautiful people would become perfect sacrifices. Planning, stalking, hunting and killing them would be a great challenge, but that didn't matter right now. Right now, the killer wanted to celebrate and acknowledge that the Dark Lord had led him to this perfect sacrifice. He didn't know why these souls were chosen. The Dark Lord led him and he had simply followed. When he prayed he was able to feel instinct and then act on it. He was a worthy servant and he knew that he would be rewarded in Hell. His work here on earth was purposeful. The knowledge that The Afterlife was real and that a spiritual plain of existence existed was powerful. The Killer understood the magnitude of this idea and lived to torment and destroy. The satanic powers driving him allowed for fulfillment without restriction. He was thankful for this gift.

Inserting the thumb-sized SD card from his camera into the card reader that plugged into the side of his Mac Book Pro, the Killer waited for his video footage to import. The screen finally brightened and the image of a painted yellow smiley face with red devil's horns digitized into clarity. A distorted voice crackled, "The next souls to be sacrificed to our Dark Lord are among us."

The camera being used tilted. The image twisted from a dark, masked face to the house across the street where—from a distance—Lance, Brock, and Brianna entered a three-story home where a raging college party was clearly going off. When the front door opened, a flat screen TV with pornographic images exposed itself from inside the living room.

The Killer's camera zoomed-in through the plate glass window and focused on an attractive blonde girl while she took a beautiful, young, tan boy in her mouth.

The Killer tapped his finger onto the keyboard, which fast-forwarded the footage until it showed Brock, Lance, and Brianna circled together in the upstairs bedroom of the house. The footage showed Brianna kissing both Lance and Brock. The camera zoomed out and then down to the sidewalk in front of the house where another young man entered carrying two boxes of cheap wine. The Killer turned the camera toward himself. His mask held the same design as the painted rock he'd displayed earlier—a smiley devil face. The computer had synthesized his voice to sound demonic.

The voice stated, "I will tear their flesh from their bones before I wrench into their souls and rip them from their beings."

The Killer laughed hysterically. "If they only knew that their vanity has killed them ... their beauty will hurt when I deform and mutilate their bodies."

The laughter continued, but the images on the computer switched to another video. This new footage was raw, real, and shook. In it, a row of three young, naked women screamed as thorny bullwhips tore their skin from their bodies. The whips cracked repeatedly until blood splattered the camera lens creating a red filter. Although hard to see through the blood, the shapes of four masked killers enveloped the naked women.

And the screams entered new heights of torment.

Chapter 6

Moving Forward

1

Lance was sitting on the couch sipping hot Green Tea and wondering why the cushions smelled like Brock's God-awful deodorant-spray when Brianna knocked on the door. He started to rise from his seat, but Brock hustled to let her in. He answered smiling, and showed Brianna to the couch where she sat next to Lance making brief eye contact. After a moment of acknowledging the cozy white twinkle lights that Brock had draped around the living room, she nodded, started to say something, but decided not to. She wore a pair of light blue jeans that conformed nicely to her ass and legs. Lance was fairly certain that she was attempting to seduce and was aware of her progress.

Brock took a seat on the chair in the corner, lifted his beer can and tapped the lid with his index fingernail in an attempt to settle the carbonation. The crack and hiss drew everyone's attention.

"Brianna, you want a beer?" Brock asked. "Lance already has his little sissy drink."

"I would like a giant glass of wine and for the time being you're going to stop antagonizing Lance. I don't think of you as more masculine when you emasculate Lance. You always do that when you're nervous. After you get my wine we're going to sit down and talk about how this *experiment* is going to go down. I want to know what the rules are and how and when we're going to ... you know."

"Understood." Head down, Brock took a sip from his beer then stood and marched into the kitchen.

Brianna looked to Lance who was staring into his cup of tea, clearly attempting to avoid eye contact.

"You know if we're going to do *this* you're going to have to look at me ... at some point." Brianna placed her hand on Lance's leg and squeezed lightly. She could feel the muscles and ligaments tensing beneath his skin. She almost smiled. Holding this much control over her friend was enthralling and empowering. She almost hated that she loved having this level of control. And when she slid her fingers along the inside of Lance's thigh and he let out a whimper she felt nearly as vulnerable as he did.

Brock returned from the kitchen with a spotted wine glass filled to the rim. He handed it to Brianna. "For the lady." His eyes fell to Brianna's hand, which was still inching its way up Lance's thigh. "We're already starting?"

"No, we're not," Brianna stated with authority. "We're going to talk about the rules and about what we each want to get out of this experience. Lance, we're going to start with you. What do you want me to do with you?"

"Why do I have to start?" Lance whispered.

"Because, if we're going to do this then you need to be comfortable telling me what you want me to do. Our inhibitions need to cease. You're going to need to look me in the eyes." She grabbed his chin and tilted his head toward hers. "And its okay to say things like, 'Brianna, suck my cock and let me cum on your face.' Does that make sense?"

Lance's face turned bright red.

Without realizing that he'd done so, Brock adjusted himself.

Lance sat up and said, "Ye ... ye ... yes, ma'am."

"You don't have to call me ma'am." Brianna leaned in toward Lance and kissed the corner of his mouth.

"And now what I want?" Brock stepped toward the couch and took a seat next to Brianna.

Brianna pushed him away and said, "No, now we're going to talk about what I want."

"What do you want?" Lance leaned forward to the edge of his seat. He licked the dryness from his lips.

"Whoa, slow down, cowboy. A little too eager," Brianna laughed.

Lance's face turned magenta. He sat back in his chair and sighed.

"First of all, I want both of you to take your clothes off."

"You first," Brock insisted.

Brianna stood and walked to the door. Without a word, she twisted the knob and left.

"What the hell, dude?" Lance barked at Brock while he sprung to his feet and dashed to the door. He twisted the knob, stepped outside, looked from left to right and couldn't find Brianna. She was gone.

2

Both Brock and Lance attempted to call Brianna over the next few hours, but her cell phone went straight to voicemail and, go figure, it was full.

"You should have let her talk," Lance fussed.

"I didn't know she was gonna leave," Brock returned.

"She was trying to make a point. If you think about this, we're asking more than a lot of her. Just the fact that she entertained this idea is crazy. Now, she's probably back at her dorm room smacking her head against the wall and asking herself why she'd even considered this."

As if on cue, both Lance and Brock's cell phones chirped with a text message. Coins and a set of keys spilled, jangled, and scattered on the floor as Brock scrambled through his pockets, searching for his iPhone.

Lance was already checking his messages.

The text read, *Be back at eight o'clock. You will both be naked and sitting on the couch in the living room. I want candles lit and a glass of red wine in a nice, clean wineglass. If the wine is cheap or one of you isn't naked then I'm leaving. Understood? Answer with a simple yes or a simple no.*

They both answered *yes*.

"What should we do now?" Lance had no instinct other than turning to Brock.

"You should go to the store and buy a fifty dollar bottle of Cabernet. I'll find some fucking candles and get this pig trough ready for action."

"Wow, this is really happening." He turned in circles and nearly fell on his ass when he tripped over his own shoelace. "Hey Brock?" Lance calmed.

"Yes?"

"Promise me she isn't just another conquest."

"Fuck you. I care more about her than you do. It's not like she isn't going to enjoy this, dude. Think about how empowered she is already. We're running around like a bunch of idiots. We're about to be sitting in the living room with no clothes on waiting for her. We don't even know that she's going to sleep with us. Thus far, she's just making us feel vulnerable while she establishes that she's in control."

"I see your point."

"You should, it's a good one. Now go get that fucking bottle of red."

Lance grabbed his wallet from the coffee table and marched out the front door.

3

Hands shaking from the excitement of what was to come, Lance strolled down the wine aisle of the local grocery store checking the price tags of each bottle of red wine. Sure, this was a cheap college town grocery store, but they'd likely have a few selections of decent wine. The kind Brianna would enjoy—something smooth, something tart. Brianna enjoyed all things tart: candies, foods, and full-bodied wines. Oddly, he remembered past Halloweens when he, Brock and Brianna would go trick or treating. She'd insisted that he and Brock give her their Sweet Tarts.

"Watcha lookin' for?" A young clerk tapped Lance's shoulder.

Startled, he twisted and nearly punched her.

"Sorry, you scared me."

"Am I that ugly?" The clerk laughed, her beautiful smile lighting up her face. Even in her work clothes she was a knock out. Her blonde hair was pulled back in a ponytail and her black-rimmed glasses accentuated her sparkling sapphire eyes. Her breasts jutted out from her tight button down. Lance glanced at her shirt where her nametag announced that her name was Natalee.

Lance took a moment to imagine a cheesy pornographic scenario with Natalee.

Maybe she'd rip her shirt open and expose her breasts while he freed her hair from the ponytail and she dropped to her knees before begging him to enter her.

"You certainly are not ugly," Lance stated, matter-of-factly.

He could tell that she was interested. Intimidating boys probably came easy to her, but she still enjoyed the sensation of a good ego stroke. Her down-to-earth attitude, which was obviously a façade, was equally attractive. After surviving the intimidation that Brianna had subjected him to, Lance now displayed confidence when speaking with the opposite sex, even a young woman as attractive as Natalee.

"Well, um, that's nice of you to say. What kind of wine are you looking for?" she asked.

"Something expensive, something tart." Lance made intense eye contact with Natalee and slightly leaned in toward her.

"Lucky girl," the store clerk blushed.

"Yes, she is."

"What's the occasion?" she asked.

"My friend and I are going to seduce a beautiful woman into fucking both of our brains out at the same time." Lance couldn't believe he'd told her the truth. It was empowering to watch Natalee become uneasy, not offended, and unavoidably seduced.

"I, um, wow. I don't know what kind of wine goes with a three way. How about this?" She retrieved a bottle of semi-cheap wine. Ironically, the brand name was *Ménage A Trois*.

She smiled through the awkward silence that followed. She and Lance surveyed the aisle to see that no one was watching and then shared a laugh.

Lance took the bottle plus another more expensive one just in case, and after he'd paid, Natalee found him on the sidewalk just outside the sliding glass doors and slipped him her phone number on a small piece of notepad paper.

"Just in case you're ever looking for a girl to laugh with," Natalee smiled before she turned and walked back into the grocery store.

Sexual enlightenment felt like the cure to his lack of confidence. Lance thought of the random store clerk as he walked through the parking lot. He felt as if his skin was glowing. He'd never been hit on by someone so good-looking in the past nor been able to reciprocate with confidence. Her attraction resonated with him. Even in the clutches of embarrassment she'd come up with humor. That was an outstanding quality. She reminded him of Brianna.

Pulling the bottle of *Ménage A Trois* from the brown paper bag, he spun it in his hand while naked images of he and Brianna flitted through his mind.

In this moment he was able to connect with Brock on a level he'd never been able to before. Being the object of attraction was a powerful sensation. He now understood Brock's addiction to it.

He returned to his off-campus house. The door was locked. He searched his pockets for the keys and then remembered he'd left them on his bedroom dresser. Peering through the plate glass window, he watched Brock hang a black bed sheet over the entirety of the window facing the side of the house. Brianna would think the cheap black sheet was juvenile, but she'd also know that Brock put it there. Hopefully it wouldn't turn her off. Placing the pad of his index finger on the doorbell, he pushed. Nothing. Titling his head to the side, Lance remembered that he'd never actually rung his own doorbell before and wasn't sure if he'd ever locked the front door.

The things you learn about your immediate surroundings while in preparation for diverse activity.

Then he pounded his fists into the front door and yelled, "Open up, dick-bag!"

Next door, Mr. O'Reilly, stepped out onto the porch and yelled, "I have to deal with your shit almost every night. Can you clean up your talk during the day, please?"

"Hey, Mr. O'Reilly," Lance returned, respectfully.

As he turned to continue knocking, Brock answered the door.

Lance was startled to find Brock naked and sporting half an erection. "What the hell, dude? You ever heard of a towel?" Lance barked and then turned to see that Mr. O'Reilly was shaking his head.

Brock stepped onto the porch, smiled, and waved to Mr. O'Reilly. "Would you like to stop over for a cup of tea and a blowjob? My girlfriend here—" Brock clapped a strong hand on Lance's shoulder. "—has a really special mouth. Fat inner cheeks."

Mr. O'Reilly shook his head and slammed his door.

Old man probably had a heart attack.

"What the fuck, dude?" Lance grabbed Brock's arm and tossed it off his shoulder.

"Don't you dare bruise my perfect arm-skin," Brock leaned forward, flexed his muscular arms. "This body is the image of male perfection," Brock informed Lance.

"You gotta be fucking kidding me."

"Get in here! Brianna will be here in like an hour." Brock powered Lance through the front door.

Once in the house, Lance surveyed the living room and was oddly impressed that Brock had cleaned the place up. Brock had dusted and a faint odor of carpet powder wafted through the living room.

He'd vacuumed.

"Jesus, the place has never looked so good, dude. I can't believe it, but I'm proud of you."

"You are proud, aren't you? There's a parade for that kind of pride."

"Is there anything about you that isn't offensive?"

"I don't even know what that means," Brock stated.

"Let's see, you're sexist, racist, homophobic—"

"Can't help who I am. Is that all you got? I think you're just jealous of my confidence, " Brock combated.

Lance was having a hard time concentrating while Brock stood—erect—in front of him. "Can you please cover up? And why do you have a boner? I'm the only one here."

"I was thinking that I could warm up on you," Brock's face remained intense. There was no joke about this expression and it scared Lance. "You know, like in that movie *Something About Mary* when the friend tells him to rub one out before he goes on his date. That way he'll be more relaxed. I figured if I fuck your mouth then I'll be one nut deep and I'll last longer when Brianna gets here. It's not gay if it's warm-up sex."

"What. The. Fuck. Is. Wrong. With. You? You'd fuck me?"

"It's not as bad as you think, dude. Your ass looks like a chick's ass. Just kind of tuck your cock and balls and bend over the hassock." Brock stepped toward Lance. "And spread 'em." His head cocked to the side and he continued, "Maybe take a shower and shave your asshole first."

"I…I…Um…" Lance was convinced that Brock was no longer kidding and so he stepped backward toward the staircase defensively. His friend had had so much pussy that he'd become gay, or bisexual. Vaginal sex wasn't enough anymore. Lance looked to the front door, ready to flee when Brock broke into laughter. His erection bounced and flopped as he laughed, which was incredibly distracting.

"Dude, you should see the look on your face. You look like Olaf just got ass hammered by Thor. I'm hard as fuck because I took two Viagra just after you left. I'm not going soft on Brianna. No way. No how." He glanced at his member and gave it a swat. "I couldn't get this thing down if I tried."

Lance was relieved, but at the same time he still felt awkward to be having such an in-depth conversation with his naked friend. This was incredibly uncomfortable. "Can't you put a dishtowel over it or something?"

"I could, but I'm trying to get over the discomfort of being naked in front of you. We're about to have a threesome with our best chick-friend. There will probably be moments when you're touching me and I'm touching you ... Not on purpose and not in a homosexual way, but it's just going to happen. It's not outside the realm of possibility that we cross swords on accident. So, strip down. We might as well get used to this."

Again, Lance hated it when Brock had a point. "You got any extra Viagra?" Lance shook his head while disrobing.

"I might get nervous."

Chapter 7

Brianna's Here

1

Naked and sitting on the couch, Brock and Lance remained silent. The situation was awkward. They stared at their iPhones in an attempt to avoid looking at each other.

When the digital clocks on their phones struck seven o'clock, Brianna rang the doorbell.

Brock turned to Lance, unavoidably glanced at his nakedness, tried not laugh and said, "You need to work out a little more, but don't worry—you look good and remember to be confident."

"I can't believe you just said that right before we open the door and possibly have a threesome with our beautiful, best friend. I'm nervous as hell, dude," Lance quipped.

Brock was aware that he'd involuntarily ribbed his friend. Thinking about what he'd said—and what it must have done to Lance's psyche—he realized that he'd been hurtful. Considering how nervous Lance was he may have given him a stigma and aided in diminishing his confidence, *if he had any to begin with.* But the show had to go on. Naked as the day he was born and fully erect, Brock walked through the living room and answered the door.

"You're happy to see me." Brianna's gaze immediately dropped to Brock's erect member.

"You asked that we be naked." He looked her over. "We are." Brock stepped aside so that Brianna could enter the house. He was aware that she would have to brush against his erection in order to get through the door.

She marched in briskly and reached out a hand to scrape the head of Brock's penis with a long fingernail before closing the door. He winced.

A cold gust of wind circled the living room and caused the candle flames to dance. "I like the candles. The atmosphere is nice." She looked to the kitchen table and stated, "You got the wine." She picked up the bottle of Ménage A Trois. "This is very clever." She looked to Lance. "This is you."

"I figured—"

"You figured correctly." Brianna set the bottle down, turned to Lance then Brock, smiled, and allowed the blue sundress she wore to fall to the floor. She wasn't wearing a bra. Her skin was red, slightly burned. It was the middle of winter. Obviously, she'd been to a tanning bed. The fresh tan lines were fairly even and barely visible around her handful-sized breasts. Her quarter-sized nipples were erect. Her fingers lightly shook as she lowered her hand to her hip and strummed the string of her black lace thong. She spun one hundred and eighty degrees so that he and Lance could see each of her perfect curves and contours. Then she bent over, removed her thong and parted her legs. All she wore now were black high heels and a silver necklace with a black heart that rested symmetrically between her breasts. She stood and turned to them, tossing the panties at their feet. Her silky blond hair was pulled back into a ponytail except for a few strands that hung perfectly to the side of her face. Clearly done on purpose. Slowly, she slid the stray strands of hair behind her ear and smiled. The faint, very expensive, perfume she wore intoxicated Brock and triggered lustful thoughts.

Having known Brianna for her entire life, Brock knew that this perfume came from a bottle that she saved for special occasions. He knew that she kept a *secret* bottle because she always conferred with he and Lance before going out on a *special* date. On special dates she wore this specific brand.

How sweet.

It was the scent of arousal.

Head down with his hands crossed over his genitals, Lance offered, "You look perfect, Brianna."

Brianna walked toward Lance until they were only inches apart. Brock suddenly felt jealous. He tried to imagine what the body heat that was undeniably felt between Lance and Brianna was like. Two naked bodies standing this close together, their body heat radiated to a comforting degree. Brock thought Lance would spontaneously combust. He was red and shaking. He could almost hear his friend's heart pounding beneath his ribcage.

"Thank you, Lance," Brianna whispered in Lance's ear and then kissed him on the lips. Then she pulled away, turned to Brock and asked, "Brock, are you wanting to do animalistic things with me?"

For the first time in a long time Brock was tongue-tied. He knew that Brianna enjoyed catching him off-guard. "Yeah, I mean…"

She interrupted, "No, you'll not talk to me like you're fifteen. For that I will punish you."

"How's that?" Brock asked while a smirk found his face.

"You will watch me pleasure Lance. And you will not touch me. If you touch me I'll leave and never talk to you again."

"Watch you what?" Brock was curious yet becoming disappointed.

Brianna squatted then rested on her knees.

Lance looked to Brock as if for help. He was scared. Luckily, Brock had given him that Viagra he'd asked for or he'd go limp as a noodle. Nerves were capable of murdering sex.

Brianna slowly parted her knees, straightened her back, leaned forward and placed Lance's erection in her hand. She kissed the tip of it and then slid her tongue along the side before filling her mouth.

Brock was about to explode. He watched her suck, tickle, stroke, and pleasure Lance. Also, he knew what a pleasured woman looked like and Brianna looked pleasured. *She liked sucking cock.* But she didn't pay any attention to him, which made him feel metaphorically naked. He looked up at Lance. His eyes were closed and he gnawed on his bottom lip. Clearly, he was about to burst. Looking like he was about to cry, an aggressive pant escaped him.

Brock's gaze tilted to Brianna's perfect, heart-shaped backside while she slowly slicked back and forth on Lance's member.

"May I please join in?" Brock felt humbled. He'd never been on the verge of begging, but he was now.

Brianna made a slurping sound as she pulled Lance out of her mouth. She slowly tugged while she turned a seductive smile toward Brock and said, "Beg, you pathetic tool."

Brock's anger melded cohesively with his attraction. He found a balance that allowed him to say, "Please, please, I'm sorry for being a jerk earlier."

"What will you do for me?"

"What do you want me to do for you?"

"Good answer." Brianna stood, still stroking Lance, and turned to Brock. "I'll show you." She kissed Lance before swaying toward Brock. "Get on your knees."

Brock said nothing. He dropped to his knees, nearly shaking when Brianna tilted her head toward him and demanded, "Eat it." Then she swung her leg over his left shoulder and rested it while shoving herself into his face.

Brock had never been this turned on in all of his life. He breathed her in. Obviously, she'd dabbed her *parts* in the secret perfume, which smelled and tasted sweet. His tongue twirled while his lips pulled and kissed. Brianna flung her head back and moaned. Brock's eyes were closed, but when he opened them he saw that Lance was touching himself. He was tempted to laugh at the ridiculousness of his friend. He didn't, knowing full well that the motion of this sacred ritual would halt if he did. Lance's feet shifted on the hardwood floor. Brock knew that Lance was debating whether or not to join them. His lust had taken over logical thought. His eyes shifted and found Brianna's. Her head was drawn backward while she looked at him. She raised her hand, pointed her index finger at Lance and told him, "Get over here now."

Lance did as he was told. When he reached Brianna, Brock became uncomfortable. Looking up, Brock watched Lance's erection sway close to his face. Comfort dissipated. Brianna's expression spoke clearly: *drop your inhibitions*. Brock stopped nibbling on Brianna and tilted his face upward, toward her face. He only met Brianna's palm.

"Did I tell you to stop?" she scowled, grabbed Lance and directed him toward her ass where she rested him between her cheeks.

"No," Brock responded and continued to pleasure her. He hadn't realized how much physical exertion he'd expended until he felt heavy beads of sweat trickle down his forehead.

"Now you can stop." She tapped Brock's forehead.

She held her hand out to Brock and helped him to his feet. "Now sit in that chair and watch us fuck." She pointed to Brock's ratty recliner.

Brock went to the chair and took a seat, as ordered. No other woman had ever, could ever, or would ever boss him around like this, ever again. But it was okay for Brianna. She was good. She'd driven him to near madness. He watched with heightened anticipation while Brianna led Lance to the couch. She bent over then propped herself onto her knees, spread her hips, and lifted her ass. Once she was on all fours she pulled Lance by his penis. Brock couldn't see details because the only light source was candlelight. The fiery glow illuminating the room diminished any minor imperfections. All three appeared golden, like royal Gods and Goddess in the orgasmic throes of a sacred orgy, their sweat like honey.

Brianna turned to Lance, smiled, and whispered, "You can fuck me silly now."

Moaning loud with undeniable vulnerability, Lance pushed inside of Brianna and immediately pounded into her softness.

"Slower." She pushed a flattened hand against his pelvis, preventing him from fully entering her.

"I'm sorry."

"No apologies." Brianna's lips curled. She wiggled backward until she was bucking at him. Slow and gentle, Lance pushed into her. The intensity of his expression revealed all.

Brock couldn't help but to rub his penis. He'd never been so turned on in all of his life.

"Stop rubbing your cock! I told you to watch. If you don't stop, I will stop, grab my clothes and leave, which means you'll have ruined this entire experience for your friend."

Brock was mortified. He glanced at Lance who silently begged him to stop. Frightened by the thought of this night and its pleasures ending, Brock stopped masturbating, nodded and said, "I'm sorry."

"Damn right, you are." Brianna swayed her hips in sync with Lance's thrusts. She turned to him and asked, "Shall we let him play?"

Lance looked to Brock, smiled with quivering lips then turned to Brianna and said, "I think he's learned his lesson."

"Brock."

"Yes, Brianna?"

"How would you like to switch places with Lance?" she asked.

"I would very much like that…" He closed his eyes and hated his friend. "If that would be okay with Lance."

"That was very nice, Brock. That's what I like. You weren't selfish for once in your life. Come on over here." She turned to Lance and ordered, "Stand in front of me. I want to know what I taste like… on your dick."

Lance stood and made his way in front of Brianna until his erection was directly in her face.

Brock made his way to the back of Brianna. Gently, she grabbed his testicles and applied light pressure. Brock moaned. Then she guided him inside of her.

His excitement heightened. She felt like warm oil. Brock felt like melting inside of her. These sensations were of no comparison to any one-night-stand he'd experienced. The overwhelming sensation of sexual bliss blended with genuine care for his friend. Sure, she was dominant. He understood that this part was *her* fantasy. He cared about her receiving joy. He couldn't deny the lustful sensations he felt when she dominated him. And the obvious joy and love he sensed when Lance experienced the woman he'd loved gave this night meaning.

Watching his friend experience pure bliss, both emotional and spiritual, he felt grateful. For the first time, he received contentment from someone else's joy.

There was no doubt that Brianna enjoyed what was happening. Her lust was intense, made obvious by her expressions, sounds, and enthusiasm. Brock hoped she felt as uninhibited and free as he did.

And then Brianna halted her movements. She extracted Lance from her mouth, stood and stated, "Take me to the bedroom."

Naked, sweaty, with a pounding heart, Brock followed Brianna and Lance upstairs. Slightly hesitant, Brianna stopped when she reached the top of the stairs. Brock imagined she was debating whose room was more suitable. It took only seconds for her to choose Lance's room.

Brock and Lance watched Brianna walk, exhausted, but seductively to the far end of the hallway. She opened the door. More candlelight bled through the space between the door and jamb and blessed her skin with an attractive glow. Her right hand rose. Her index finger retracted then flexed as she motioned for the boys to follow her.

Brock shared genuine appreciation with his friend before they filed into the bedroom. Brianna's backside looked impossible.

Entering, Brock was amazed to acknowledge the immaculate state of Lance's domicile. Sure, Lance had always been clean, but this—the state of immaculate shape that his room was in—was something more than neat. His vanity mirror had been wiped spotless. The sheets dressing the bed were pulled taught and tightly tucked into the corners of the mattress. A hospital nurse from the 1950's would be proud to place a patient in this bed. Even the carpet was vacuumed. The dressers had been wiped clean with pine scented *something*—something nicer than the

Pledge that had cleansed the downstairs rooms. The candles released vanilla scented aromatherapy. Even the photos and posters lining the wall were symmetrical and hung evenly. Brock was proud of Lance's cleanliness and the scent was calming, relaxing.

Brock and Lance watched Brianna pull the bed sheets back and then slide beneath the soft fabric. Rolling onto her back, she looked from Lance to Brock and with an intense scowl she stated, "Now, we'll make love."

Brock knew better than to laugh when Lance groaned. He was simply unable to abstain his sexual intensity.

What a poor, lovesick puppy.

But Brock respected Brianna's decision to change the tone of their experience. They were experimenting new avenues of sexual bliss. He too needed this emotional continuation, which extended sexual variety to their evening.

Lance rounded the bed from the right while Brock marched along the left side. Brock felt the warmth of Brianna's skin. He felt her heart hammering beneath her bosom.

"What would you like me to do?" Brock asked in what he'd hoped was a low, comforting voice.

"Be gentle. Care, Brock Hills," Brianna whispered back. The slight tremble to Brianna's voice gave away her vulnerability. "Then slip inside me from the front."

"I can't wait, Brianna Zastrow." Brock felt and sounded genuine, true.

Brianna moaned, closed her eyes, and swayed her hips in perfect motion with Brock's pelvis.

After a few moments, she opened her eyes, turned toward Lance and whispered, almost stuttered, "Slide into me from behind." She noticed the confusion on Lance's face. Gently sliding her hand along his penis she directed it below her vagina and into the *other place* then said, "It's okay. I promise."

Lance nodded, groaned again and then entered her anus. In the heat of this moment he didn't mind that he could feel Brock through the thin wall separating Brianna's vaginal canal from her anus.

Brianna nearly cried as he fully entered. Slowly, the three best friends made real, true, uninhibited love. It was sweet and it was respectful and it was everything that Brianna, Brock or Lance had experienced.

Brock paid close attention to Brianna's pained face as her men filled her completely. He thrust into her—with her—in a fashion that he felt wouldn't hurt her. He only cared for her pleasure.

Also, Brock noticed Lance trying not to lose control. His excitement was clearly heightened. Brock recognized the eagerness and lustful pleasure that Lance fought. An intensely loud and possibly embarrassing moan escaped him. Brock knew that Lance was terrified of embarrassing himself. When Brock and Lance made eye contact, Lance nodded, clearly signifying that he was ready to climax. Then Brock looked to Brianna. She quickly nodded in succession. Tears formed in her eyes. The movement of their hips succeeded in rapidity. All three nearly screamed in the deep throes of ecstasy. Brianna extended her elbow, reached far behind her shoulder, grabbed Lance's medium length hair and yanked. "It's okay, cum inside of me. Both of you."

They did.

2

Exhausted, still excited and with strumming hearts they tightened to each other. Silence. No one needed to say anything. Neither Brock nor Lance extracted their penises from inside Brianna and she was thankful for that. Her muscles and insides needed to relax before extraction. Both penises slowly became flaccid while nestled inside of her. And there was that *other* thing: she wanted to remain held tightly between the men she loved dearly. Brock had been right. This experience had heightened their friendship and their love for one another. Guilt hadn't lifted from the experience. Not yet anyway. Without consideration for convention, what they'd experienced was right. It was moral. Acceptable. Good.

Brianna felt that God or the universe or whatever higher power existed was not frowning on them because what they'd done was good. What they'd done was deeply spiritual. She was thankful that their inhibitions had ceased. Their artful bodies had been respectful with one another. Their souls had intertwined.

Just thinking about how she'd dominated Brock continued to arouse her and she'd not noticed that she was running her index fingernail along her right inner thigh. No way in hell would she even consider making love to her boys again, not tonight. She'd exceeded her physical limits. If they went again they'd cause physical damage.

"Is it okay if I pull it out, Brianna?" Lance asked. His voice was that of a small boy asking his mother if it was okay to play outside for a short while after dinner.

Brianna smiled, ran her hand along Lance's cheek, leaned in and kissed him passionately. Even her lips hurt when she kissed him. Once their lips parted, she slid her hand around back to the bottom of her ass and assisted Lance in extracting his penis from her. He slid out with ease. Clean. She gasped as he fully exited her. Brock followed suit and then Brianna rolled onto her back and shouted, "Oh my God! That was amazing!"

Brock burst into laughter and then rolled upward onto his forearm. He faced Brianna. Their lips met and he ran his fingers through the dangling strands of hair in front of her face. "I've never felt something so deeply before, Brianna. I'm not just saying that. That was special."

She touched Brock's face, which was something she hadn't done since they were very young. "You changed during this. Something will never be the same with you, will it?"

"No, but I think ... I know that I'm better for it. Thank you, Brianna and Lance. This was right."

"It so was. Thank you for letting me act out my fantasy with you at the beginning, Brock." She shook her head and smiled, clearly reminiscing about what had happened. "I had multiple orgasms. That's never happened." She rolled over to Lance and said, "I've never let anyone ... you know. Back there."

"Did you enjoy it?" Lance asked. He almost looked ashamed.

Brianna kissed him, parted and then said, "I had no idea that I could receive so much pleasure from anal sex. We'll be doing that again."

Lance smiled. Brianna and Brock cuddled and laughed at Lance's vulnerability.

"I love you both." Lance said.

Brianna nodded, placed her hands between their hands and said, "I love you both."

Brock squeezed Brianna's hand hard then patted Lance on the shoulder and said, "Me too. I love you too."

"We have so many more adventures to plan, boys. But for right now I think we need a nap."

3

Legs intertwined with arms overlapping, they fell into deep sleep and felt the warmth of each other's naked bodies.

A few hours later, Lance woke up and stared at Brianna. A sliver of moonlight slashed into the room and illuminated her face. She was so beautiful. He felt close to her—*so close*—and he'd achieved his fantasy. Not just the physical aspect either. Sure, the sex was amazing, but the connection he'd now established with her was unbreakable.

For a quick moment, his thoughts of Brianna parted. He glanced at Brock, lying on the opposite side of Brianna. He couldn't deny that his feelings for Brock had deepened. Not in a sexual sense, but an indescribable intimacy had refined their friendship. For that he was thankful.

Rolling out of bed, he crept downstairs to drink a glass of water. His thirst was ravenous. He filled a clear plastic pitcher with ice, grabbed three glasses from the cupboard and made his way back upstairs. He knew they would awake soon and experience a similar thirst. When he entered the bedroom he found them awake.

"I've never been this thirsty in my life. Thanks, man," Brock sighed. He grabbed a glass. Lance poured for him. He slurped and gulped the entire glass.

"Thank you, sweetie." Brianna gulped the water. They finished the pitcher before crashing into slumber again.

4

A sinking sensation struck the pit of Lance's stomach when he awoke in the morning to an empty bed. He listened to the silence, but only heard the howling of winter wind shuttering across the frozen window frames. He was sad, but equivocally felt relief. Morning rituals were an important part of Lance's daily routine. Plus, on this particular morning he had nothing to do until after noon. He'd lie in bed and watch a movie.

Ordinary People was his favorite, but today the film was simply background noise. Lance's focus was on the memory of last night. It had actually happened. Outwardly, it had been a threesome. A risqué physical experience, but introspectively it had been so much more. It had been innocent. It was an experience built on the foundation of love, *an early Christmas present*. There had been too much emotion involved for the experience to be considered hedonistic. Sure, elements of it were animalistic, especially at the beginning, but it needed to be that way. Once they had become comfortable and gone to the bedroom the experience had evolved into something much more passionate and heartfelt. The sex had come natural as though it *was* natural. Meant to be. There *couldn't* be anything wrong with it because it was right.

Brianna was Lance's drug. His addiction. He didn't want to wait for next time. A small, but powerful fantasy manifested in the deepest arena of Lance's thoughts. At some point, he'd want to be with Brianna alone. There was no animosity toward Brock. In fact, Lance was thankful he'd brought last night to fruition. But he was in love with Brianna and he wouldn't want to share her forever. Maturity took over and Lance allowed his fantasy to diminish with his thoughts. He and his best friends had elevated their friendship into something physical. Their life would always remain together. It had always been the three of them.

Unless something bad would happen to Brock.

"Stop." Lance whispered. He hardly realized that he'd said it out loud.

He also couldn't deny that the idea and thought of he and Brianna grieving the demise of Brock wasn't unpleasant.

Chapter 8

Troubled Waters

1

Standing near the entrance to the Quarter and glancing in the direction of the disruptions at the bar, Ricky Mack couldn't stand to watch Nick Benson stumble into one more plastered rip-head or sexually harass another college coed. Usually, Nick was a happy drunk. Tonight, he was a stumbling idiot and every patron of the bar took notice and found his inebriation unfit. Puffing his chest out and placing a scowl on his face, Ricky made his way to the end of the sticky, liquor-drenched bar where Nick slurped beer and fingered the bartender's garnishes. Cherry juice dripped from Nick's chapped lips, ran down his chin and stained his shirt. The light brown beer—intended to connect with his lips and soar down his throat—also ran down his chin and darkened the fabric of his blue T-shirt.

"Nick, come on man. Let me call you a cab." Ricky clapped a massive hand on Nick's shoulder, which unintentionally guided him, chest first, into the bar. More beer slushed from Nick's mug.

"What the hell, man?" Nick wobbled then straightened his position. His head swiveled until lucid eye contact was established. Nick closed one eye as he attempted to focus. His sight stuttered on random onlookers. Ricky settled when he realized Nick's shame.

True alcoholics always felt shame.

"I'm *that* drunk, huh Ricky?" Nick mumbled.

Ricky looked to the bartender who nodded his vote of approval to remove Nick from the crowded bar. A clique of sophomore girls pointed and laughed with cruel intent.

"Can I call you a cab?" Ricky slouched his chest and dropped the scowl. Nick's drunken demeanor reminded Ricky of his father before he'd died from liver disease.

"Nah, I'll walk back to the dorm. It's just across the bridge." His head bobbled. "I could use the fresh air."

"I'd feel better if I called you a cab." Ricky was genuine, concerned.

"Please, Ricky. I respect you, but just let me stumble out the back. Please? I'm embarrassed."

Ricky didn't know if he preferred the shameful drunk or the mean drunk. The shameful drunk could tug at the heartstrings, which was harder to hate. Sure, the mean drunk's were easier to handle than the loudmouth frat-type assholes. Those assholes traveled in packs and always looked for a fight. He usually had to deal with them at the end of the night. "It's your call, Nick."

"Thanks. You mind if I take a piss first?"

"Sure thing, just don't pass out in the stall again."

"Check on me in a minute, would ya?"

"Sure thing."

Nick made his way down the narrow hallway to the men's bathroom, located near the back exit where he could sneak out when he was done with his business.

The bar-back fist bumped Ricky and said, "Gotta love a cooperative drunk. I like that dude, but he's fucked if he keeps drinking like that."

Ricky nodded while watching Nick exit the bathroom. "You just look at him and know *the drink* is gonna kill him."

"Sad." The bartender downed a shot before walking toward a brunette that flagged him down with a shout and chest jiggle. Her shirt was navy blue with deep cleavage.

Ricky watched Nick bump into both sides of the hall like a pinball before exiting into the icy winter night.

2

The Killer stood in the shadows of the bar near a small round table littered with glasses filled with the remnants of spirits. He watched intently as Nick Benson stumbled outside. The Killer's smile wasn't visible from this dark corner. People were magnetized by smiles and The Killer didn't want magnetism or attention, but couldn't refrain from grinning. Smiling was an involuntary action that drew people close. He didn't want anyone to notice nor approach. Not now.

About a minute after Nick left, The Killer slid out the front door, unnoticed, bundled his black winter coat and swiftly b-lined to the black van parked two lots over beneath the cover of a leafless Maple tree. He wasn't worried about losing track of Nick. He'd been observing Nick and studying his patterns for the past few weeks. He was aware of Nick's routines.

Tonight, Nick wasn't going to reach home.

3

"Fuck, it's cold out here!" A voice called out from the icy darkness.

Stumbling, eventually tripping over his own large left boot, Nick spun, surveying his surroundings in search of the voice.

Maybe it was just the wind? Maybe just his mind?

The cold bite that stung Nick's ears was becoming a fearful reality. The cold air pulsated with what felt like freezer burn. "Who said something?" Nick spun until his outlook halted on the outline of a person that stood at the base of the bridge where the railing ended and the street began. Along the west front, a short cement hill slanted downward to the river.

"You okay?" the shape called.

Lowering his head, Nick hurried toward the shape, hoping for a friend. "My ears are fucking popsicles, man. What's up?"

"Nothing. Just saw you walking. Thought you might want to, um ... " He held up his hand. "Smoke up ... kill some of this cold. I think it's gonna snow tonight."

Nearly forgetting about the pain in his pulsating ears, Nick's adrenal gland produced ability, and he spoke with mild coherence. "You got smoke?"

"I got a little Purple Cush." The shadowed figure returned while he extracted a tightly rolled joint from his pocket. From his other pocket he pulled a small torch—blue—that maintained its flame in the gusty wind.

The figure walked toward Nick and sparked the joint. The cherry burned like an ember when he inhaled. Close now, the figure came into focus when he extended the joint to Nick.

When Nick inhaled, the man laughed.

Nick lowered the joint and asked, "What's so funny, dude?"

"Your face."

"I'm drunk, man, but I ain't gonna take any shit."

"Bullshit, I'm gonna fucking kill you and you're not gonna do a fucking thing about it."

The black van slid sideways then halted near the curb. The sliding door whipped open and a man wearing all black with a silly rubber Devil mask popped out. Involuntarily, Nick would have laughed if the man hadn't slammed a metal pipe against the side of his face. The shadowed figure puffed deeply on the joint before stomping it out and placing a black plastic bag over Nick's head. Quickly, the figure retrieved a piece of thin copper wire and wrapped it around Nick's neck. Both men grabbed Nick while he struggled drunkenly. Then they threw him into the van. His head slammed against something metallic. *Maybe a toolbox?* A blinding white pain shot across his forehead. It felt worse than the migraine that had put him in the hospital a few years back.

The street darkened as the snow fell heavy now and the van's headlights disappeared into the night.

The van was not to be seen.

And neither was Nick, ever again.

4

Frozen, tiny beads of ice pelted the van's windshield, diminishing visibility. Whether the high beams were on or off, the succession of snowflakes dashing forward prevented safety.

The Killer instructed the driver, "Turn left." He pointed to an industrial park at the end of the street. There were a few glowing florescent lights illuminating the dark from a distance, but other than those dimly lit bulbs the structure was unseen.

"I can't see shit, man." The driver leaned in close to the windshield as if his actions might aid with visibility.

"Keep driving straight," the Killer stated.

An aluminum metal garage door opened. More florescent light splashed outward into the night revealing another two figures wearing the uniform: all black with Smiley Devil masks.

The Killer smiled, pulled the plastic bag off of Nick's head, broke open an ammonia-based smelling salt, and placed it beneath his unconscious nose. "Wake up, sunshine."

Nick shook to life. Punched and kicked.

This reaction was nothing The Killer hadn't dealt with prior and he was prepared.

"What the fuck, man!" Nick slapped his palm to the bleeding gash on the right side of his face where the pipe had torn skin. "What did I do? Why is this happening?"

"You met the criteria. That's all," the Killer explained, calmly.

"What?"

"You met the criteria. You're an athletic, in-shape, Caucasian male with the ability to resist being murdered. A challenge," He continued. There was a less-than-calm edge to his voice as if he were losing his patience.

The surrounding figures wearing black clothes and Smiley Devil masks had gathered around the van. They turned to each other before nodding their approval. They dragged Nick out of the van. Abruptly crashing to the cement floor, they subdued him. "Please, my mom won't know what do."

"Sorry bro, we like that. In fact, that's one aspect to all of this that I enjoy focusing on. The pain of all the others that know and care about you provides me with strength and inspiration. You should be thankful that you've become important. You're an offering."

Nick slid his foot free from beneath one of the masked men, shot upward with all his strength and slammed his boot into another masked face. The figure stumbled backward and grabbed at his mask, but the Killer prevented the figure from removing it.

Nick freed one of his arms when the other masked figure stumbled backward.

Lunging to his feet, Nick ran instinctually pulling his cell phone from his pocket. From memory, he thumbed in his brother's contact. The pain throbbing from his wrist was intense and prevented mobility. He was certain that it had been broken. The phone fell. Nick's stomach felt like it had filled with ice. The rectangular, plastic communication device—that had meant so much to him— slid beneath a stack of wooden pallets that lined the tall cement walls, which appeared damning. He only hoped that his call had connected and that his brother would answer, hear the struggle, and notify the authorities— before these maniacs killed him would be convenient, but wishful. For now, he would prepare to fight. Survival mode would need to kick in.

To the front of him, a small door behind a neatly aligned row of old, broken down cars became visible. Setting his sight on the door, he thrust his legs forward and sprinted harder than he knew he could. Earlier, he'd downed many drinks and had been drunker than hell, but right now he was sober. His vision was clear. Tongue dry and swollen, it stuck to the roof of his mouth, which made it hard but not impossible to breathe. The only thing that mattered was reaching that door.

The obnoxious crashing of boots chasing him rose in volume. The vibrations of their murderous feet tore at his sanity.

The skeleton of a car resting in front of the door—his salvation—didn't deter his focus. Head first he slid underneath the car. His skin screeched and tore as the damp cement tugged it tight. Then he crawled forward.

The stomping boots halted.

A glimmer of hope couldn't resist expanding in his gut. Then hope diminished when he heard the creaking of metal above. They were running to either side of the car and on top of it.

It was now or never.

Nick knew three things: 1) these maniacs wouldn't stop; 2) this was going to hurt; and 3) they intended to kill him.

He scraped the skin off of his elbows while dragging himself out from under the car. He looked up and saw the metal doorknob. He rolled to his feet, grabbed the knob, and twisted.

It was locked.

"What? What the fuck is this?" Nick begged for an answer.

"It's just a game. You're a random pick, bud. Sorry," one of the masked figures said with eerie calmness. Then a wet towel whipped across Nick's face. The soaking wet tip of the towel snapped into his naked right eye. A million nerve endings exploded painfully. The scream came from his soul. The lens of his right eye ripped free. No one saw it and no one cared. They dragged him away from the door toward the metal tub at the entrance to the warehouse. A strong metallic odor stung his nasal passages. He knew the towel had been soaked in some form of chemical. His eye burned badly. Stars, white dots, and then blackness clouded his limited vision. He fell from consciousness. After some discomfort he was being submerged in freezing cold water. He saw all colors. A rainbow of different colored clouds erupted before his black vision. A euphoric sense surrounded him. He felt lucid like he'd taken morphine. He was suddenly comforted.

Blackness found him.

5

Nick's brother, Tim, hadn't been sleeping, but he wasn't awake either. His evening had consisted of more than a few drinks and topped off with cheap Mexican food that gave him horrid gas and heartburn. The struggle over whether or not to answer his cell phone had landed on yes.

"Nick, I'm too drunk to pick you up, dude. Take a cab." He started to drift into sleep with the phone stuck to his ear. Then dread coursed into the pit of his stomach when he heard his brother's faint screams. The sloshing of water melded with the laughter of at least four people. Those icy cackles filled him with terror and the threat of loss. He couldn't help but to cry. On his landline, he dialed 911.

"911, what's your emergency?" dispatch asked.

"It's my brother, he's being attacked, he's being ..." he couldn't bring himself to say the truth. He looked to his cell phone, which was still connected to Nick's phone. But his brother needed help. Tim pulled it together. Saying what was wrong brought horror into reality. He didn't want to accept that his brother was being harmed. To feel that torturous emotion would be too much, but he had to. So he said, "They're killing my brother. He called me and his cell phone is still on. I can hear them. Is there any way you can track my brother's cell phone?"

"Sir, please stay on the line, I'm sending an officer, right now."

Tim stayed on the line until the police showed up, which didn't take long. Scared as he was, he had to admit that the police were impressive. They showed up in less than five minutes and didn't waste any time. They saw the phone, called some kind of service to have the device tracked and then sent more police to the location of his brother's cell phone.

6

The Killer's attention was honed into the faintest echo of someone yelling from somewhere near, but hidden. His head swiveled to each corner of the building. Glancing at every stack of pallets and every nook of the warehouse he finally found the cell phone that had been thrown under a metal shelf full of tools. He picked it up and listened. Whoever was on the other line had called the police. He picked up the phone and placed it to his ear. A shaky voice spoke with the dispatch.

The Killer looked to the others and yelled, "Out! Now! Take the vile thing!"

The masked man that stood behind the tank suddenly dropped his camcorder on the floor.

"Dude, pick that up! You fucking idiot! You better not have lost any of the footage."

"Take it easy."

"I'll take it easy once we're out of here!" the Killer screamed.

They pulled Nick's lifeless corpse out of the metal tub of water, dragged him to the van, tossed him into the back, killed the lights, and drove away from the industrial park.

Less than ten minutes later the Smiley Devils stood silent in an abandoned house off campus. Nick's body was slumped on the floor and leaked water onto the hardwood.

The Killer watched through the upstairs hallway window as three police cruisers parked at the warehouse where they would find nothing unusual except an overturned industrial-sized metal tub. Fifty gallons of water spilled on the cement floor.

"Are we good?" one of the masked men asked.

"We'll be good once this is over," the female voice chattered through the rubber mask.

"We need to get him to the bridge. Quick," the Killer demanded.

7

The rear tires slid as the black van weaved along the backstreets of town like a drifting shadow. Finally, the van ended up at a small parking garage where the four men tossed Nick's corpse from the van into the trunk of a cheap Ford Tempo. After removing their masks and placing them in an empty plastic trashcan they poured a quarter gallon of hydrochloric acid over the evidence and waited for the acid's sizzle to become audible before they separated into two groups.

The Tempo drove through town, stopped at the edge of the bridge, and killed the headlights. The Killer exited the car, glanced both ways—saw that no one was coming— then discarded Nick into the icy waters of the river below. Smiling, The Killer zoomed his camera on Nick's corpse as it sank below the water surface and then traveled with the current. It wasn't long before the camera image of Nick's bobbing head disappeared into the blackness of this icy river.

8

In the upstairs bedroom of a rundown Victorian home near campus, sitting at his desk, The Killer removed the SD Card from his video camera, inserted it into the card reader that was connected to his Mac Book Pro via SBC cord and then imported the footage of Nick's demise. Once the footage was imported he quickly edited the clips together and uploaded the artistic demise of Nick Benson onto the Dark Web. A quick ting struck. Scrolling his eyes along the side of the computer screen he found that bit coins had been deposited into his account. As always, The Killer saved a copy of his work as a souvenir. It would be a good edition to his collection.

Sitting back, The Killer ran his hand through his shaggy hair and then reached for the aged scotch that rested in the cabinet above his desk. He poured it into a neat whiskey glass and sipped from it. The first sip was the best. It scorched down his throat and eased his mind into a relaxed, reflective state. The next part of his ritual was the crystal. He broke off a chunk of the clear white rock and stuffed it down the straw at the end of his glass pipe. His torch lighter hissed, ignited, and he held the flame beneath the glass bulb. He watched the methamphetamine melt and create a ribbon of smoke that he then inhaled. He was always impressed with the amount of smoke expelled from his mouth when he exhaled this drug. Something about the toxic recipe created an abundance of smoke—more than with any usual narcotic substance. Now—he thought to himself—this is only after a completed kill. Meth was very addictive and very intense—a wonderful drug that heightened the experience of a kill and added an orgasmic sensation as a cap.

After he'd smoked a bowl of the smooth Russian ice, his brain felt quenched in fire. He sat back and watched the murder he'd committed while offering prayer to his Dark Lord. When Nick's agonized face showed signs that his life was diminishing, The Killer would pleasure himself. Masturbating while viewing a kill was majestic, especially on meth. He'd spend at least three hours doing this before downing a few tabs of Valium to ease out of the amphetamine high. Then he'd relax, settle. But that would come later.

When Nick died on camera, The Killer ejaculated hard.

The trajectory of his spray was guttural and felt like Heaven, if Heaven was Hell. He finished his scotch and then settled into bed and watched a few of his past victims lose their lives.

Technology was great. He could watch these videos in the highest quality.

Chapter 9

Breakfast Chit Chat

1

Brock arrived at the cozy off-campus diner, hurried into the building, and grabbed a booth at the farthest corner of the restaurant specifically because the topic of conversation between Brianna, Lance, and he would be unsuitable for ears of decency. Hoped so anyway. Naughty would be good. In a sense, their banter would be comical, maybe disturbing—to the uninvolved ear. For this reason, they needed to meet at a secluded diner to discuss. Attempting a mature discussion about how and when to execute their heathenism was excitingly humorous. Brock took his seat, scanned the near empty restaurant, and waited.

Brock had only settled when the cheap, rusted bell above the entrance jingled and Brianna walked in with Lance. Both were laughing at something Lance had said. And Brianna kept touching Lance's arm, which caused mild jealousy. Quickly dismissed. Both surveyed the diner before spotting Brock at the far corner, near the restroom. Connected, they're smiles were contagious and laughter was involuntary.

Excitedly, Lance and Brianna shuffled to Brock's table.

"Hey stud," Brianna said as she sat then inched toward him.

Their legs touched and their fingers clasped together briefly.

Brock glanced at their hands. Lying parallel to each other, he thought Brianna would close her grip around his. She didn't. Glancing at her face, he wondered if at some corner of her thought process she assumed they'd entered into a romantic relationship—the kind of relationship where holding hands at the dinner table was an expression of affection. He despised that brand of a relationship. Nothing about it attracted him.

Lance took a seat across from Brock, fist-bumped him, and then nonchalantly glanced at the menu.

A waitress with dark circles beneath her exhausted red eyes strolled over and took their orders for coffee and water. She never made eye contact and a queer grin never left her mousy mouth. "Ya'll need a minute?" she whispered.

Oddly, Brianna lost her train of thought when the waitress finally made eye contact, but managed to say, "Yes, please."

The waitress glanced at Brock. Her lips twitched. Then she turned, abruptly, and left.

"She's chipper." Brianna shook her head.

"Did you hear that some dude drowned last night?" Brock steered the conversation away from the quirky waitress.

"That's like the fourth drown victim this year. It's that creaky old bridge, man. That and drunk people fall," Lance expanded.

"What do you mean?" Brock sounded interested. "Did we know him?"

"I mean dudes get hammered drunk at The Quarter. Stumble home to the dorms across the bridge. They take that shortcut at the edge of the bridge and fall into the water. End up drowning," Lance rambled. "And it was Nick Benson. I didn't know him, but I'd probably recognize him at a party."

"Huh, I thought they pulled his body out of the river over by that generator factory," Brianna added.

"They did, but he fell in at the bridge," Lance informed.

"How do you know that?" Brock asked.

"I read it online."

"Which article?" Brock pushed.

"I don't remember. Google it." Lance separated eye contact with Brock.

"Huh, that sucks." Brock didn't force the issue, but—oddly—thought that Lance was lying.

Brianna broke the awkward moment. "How are we going to talk about what happened? If it's gonna happen again? And what everyone thought about it?" She smiled.

Brock knew she was nervous and excited, which was promising. Their sexual adventures would continue. And he was glad she'd been the one to bring it up. He and Lance were clearly insecure about how to broach the topic. Women had more power when it came to illuminating sensitive topics.

"Those are excellent questions." Brock found his words comical. He was excited to dive into this subject. "Can we talk about it right now?"

"I'd like to." Lance was unable to control the smile sprawling across his face. His cheeks flushed red.

"I really haven't been with too many guys ... just boyfriends and a couple of one-night stands. You both know my entire sex life." She lowered her eyes while a smile widened across her face. "But last night I was free.

That was the most liberating, intense, amazing night of my life. I think." She must have realized that she looked overly excited because she suddenly placed a flat hand over her mouth as if ashamed. "I don't mean to put any pressure on you guys if you didn't feel the same way. It's totally cool if that was like a one time deal."

"Is it wrong for me to say that it was amazing and that I really hope we can do it again?" Lance spoke fast. Usually, he wasn't talkative, but on this morning he sang like a lark.

"Sounds like we all feel the same. Brianna, when you dominated me and made me feel jealous of Lance ... that made me so horny that you could have told me to kill someone and I would have done it ... just to please you."

Brianna swallowed and then scratched Brock's palm with her index finger. Then she surveyed the diner to see that no one had witnessed this. "I couldn't believe I had the balls to do that to you. It felt amazing. And then to have Lance fuck me in front of you ... wow. We've come a long way since the days of kick-the-can."

"The bedroom got me," Lance said.

"I didn't know that getting fucked from ... *back there* ... would feel so good." Brianna bit her lower lip, embarrassed.

Brock rubbed his hands together successively before asking,

"When can we do it again?"

"Can we, like, plan out a scenario?" Brianna smiled.

"What kind of scenario?" Brock asked.

"I want to make you guys breakfast while wearing just a thong and an apron." She laughed. "I'm serious. And like one of those thongs that chicks wear in porn movies. The ones that are *just* strings, T-shaped." She bit her lip again and Brock wondered if it hurt.

"Breakfast *in* you. I'm in." Lance nodded.

"I want you to make me eat everything." Brianna rubbed her hand over Brock's groin while she extended her foot beneath the table and rubbed it over Lance's erection.

"I so can't believe we're doing this. It's so exciting." Brianna stopped moving when she realized what the waitresses and cooks would think if they saw her gyrating like this.

"I guess we should talk about being secretive," Brock mentioned.

"Good point," Lance chimed in.

"What are you going to do about Grady?" Brock asked. Brianna looked surprised that Brock was concerned, which he really wasn't. Appearing concerned would allow Brianna to think that he cared, which would rile her up, sexually. He thought.

Brianna glanced around the diner and then returned her gaze toward Lance and Brock. She opened her mouth to talk, but didn't.

"That's my job to do that." Lance smiled.

"Do what?" Brianna looked confused.

"Open your mouth to talk and then not say anything." Lance smiled again.

"You definitely do that. I just ... "

Brock reached across the table and placed his hand over the top of Brianna's. Defensively, she tugged her hand away, but Brock didn't let go. "Tell us. Whatever you want to say, you need to tell us. Our friendship just elevated to the next level and if we can't tell each other exactly what's on our minds at all times then this is going to fail and so will our friendship."

Brianna nodded then looked to the tabletop, ran her finger along the edge of a deep gash, and twirled her thumbs. "I ... I, um ... it turns me on to have a boyfriend ... and cheat on him."

Brock smiled.

Lance nodded.

"It feels good to be honest about those deep feelings, doesn't it?" Brock whispered.

Brianna smiled. When her lips quivered, Brock knew that she was fighting the urge not to smile.

"It would turn me on to fuck you behind his back and make him out to be a total chump," Brock continued. He was serious. His sly grin was a telling expression.

"I like that I like Grady as a friend, but that I'm having sex with his girlfriend." Lance took a deep breath.

The only sound was their breathing.

Then they began laughing hard and guttural. The waitress was alarmed.

"We're so deplorable," Brianna continued laughing.

"God it feels great to be honest about this stuff." Lance inhaled deeply and laughed so hard that the manager exited the kitchen to see what the noise was about.

Brock glanced at the manager and silenced himself, embarrassed. Lance and Brianna followed suit and soon the table was silent, red in the face, trying not to laugh. It felt like they had nearly been caught. *Thrilled.* The waitress returned with their coffees and water. They thanked her and ordered the sampler platter.

"So where and when do we have our next ... excursion?" Lance pried.

"A nice hotel?" Brianna was still flustered.

"You have to stop looking so embarrassed about what you want to do. This is we, and we can do anything," Brock stated.

"You're right." I want to get a room at the Marriott. Downtown. Top floor. I want Brock to fuck me from behind while he shoves me up against the glass with the curtain open. And I want Lance to watch from the bed." She was smiling ear to ear.

Brianna reached over and rubbed Lance's shoulder. "What do you want? Honest."

Lance glanced from Brock to Brianna, smiled, and said, "I want to fuck your mouth, like hard. We can make up a safe word so that I know to stop if it gets to be too much. Is that okay?"

"That's more than okay, that turns me on. In return, I want you to lick my asshole while I'm propped up on all fours on the bed. Is that okay?" Brianna returned. "I can't believe we're talking like this."

"Me neither."

"I'm super turned on right now," Brock stated.

"Fuck it." Brianna stood from the table, threw down a twenty and marched outside.

2

Soft panting melded with deep groans and echoed from the nearby woods behind the university practice football field where Brianna leaned forward against a thick elm tree with her jeans bunched around her ankles.

With rapid succession, Brock thrust into her from behind while she took Lance in her mouth. Eagerly, Brock and Lance switched positions. All three nearly climaxed. Afterward they clung to each other as if they were unable to separate.

"Oh, my boys, my boys." Brianna held them both.

3

The Killer rested his back against the bark of a thick poplar tree fifty yards away and watched. Covering the black box-like shape of his camera body with his palm, he zoomed in and focused on the fornication happening in the distance.

Pressing the display button on the camera's digital menu, he saved the footage from the diner. Then he ended the recording. He'd been sitting in his black Chevy van, which was parked across the street while the misguided youths sipped coffee. He'd filmed them through the window at a distance. This would make a nice establishing shot.

Now, seeking cover behind a gaggle of poplars and elms, he was filming cover footage. Little shots that could fill time and add depth to his video. His surprise pleasure was in the discovery of this love triangle, which added an erotic dimension to his masterpiece. He was ecstatic that he'd been guided to such intriguing people, and at random. These sacrifices were an intervention from his lord.

Had to be.

He didn't want to share these victims with the others, but he would. This was more powerful than the other sacrifices. He could feel that he was being rewarded. These three would not be drowned. That wasn't enough. This sacrifice was a gift and he would savor it with sweet sorrow. Also, he didn't know if he'd share all of this footage on the dark net. He'd have to edit a theatrical cut. This film was spiritually enlightening. It was to be shared between he and the Dark Master. This was the category of sacrifice that would ensure a place of rank in Hell. Sure, he enjoyed the company of his enlightened friends, but they weren't as dedicated or as loyal. In fact, the members of his secret club could get him in a lot of trouble if they were to ever open their mouths about what transpired.

The Killer recalled the experience of that day. The day he'd found the others. The meeting in the desert had been terrifying yet orgasmic and thrilling.

His desire to end a human life had become a maddening itch that needed to be scratched. The itch had snowballed since his young body had begun developing, sexually. His heart would race when images of desecrated flesh flashed in his mind until he felt like it would burst. He would kill a neighborhood pet. At the time, it was the only way to sooth his internal desire. Cracking a kitten's neck and then skinning it would bring out intense sensations. Love and hate and anger all built into twisted release. His insides revved high and his desire to kill a human being boiled to the point that he was consumed. One morning, while surfing unconventional porn sites on the Dark Net he'd discovered the Smiley Devils. He didn't think much of the Dark Net at the time. It was underwhelming. He'd only heard rumors that you could purchase anything you wanted with bit coins. It was easy enough to login. There was a YouTube video that explained how to enter. Furthermore, there was a nice infomercial detailing the legalities of how the Dark Net could not be monitored by the government or law enforcement. So he'd browsed the items on the various sites and he was pleasantly surprised, very enthused, and ultimately excited to discover that he could use the site to benefit his hidden desire. The Smiley Devils drew him in. There was something spiritual calling to him. He couldn't resist the magnetic force driving him to check out this group. Their page was a recruiting site. Really, it was a job posting. Live videos of actualized killings—that *you* committed—could be uploaded to a designated portion of the website and viewed for a price. *Snuff films.* If you uploaded a real video that was verified by an unknown source then your account was credited with bit coin, same as money.

The Killer enjoyed committing murder. Filming his vile acts created paranoia at first, but once he became skilled the paranoia diminished. Filming these videos became a necessity. Watching the movies, afterward, he relived the experience. He became a polished editor. With neatly composed shots, The Killer created real storylines. He would read film writing books about the Hero's Journey and script structures and before he knew it he could stalk, stage, create, and structure live action snuff films. But the aspect of the Smiley Devils that he enjoyed most was the comfort he felt that there were others like him, walking amongst the ordinary. Suburban maniacs committing home invasions, urban torture videos, and rural human hunting were common themes. They were real and the people committing these acts were connected via this Dark Net. Once comfortable with his craft, he arranged a meet with some of these likeminded murderers. The relationships he developed with these murderous churchgoers, accountants, factory workers, lab geeks, and all other walks of life bloomed. The Killer had found his life's calling. There was a deep spiritual side to these people. The Dark Lord had gathered them. It was involuntary. They were serving a purpose that was much greater than any one killer.

He was happy.

Leaving rocks with painted Smiley Devil's on them was an antagonistic, self-serving, magnificent signature. Worshiping one's self was righteous. It heightened the experience and added to its orgasmic effect. Leaving the signature was necessary. It bound the group and it was simple. They left a simple painted smiley face similar to the *"Have a Nice Day"* tee shirts found at hobby shops. The only difference was that the Smiley Devil's drew red devil horns on theirs.

The Killer recalled his first encounter with others like him. The Dark Net had chat rooms that allowed for like-minded discussions without worry of legal issues. Still, he never entered a chat room using his own computer. He would use unattended computers at the library or college parties. That or he'd break into a fellow student's dorm room while they were out. When he joined the group on murderous discussions it was enthralling. It was therapeutic to speak freely. The group shared snuff films and talked about specific emotions and feelings felt before, during, and after a human sacrifice. It became inevitable that the members would need to meet at some point. The Killer had become overly excited and couldn't wait to meet his peers. They organized a meet, quickly.

The private rendezvous had taken place in a small Arizona town, a completely neutral zone. Sure, The Killer would have to drive a great distance, but he found long drives to be enjoyable. The Killer appreciated the scenery of this great country. And The Killer was cautious. Parking over a mile away from the hollowed and rotting abandoned motel—that had been agreed upon—he'd ended up performing a reconnaissance. This happened a few days prior to the meet. He'd camped out in the blaring desert with only a camouflaged blanket, binoculars, water, and canned food. He'd dug a hole three feet into the sand and camouflaged it with tumbleweed and brush. The day prior to the meet, he watched as a rust trodden pick-up truck parked near the motel. His heart had been beating out of his chest. His hands shook. Looking through his binoculars, he saw two men and a woman in the cab of the truck. They parked near the motel and then covered their vehicle with a camouflage tarp and tumbleweed. They removed bags of bulky items from the truck bed and then loaded them into the motel. The Killer thought that the bulk was bedding, but he also saw an altar.

How appropriate.

He crawled forward for a closer look.

Close to the ground, The Killer dug his elbows and knees into the earth and dragged himself forward to the abandoned motel. Over the course of the thirty-six hours since he'd arrived he hadn't seen any vehicles accept for the pick-up truck. He needed clarification that the driver wasn't law enforcement. Once he was within fifty feet of the burned structure he lifted his binoculars and surveyed the site. Luckily, the moonlight illuminated their faces. Enough that he knew they were young, probably early twenties. Long silky brown hair flowed from the woman's shoulders. Slivers of moonlight stabbed through the burnt and rotting windows and highlighted her figure. It was clear that she had a sharp facial structure judging by the slanted contours. It was dark, but when the sun rose in the morning he hoped for an attractive display. For the moment, he allowed his imagination to take control. He envisioned her as perfect—a gorgeous, smart, murderous girl that shared his methodology and darkness.

The two men were large. They weren't slim like fashion models with molded contours. Even in the dark, The Killer knew that they held real mass. Both were tall and wide, not fat. They could inflict damage. Judging by their presence at this meet, The Killer assumed that these men had conducted violent crimes.

The men laid out three Army style cots, lit a small bonfire, and then cracked open a bottle of liquor. The Killer thought to join them, but knew better. He decided to continue with his reconnaissance.

"You worried about tomorrow?" A woman's voice drifted into the night.

"Lisa, if it don't turn out ... we'll leave. No worries," One of the men replied.

"And what if the police show up? Don't they monitor the web?" Lisa asked.

The second man spoke up with an anxiousness shake to his voice, "We know this area. We know the website and we know the people showing up. If they don't provide their videos then we cut 'em to pieces, fuck their corpses and bury 'em."

"I second that, Rudy," The first man said.

The Killer contemplated the cumulated intelligence of these three. They hadn't spotted him. He was more intelligent than they were. Also, he didn't want to be involved with moronic killers. They would only get him caught. The Dark Lord wouldn't properly reward these fools. In fact, more than likely they didn't understand what they were worshiping. They certainly didn't understand the importance of their actions. Maybe it would be best to stake these people out and kill them, leave them as a sacrifice.

What would the chat room folks think of that?

He knew how anxious the community was to find out about this meeting. They were all checking in online—probably—waiting to hear the gory or not-so-gory details of what transpired.

"Do you think we'll be rewarded?" Lisa whispered.

"Lisa, listen to me. How good does it feel when you take a person's life? The sex we have afterwards. You don't think that the explosive orgasmic feelings that last for days aren't the work of *Him*? Come on. We're rewarded every time we commit an act of heinous evil."

"You're right," Lisa said.

The Killer watched Lisa's mouth form into a smile. The Killer liked this smile. It was sinister and it attracted him—so did watching three beautiful young people have sex in the abandoned motel.

Standing, The Killer took a deep breath and whispered, "What the hell." Logic and reason were important. These were qualities that he needed in order to execute the Dark Lord's will. But then he remembered that to have faith meant believing in acting on faith. This situation was not in his control. He believed in this idea one hundred percent. With faith in his black heart he stepped forward and made his way into the abandoned motel.

He entered through an opening that was once a doorway, but now a vacated hole in the wall. "Look at you, Smiley Devils." The metallic click of a gun being cocked rang crisp in the darkness. His heart raced. After a few brief seconds The Killer realized that his racing heart was exhausted. Any fear had diminished. The Dark Lord was going to reward him for his faith. He gave thanks.

The icy eyes of another killer illuminated the dark. This man held a shotgun trained in The Killer's direction. "I come in peace to rip bodies into pieces," the Killer said with charmed conviction. This phrase was the secret password agreed on to admit entrance. He felt confident now. The Dark Lord was rewarding him.

The shotgun lowered. The girl, who was exponentially more attractive up close, didn't attempt to cover her nakedness. She remained on all fours, staring at The Killer from behind. "Want a ride, Smiley Devil?" The Killer looked to the man holding the shotgun.

The man nodded.

The Killer removed his clothes and mounted the female Smiley Devil.

"She's amazing, isn't she?"

"Oh, fuck yeah." The Killer quickly climaxed.

They were silent for a few moments as he finished and caught his breath.

"Have a seat. Tell us about yourself," a second man said as he sat on a burnt, blackened wooden chair.

The Killer pulled his jeans on and said, "Well, I'm satan@666die." He knew these men would be easily controlled. He also knew that they were nothing to the Dark Lord. The Dark Lord demanded loyalty and worship. These idiots were only in this for the shallow thrill of killing and hedonism.

Such fools.

"Wow, man. I dig your videos. That one where you cut that old woman's tongue out ... that was my favorite," the Smiley Devil holding the shotgun announced.

"She was a worthy sacrifice." The Killer looked down at the Smiley Devil. "She offered me a butterscotch not to cut her tongue out."

Laughter soaked into the walls of the burned motel lobby. The Killer knew that the silly bond of humanity had been established. He would control these fools and offer them as a sacrifice before this visit concluded.

Lisa inched closer to The Killer and asked, "The Dark Lord rewarded you for that sacrifice?" Her eye contact was intense. Even in the dark The Killer knew that she was sincere in her faith. Maybe he'd been wrong about her devotion.

She looked to all three men and said, "I'm really fucking turned on. You guys want to run a train on me?"

The Smiley Devil's looked to each other and then swarmed her. She was triple penetrated at one point, but the sex didn't last long. The men took turns coming on her face. She begged to be degraded and she thanked the men for it.

Once they were cleaned up, the Smiley Devil that had praised The Killer's elderly video pulled out his glass pipe, filled it with crystal meth, placed the lighter beneath the glass bulb and inhaled the potent clarity.

Lisa inhaled deeply and exhaled a large plume of smoke. "I love this group because we stay hidden. It's true. To do the devil's work you have to make it appear that the devil had nothing to do with the act. The drown victims are the best."

"It makes sense and it makes people wonder whether or not the deaths are the result of a killer or substance abuse," The Killer stated.

"It's a little of both, if you think about it." Lisa eagerly grabbed the pipe.

"That's the model."

The Killer moved to the edge of his seat and asked, "Why is that the model, anyway? Does anyone know or is it just something that works?"

"Only the Dark Lord knows," the Smiley Devil with the shotgun stated.

The bearded Smiley Devil began laughing as if the last statement was funny and for that The Killer slammed the shotgun into the side of his face. Blood and teeth erupted from his mouth.

"Hey fuck you, man! You don't believe in that Satan shit. Not for real, do you?" Blood pulsated from his mouth and ran down his face. The crimson fluid clumped to his thick beard.

Lisa stood, removed a hatchet from her duffel bag and then slammed it into the bearded Devil's forearm. The Smiley Devil screamed gutturally.

The Smiley Devil holding the shotgun laughed. "Now that's funny, you stupid prick. And yes, I believe in the devil, I believe in Jesus and I believe in God. And if you don't ... then I must convince you." He looked to Lisa as she retracted the ax from the man's nearly severed forearm. She raised the hatchet high above her head.

"Please don't. I believe, I believe, I believe ... " he continued until the hatchet blade slammed into the top of his head. Even in the dark, The Killer saw a heavy expulsion of blood-drenched mist.

"Let's rip him apart," The naked woman suggested. "I want you to fuck me while we rip him to pieces."

The blood orgy lifted illicit sickness and twisted pleasure. The experience was new and orgasmic and he experienced extraordinary sensations that he appreciated. He truly believed this to be the work of God or Satan, which to The Killer had been both. Now, as their religious awakening developed, they desecrated the deceased and fucked in his blood. The Killer's belief was heightened by this act, consummated into darkness. His destiny to serve the Dark Lord had been fulfilled. His destiny, loyalty, and pursuit of pleasure now belonged to Lucifer and with devotion he would earn his rank in the sensational demonic realm of Hell. He was glad that he'd met these new people and that they'd shared the sacrifice—insulted the flesh of a less devoted follower.

Afterward, The Killer and his spiritual mates received pleasure in dismembering the unbeliever. They removed his head with the small hatchet and experienced camaraderie when insulting the dead with panache. They used the severed head in similar fashion to a ventriloquist—opening and closing his mouth—having him speak nonsense. Then they gifted each other via a hands-on anatomy lesson. Removing the top portion of his skull, they examined his brain. The grey matter was interesting up close and freshly dead. The Smiley Devil's contemplated their shared thoughts, pains, emotions, and memories as they prodded at the jelly-like brain. Upon completion, they burned the corpse and inhaled the sweet smoke and imagined they were reserving his twisted soul. With excitement, they spoke of the torment they would impress upon the souls that the Dark Lord would permit them in Hell. The night would soon conclude, but their renewal and strengthened faith would last. The meth aided in their experiences and heightened their enjoyment. The amphetamine allowed for the escalation of thought as it widened the intricate canals of the brain and sparked electric impulse.

The drug insisted they stay awake for the following days, but the morning after was when they received rest. Twelve more Smiley Devils arrived. Each brought ingredients of hedonism. Powerful drugs. Acid with meth allowed them to enter the realm of existence between the material world and the spiritual world. They concocted strong drink—one part alcohol, one part mescal. An excommunicated Mormon from Utah had sprinkled meth with fresh fruit into this mix of mind enhancer. The elixir siphoned the demonic rage. The brain serum was blessed. The Dark Lord had cast his sick blessing. Once all had drunk from the Holy Water, they gathered near the warmth of the desert fire. With tears in their eyes and diminished inhibitions they confessed their true feelings about life and pain. The stars above shined red like blood in honor of the darkness. With each confession the Smiley Devils achieved power and control. A movement was born. There was much more to discuss. The rules were made to protect the tribe. The sacrifices wouldn't be weak prostitutes that wouldn't be missed, in a societal sense. The Smiley Devil's would seek out strong athletic males that were capable of defending themselves. And they would find these young men at college bars where false safety and comfort came easy. They would wait for the victim near a body of water, a river or lake. An accidental phenomenon is what the authorities and media would reason. But in the back of their minds they would know that something sinister was spreading beneath the epidermis of their communities. The victims would leave of their own accord. Their friends would attest to this. Once the sacrifice was isolated, the Smiley Devils would stalk, capture, and torture these pathetic beings with water. Baptize them in the waters of death.

They would execute this task in a separate location so that autopsy reports would be inconclusive and examiners would be baffled by inconsistencies found in the corpse. The water elements in the lungs would not match the elements found in the bodies of water where they'd be found. Most would think that the cause of death was drowning by drunken college kids. A drunk, young adult that had consumed too much had fallen into the river. The Smiley Devils would stamp the Dark Lord's fingerprint into these small college towns.

The Dark Lord would reward them by dooming the affected communities with dread, anxiety, and fear. These like-minded individuals would enjoy their craft. The only aspect of the sacrifice that would be difficult and considered mildly sloppy would be the recorded videos. These recordings would be necessary evils. They would share the joy of sacrifice with the church of the Smiley Devil. The Devils would not be an isolated group. It would be a nationwide and then a worldwide organization. The Smiley Devil's would leave a signature—a painted rock placed near the water's edge. An officer's common sense would conclude that this was a signature of sorts, but the signature would be too mundane to use as evidence.

Somewhere, there was a head to this organization. Whoever this was they had created the Dark Net chat room. This individual existed. The Smiley Devils knew this because when a recorded sacrifice was uploaded, the account that uploaded would receive monetary reward in the form of Bitcoins.

4

Two days passed and when all members of the Smiley Devils had finished their convention, of sorts, they piled into their vehicles and left. No phone numbers or email addresses were exchanged. This secret sect of society would remain that way. Their communication would remain on the Dark Net. That way they could not be connected and it would be harder to track them down, find one of the members and interrogate answers from them.

The Killer drove to Wisconsin where he began collecting possible victims. It was fun to stroll the campus and look at the athletic, handsome males that had no idea a killer was watching them, considering them as a sacrifice to the devil. The Killer smiled when he thought about what it would be like to know—to have the psychic ability to realize that you were an ordinary human attending college courses on a safe campus, but that you were being considered for sacrifice to Satan. The Killer vaguely remembered the Satanic Panic of the nineteen-eighties. Most of it had been bullshit, but hidden in deep wells of dark hearts some of the crimes that had been committed were real. Some were carried out.

The Killer enjoyed watching his new victims: Brock and Lance. He had something very special in mind for them. His small movie was coming together well. The experimental threesome that they had planned and executed added a nice element of eroticism that hadn't been explored before.

The Smiley Devils would enjoy this film more than the others.

Part 4: The Season of Giving

Chapter 10

Planning, Planning, Planning

1

Brianna thirsted for passion. Her excitement burned and it was unquenchable. The permanent smile embedded on her face wouldn't diminish. Her cheek muscles cramped and the thin skin below her eye twitched when she thought of what her boys would do to her. In only a few days—together—they would experience sexual bliss. An ideal hotel in a nice part of downtown was the perfect setting. Saturday was only a few days away, but hours felt like months. Already, she'd called Grady and lied about her weekend plans. She, Brock, and Lance maintained the same lie. Grady was under the impression that a family Christmas party in their hometown took precedence and they wouldn't return until Sunday evening.

Oddly, she had hoped he wouldn't be offended for not being invited. If he discovered the truth he'd be more than offended. He'd be devastated. She thought so anyway, assuming that he was *into* her as much as he professed.

Saturday would be enigmatic. She didn't care that she'd spent too much money on the hotel room. It would be worth every penny to get fucked silly by her precious boys. She couldn't wait to feel Brock's hands invade her every opening. The image of his strong fingers jammed in her mouth drew perspiration. Tormented, she needed Brock to bend her over and thrust into her. Dominating the unattainable man would bring true ecstasy into full bloom. She experienced true enlightenment when Brock adhered to her, when she'd ordered him to beg. Commanding him to do as she pleased was enough to shake her knees and quake her heart.

And then she thought about Lance. She felt guilty for the lack of excitement in regard to Lance. But she remembered what she enjoyed about him. She enjoyed that he worshipped her. While she was receiving intense physical pleasure from Brock, she also received adornment, soul, passion, worship, and devotion from Lance. Lance made love to her while Brock fucked her. She sustained pleasures rooted from both aspects of their intimacy. *Synchronicity.* Being intimate with two men and expelling all inhibitions allowed her to attain complete intimacy. Conflicting emotions complicated this arrangement. The fact that she loved Brock, but Lance loved her, and she didn't love Lance, while Brock didn't love her was hard to clarify with any sense of preciseness. But together, the dots connected. A superlative combination was aligned. The relationship functioned on levels that society wouldn't condone. Their friends would call them perverts and their relatives would consider them deviants. But they were inhibited. Their perception was inaccurate and misguided. The sexual bliss experienced was tender, genuine. Three people providing each other with physical and emotional connection was something many people would attempt and fail at. All three needed each other.

Brianna found herself wondering how long this relationship could last. *Why not?* The sensations they'd shared allowed real freedom. The relationship felt right even if it sounded wrong. The openness of their private world—that very few people would ever achieve—was pure. While the exterior display of their actions was categorized as wrong it simply wasn't. There was only love and pleasure. No hatred or resentment. Their relationship was special because of its complicated maturity.

And then Brianna remembered Grady. *How could she have forgotten?* What about Grady? She would need to break it off with Grady. If there was a negative energy involved in this experiment it stemmed from Grady. Guilt would eventually consume her for which she was aware. Therefore, she would need to end her relationship with the California boy.

Glancing at her reflection in the mirror, a sly grin curled her lips. She focused on the raw consequences and brutal truth that she enjoyed cheating on Grady. The thought of Grady blabbing on about his daily activities while she smiled, pretended to care, but only thought about being ravaged by her boys, not Grady, thrilled her. The sheer notion of being naughty shook her inner thighs. Her breaths came hard and she perspired again. Jeez, she'd need to take a shower after groveling over her thoughts. The shower nozzle would double in purpose—maybe the Jack Rabbit for a little extra support?

Startled, Brianna twisted toward the door when someone pounded their fists into it. After a quick minute, she shook her lustful thoughts. She called out, "Who is it?"

"Me."

It was Grady. Oh shit.

Brianna's nerves revved. Lifting her hand, she extended her shaking hand. Her cheeks were heated, soft embers. Dashing to the kitchen sink she splashed cold water onto her face. Her knees still shook. *It was happening.* She was clearly in heat. "Just give me a sec!" she hollered before darting into the bathroom.

"Okay." She heard Grady's relaxed California drawl.

In the bathroom, she approved of her hasty appearance, whisked her hair over her ear, dabbed some perfume on her privates, slid some deodorant on, and then ran to the door. On her way, as her hand extended to unlock the door, she completed a thought: *I'm going to fuck the hell out of Grady.* This act would settle her lustful nerves. Afterward when she was relaxed she'd be able to converse with Grady like a normal human being. Not a lust-sick idiot.

Opening the door, she observed a shocked expression etched to Grady's face.

"Everything okay?" He took a step backward.

"No, get in here." She pulled the sleeve of his white tee shirt.

Once inside, she pressed her lips to Grady's and eagerly dipped her tongue into his mouth.

"Whatever's up with you—I'm down." Grady slammed the door and marched inside.

"Lock the door," Brianna insisted. "Now!" She enjoyed bossing men around.

"Yes, ma'am." Grady turned and locked the door. Brianna noticed that his hands were shaking. "Whatever you want."

She grinned coyly and asked, "Whatever I want?"

Grady looked scared. "Yes?" he was probably uncertain so stated a question.

"Bend me over the couch and eat until I say it's okay to come up for air."

Grady smiled.

Brianna slapped his face and instructed, "No smiling."

Grady pushed her toward the boring, standard issued couch that the college provided. It was drab, grey and didn't add flare to the room. Nor was it comfortable.

Brianna kicked off her gym shorts and then tugged her thong off before bending over the couch. She turned to see that Grady's face was beet red. His appearance was a cross between a timid student delivering a public speech and a comedian trying not to laugh at his own joke. She didn't care. She was too turned on. She grabbed Grady's shaggy hair and stuffed his face between her ass cheeks. He wasted no time. She could feel his tongue whirling and twisting in both holes. And she moaned with extreme pleasure while he did this.

2

The red light on the digital camera set on the tripod in the building across from *that slut* Brianna's dorm room blinked on. The lens zoomed in on the boy cleaning Brianna's crack. Footage like this hadn't been recorded prior. Not by The Killer. This footage would play nicely into the lineage of his murderous video. The story was robust. The Smiley Devils would adore his artistry.

3

The front door creaked open. Lance inhaled the chilly December air, acclimatized to the cold and kicked off his four-mile run across the college town of Oshkosh, Wisconsin. His thoughts—like he assumed his best friend's thoughts—were twisted, maddening and spiraled like a Midwest tornado. Being this in love with Brianna caused relentless anxiety. Reality struck. He was honest with himself: Brianna didn't love him the way he loved her. She'd never love him because he knew how she felt about Brock. Still, Lance was a romantic. He'd never give up on love. There was always a way. He'd fight for Brianna. Maybe Brock's vanity would eventually run out and his antics would age poorly.

Horrible ideas polluted Lance's train of thought. Visuals of Brock getting into an accident spawned joy. Any kind of accident that would damage his perfect face would suffice.

Maybe he'd get drunk and fall into the river like those other drunken idiots?

So many awful—good—thoughts of his friend's demise surfaced upward from the blackness of his subconscious.

Now his thoughts drifted down river to the drown boys of this college town, *such an odd phenomenon.* Lance couldn't understand why a fence wasn't erected around the bridge.

Was the town budget that tight?

Four drown victims this past year was too many.

He continued thinking about Brock's face meeting the end of its vanity. He hated his desire to think like this. The crashing waves of guilt saddened him. Simply put, it was wrong to entertain these thoughts. On the other hand, the joy of private resent-filled thoughts colored his soul. He allowed his fantasy to unwind. He created images of Brock dying at the hands of some accident. It would be best if the accident would be caused by stupidity. If this happened, eventually, Brianna would have a hard time sympathizing with his demise. She would only be angered. This idea coupled with the fact that she couldn't be attracted to his deformity would steer her devotion toward Lance. Lance's opportunity to intervene and win Brianna's heart would present itself. He'd score the girl. *His girl.* Sure, he'd remain friends with Brock. He'd be there for him. He'd lend his shoulder to cry on. Then he'd gladly take the girl.

Another wild idea struck: Lance wondered if he *could* hurt his friend.

Like, for real, as Brock would say. These violent thoughts were silly yet troubling. Lance wished he could whisk away these troubled desires. Toss them into the wind like cremated ash. But he couldn't. He knew that his mounting jealously would worsen. Jealousy was powerful. Eventually, these thoughts would possess and destroy him.

Lance couldn't help but to think about drowning his friend in the cold river on the other side of the bridge.

4

Brock's thumb applied pressure to the small plastic switch on the clippers that buzzed loudly as he pressed the hair trimmer against the skin below his abdomen. Sparse pubic hair sprinkled downward to the tile floor. Brock's member was bald now. He lathered the tender, raw skin with feminine lotion so that the razor burn would heal. Standing back, he inspected the details of his appearance in the vanity mirror that was tucked into the right corner of his bedroom. His chest hair, pubic hair, armpit hair, and some of his forearm hair had been shed—shaved skin close. After applying lotion and patiently allowing it to soak in, he sprayed himself with Australian Gold sun tan spray—this brand held a touch of artificial bronze. The spray was oil and gave the skin a smooth, shiny, polished appearance. Plus, it smelled of sweet summer beach. He wanted Brianna to be overwhelmed by his physical attributes. Glancing at his shaved ass in the mirror, Brock smacked his left butt cheek and continued to the bathroom. Now he'd bathe with baby oil to enhance the shimmer of his youthful skin, adding a glistening effect. Laughing as he sat in the hot tub, he acknowledged the silliness of his actions. Preparing for this night was more work than he'd anticipated. H had a sudden appreciation for women. Precious females adhered to this process regularly. Regardless, he was excited for this weekend's sexual recourse. He'd not been this turned on since he was much younger and sex was new. He hoped that Lance possessed enough awareness to prepare in a similar fashion. Brianna would appreciate the sentiment.

An hour later, Lance returned from his jog. Huffing, puffing and red in the face he nearly choked at the sight of Brock's hairless nakedness. Curling his body at the core, Lance laughed hysterically, which sent him into a fit of intense coughing.

"What the hell, man? I hate stereotypes and labels, but you look gay as hell. You gonna go shoot a gay porno movie?" Lance doubled over.

Brock seemed genuinely happy to see that his best friend was enjoying this sight. It was nice to see such an intense person cut loose and *lose his shit*. "I'm glad I can amuse you."

"Me too. What's the deal?"

"I'm getting ready for Friday night, dipshit." Brock smirked.

"You're getting ready for Friday night by shaving your entire body and walking around the house naked?" Lance asked.

"I'm doing you a favor."

Lance attempted to sip from his bottle of water, but spit-up onto the floor and asked, "How is this doing me a favor?"

"You should strive to look like this for our date with Brianna. That and you need to develop a new level of comfort."

"You think I should shave my cock, balls, and rub baby oil all over my asshole? Is that what you're recommending, oh-Zen-pussy-master?" Lance maintained his laughter.

"Something like that." Brock's glee diminished. Tone stern, he contributed, "Dude, I think I know a little bit more about what chicks appreciate... than you do."

"Do you?"

"Um, look at my track record... comparatively."

"Why?"

"Because you'll see that I get way more 'tang' than you."

"You bang nasty skanks that probably give you sick diseases. Sure, they're attractive, but there isn't one of them that would enter into a meaningful relationship with you. Plus, you probably have AIDS."

"What the hell does *'entering into a meaningful relationship'* have to do with anything? Do you think that what we're doing with Brianna is some kind of meaningful relationship?"

Lance was silent.

Brock recognized his friend's silence and accepted the shallow nature of his words. "Let me take back what I just said. I forgot about what this argument is all about."

"Please clarify."

"I was just trying to let you know that it might be nice for you to trim your goods prior to our next date with Brianna. That, and get comfortable being naked around me. She might like it if you go the extra mile."

"You mean shave the extra inch?"

Brock forced a laugh before admitting, "That's pretty good."

"You set me up for it." Lance sat on the ratty reclining chair. "You really think she'd appreciate it if I trimmed up a bit?"

"Yeah, man. That's all I'm saying. I guess I really didn't get my point across. I thought it would be funny if I ... " Brock looked down and was reminded of his stark nakedness and the fact that he was rubbed down in baby oil. He'd not attained the comedic effect he'd aimed to achieve. "I look like a total fag, don't I?"

"You shouldn't say 'fag.'"

"Fucking millennial-word-police-generation. We're such ass-hammers," Brock retorted, involuntarily.

"Point taken. I get it. Now, can you please cover yourself?"

"Sure thing." Brock turned and headed upstairs. His friend's laughter continued at him, not with him.

Chapter 11

Encounters

1

The front right wheel of Brianna's shopping cart spun lazily as she strolled along the home décor aisle at Scent Store—an aromatherapy hobby-shop located at the downtown mall. After every few steps, she'd halt and inhale the smell of a candle or some exotic oil. According to Brianna's perception of tonight there were specific scents that needed to accompany the experience. The hotel room would need to smell appropriate, sensual, and sweet. The candlelight would add a bronzing to their perfect bodies, but the smells would assist in the release of pheromones. These details would amplify their sexual desires, prowess, and lift the physical experience to heightened, pleasurable levels. The night needed to be perfect. No detail could be spared. An odd thought struck her: she hadn't studied all week. Her mind was consumed with thoughts of naked flesh and lust. The hotel excursion was an unquenchable affair, perfect. She'd already bought two bottles of champagne, a case of water, and beer for the boys. Also, she'd purchased an eighth of weed and a few pills of Molly. If in the morning they felt awful, she would distribute the remainder of her Percocet to knock away the hangover. There were still ten round pills in the bottle she'd been prescribed earlier in the volleyball season.

No detail would be spared.

After shopping, Brianna called her father. She'd not spoken to him in two weeks. Sex had preoccupied her thoughts, her brain, and her reality. Well, that was probably a lie. The truth was that she wouldn't speak with her father while her thoughts basked in sexual exploration. Those two ideals didn't meld well. She couldn't bare the idea of speaking with the man who'd spent countless hours reading her wholesome stories—to include the bible— while she thought about being violated by her childhood friends. He'd raised her in the church. Brock and Lance were like sons to him and he expected them to protect her. Brianna didn't want to speak with him now, but it had been too long and he'd left many messages.

Well, Brock and Lance did protect her. That was true.

If ever she were in danger, Brock and Lance would lay down their lives.

For now, they would lay her down in other ways.

She laughed.

Her fit of schoolyard laughter halted. She stood and straightened her posture.

Would they kill for her?

Probably not.

But maybe?

Another hypothetical thought struck: If she were at a party and some douchebag slipped a bad batch of GHB into her drink and then attempted to have his way with her—what would *her* Brock and Lance do to said gentleman?

She smiled.

They would kill him. She knew it. They would beat him, drag him to the trunk of the car, drive him out to the middle of nowhere and kill the rapey-prick.

Her face heated. Anger broiled her blood for a quick moment, but it was needed.

How the hell could she smile at this dark thought?

As of late, so many aspects of her life were changing. Her innocence was shedding like snake's skin.

Would she end up a bad person?

The confusion was daunting. The times were daunting. Here she was, engaging in unconventional sexual activities with men that she cared for far too much to be doing these things with. At least she acknowledged her pleasure. Worse, she enjoyed cheating on her boyfriend. Her smile faded. Another question popped like bubble gum.

Why is this wrong?

If it didn't feel wrong then was it wrong?

This question weighed six tons and she could only hold 100 lbs. If she enjoyed doing these pleasurable acts with her friends and nobody was getting hurt, then was it truly wrong? The questions continued, redundantly. The question would stop if she could answer, but she couldn't. Who made the rules? Why were the rules right? She couldn't think of an honest answer.

She scrolled through the contacts in her phone until she found her father.

She traced the edge of the phone with her index finger for a long moment before hitting the send button. He picked up after only one ring.

"Hi daddy, how are you?" She attempted to sound clueless like a young, innocent girl. The young innocent girl that her father believed she was. But she was anything but innocent as of late.

"Well, holy guacamole, I thought you'd written me off for dead. I miss my little pumpkin. Are you okay? Why haven't you called or answered my calls?" he asked, the excitement draining from his voice the more he spoke.

Lowering his voice meant that he was choking back tears. This was a lesson Brianna learned early. Sure, he was a tough guy and looked like a biker, but when it came to his little girl—his Brianna—he was soft as bunny fur.

"Daddy, I'm just... I don't know. I don't want to make you worry."

"You haven't been... you know... there hasn't been any boys that have gone too far or... " Agitation stole his tone.

"No, no, no, daddy. Nothing like that. I'm just busy with volleyball and my studying. And I'm trying to exercise... "

"You're going to parties when you get a minute. Having some fun?" He finally relaxed into the conversation.

"I go to *some* parties. Brock and Lance take good care of me."

Damn right they do.

Stop it. Stop thinking about what those boys do to you and how much you like it.

"You there?" Her father asked.

Brianna hadn't noticed that she was sucking her thumb. She popped it out of her mouth and said, "I'm sorry. I lost my train of thought."

Trained by two boys at the same time.

Again, stop it, Brianna!

"You're not taking drugs are you?"

"No, daddy. Nothing like that."

Unless two dicks in my mouth is a drug.

Stop. Stop. Stop.

She nearly hung up on her father. She couldn't bare the overwhelming guilt. Thoughts of confessing rattled her mind. She laughed out loud. Not that confessing was funny. But the oddest image of Brock's cock punching her brain wouldn't leave her image sensory.

"You know you can talk to me, right? If you ever have any trouble... that you need to talk to me about, I'm here. I'll never judge you. I promise, pumpkin."

There it was. Now she was going to cry. Her father's heart was going to break if he ever found out. He wouldn't banish her from his life, no. Nor would he condemn her. There probably wouldn't be any judgment if she came clean about her sexual prowess, but she *would* smash his heart into a million pieces. Hell, she might kill him by way of a heart attack. She couldn't. And on a high note, she couldn't hold these silly, girlish thoughts anymore. She had to stop.

"Daddy, I'm just stressed, but having fun. My grades are good. Brock and Lance watch out for me, but it's just a lot. I'm overwhelmed. College is different and I'm... adjusting. Trying to figure out who I am. What I want out of life."

"Baby, I completely understand. That's what college is for and I don't want to add to your stress, but promise you'll give me a call once a week? Even if all you do is call me up to say, 'Hey, I'm alive. Don't worry about me.'"

"I can do that, daddy."

"That's all I ask."

"I love you, dad."

"Not as much as I love you, pumpkin. I wish your mother were here to see you."

"She does." These words stung.

Once she hung up, she marched to the bathroom, pulled her shorts off, turned the hot water on, sat down in the tub, removed the nozzle, pulled it down and slowly rotated the showerhead around her wet parts. And she enjoyed it. When climax approached, she removed the spray and took quick breaths. She didn't want to orgasm. She'd save that for tonight.

2

The Killer sat at his desk watching his new video footage. The image-texture was grainy. Biting his lip, he wished the iris on his camera had been more open. While editing these fresh clips he thought about the soundtrack. What kind of music did he want to play over the footage? Music really set the tone of a video. Candle Box, a nineties band, blared from his iPad. This video needed the images to sync with nineties grunge. For whatever reason, he loved listening to this sentimental era of music. The songs held a grit-value that resonated. The beats and ballads were emotion invoking and raw. Kurt Cobain, Eddy Veder, and Chris Cornell led the pack. The gratuitous sex described in the lyrics provoked a specific brand of illicitness that he sought. Sex was everything when melded with violence. This new video was special. It cut together in the most perfectly twisted way. A montage of sex, drugs, rock and roll, then strung together with sweet young adults. Soon the video would contain violence. Extreme violence. Violence would define the content. The Smiley Devils would savor this sick film. The Dark Lord was satisfied with his work.

The Killer would savor each moment as he desecrated these boys. He wasn't sure what to do with the girl. She wasn't the subjective victim. There were rules. Caucasian males with athletic builds were to be drowned. That was protocol. This sacrifice was greater than the rules. He would gut and destroy these pigs. The girl wouldn't qualify, but at this point The Killer didn't know if he could exclude her from his masterpiece. The Dark Lord presented this sacrifice as a gift for his loyal service. He wanted her insides exposed. Cannibalism was an evolving idea. His masterpiece video demanded this content. Cutting her out from the Smiley Devil version of his film—the edited-for-television cut might appease his pallet. The uploaded version would include Lance and Brock, not Brianna. But the extended director's cut would include all three. The gruesome nature of his capabilities would shine. *Burn, really.* He would murder her in a special way. Maybe he would keep her. There were places in this massively forested portion of the Midwest where he could find an outpost and bind her. Keep her at his disposal for sexual purposes. Shaking this thought, he focused on the work. Best to leave these thoughts for another time.

Right now, his priorities were to set the trap for Brock and Lance. Lure them into his web and then attack their helpless beings.

How would he get them to a bar?

When could he find them alone?

This shouldn't be hard.

They were constant patrons at The Quarter.

Somehow, he needed to get them inebriated. Then he'd need to bait them into the cold winter night. They'd probably taken the bridge route a million times. Taking this route would be beneficial. The killer imagined his scenario. In his vision he saw Brock crossing the bridge. It would be his final walk.

Aware, he knew that this sacrifice would be a challenge. Brock was fit. He was a skilled fighter. Lance wasn't physically threatening, but he was intelligent—also a threat. After a couple drinks, Lance would fall. One Smiley Devil would suffice for his apprehension. A plan to render him defenseless and unconscious would need preplanning, but was executable.

The first week of the winter semester was his best option. During that week, the students held more parties, drank more, packed into all the bars and thinned out police resources. As for an appropriate establishment, The Quarter was the option with the greatest projection of success.

This idea was what he'd go with. The first weekend of the new semester would be the weekend that Brock and Lance's days on earth would end.

The Killer smiled wide. Striking the space key on his keyboard, he paused the editing system on his Mac Book Pro. The image on the computer was of Brock. The Killer leaned forward until his lips nearly touched the computer screen.

"You're going to be my greatest challenge." The Killer placed his index finger on the screen, directly above Brock's arrogant smile.

For the first time in many years, The Killer experienced fear creep along his spine and he enjoyed it.

The Killer somehow, someway, knew that this kill would introduce challenges. Hell, he might not walk away from this sacrifice. But the fear of death excited The Killer. If he were to die killing, then his lord would reward him in the eternal fire.

The Killer smiled the smile of a Smiley Devil.

Death hovered like a looming crow.

3

The boxing gym that Brock frequented smelled of stale sweat and left a chalky layer of dust at the back of his throat. Loud grunts and moans of agony echoed off the brittle walls as men fought and trained. Brock's forehead poured sweat in plump beads while wailing on the duct-taped heavy bag. Hands taped, with each strike of the heavy bag—one strike after the other with great succession—his anger would build and then purge. He couldn't understand where this aggression stemmed from, but at least he was present at a suitable venue for his release.

With his left foot, he pushed off the short-carpeted floor. His right foot slammed into the heavy bag and sent it soaring off the hook. The two men—off-duty cops wearing Oshkosh Police Department shorts—aged with bad mustaches—sparred in the adjacent ring. Both turned toward the commotion. Brock's loud grunt, as he kicked the bag, had been purposefully obnoxious. He desired negative attention.

"Whoa there, killer. Don't snap the bag," one of the men protested.

"One of you guys wanna spar a few rounds?" Brock asked while smacking his left fist into his right palm. His adrenaline coursed adventurous like a whitewater rampage. Brock desired to hit something live, not a punching bag.

The elder cop that clearly thought he possessed youthful stamina would do the trick.

This current behavior was primitive. Brock marched toward the second boxing ring centered in the warehouse. *This was considered a gym?* He pulled the ropes up, ducked under, and jumped from foot to foot, adjusting his rhythm into sync. He tossed his head side to side, loosened his neck. Looking to the older man, he nodded before making his way to the center of the ring. Brock and the cop bumped boxing gloves signifying *let's go.*

"You sure, old man?" Brock remembered that this was supposed to be friendly. Still, he knew the answer. Sensing aggression, anger, and humiliation in the middle-aged man's red streaked eyes came easy. This man held the eyes of a cop—strong exhaustion melded with alert focus. Plus, this man clearly wanted to punish Brock. Beat the adolescent arrogance from him. Unfortunately, he was in for a painful awakening.

"I think this old dog has a few new tricks," the man said, backing up and curling his shoulders in small circles before shadow boxing in the corner.

Someone at the back of the room rang a bell.

Brock moved forward, cocked his fist and struck the man in the face. Next, he sliced an uppercut through the officer's chin, clearly dazing him. The alert focus shook from those intense cop eyes. Brock smirked with the intention of psychologically dominating his opponent. This next punch would end the fight. But that wouldn't be enough. Brock would deny his opponent the objective. Personally, he wasn't conflicted with this man. He'd seen him around. The fact was, Brock wanted to hit something, someone, anyone. And this man fit the bill. The cop was a living thing and therefore needed to be hit. And then Brock's quick hands succeeded into the officer's face. Brock punched repeatedly until the officer bled from his mouth, nose, and bellow both eyes. His face was a mess. Visible through his sparring mask—made of heavy foam—blood spilled down along the red padding. His face continued to absorb the brunt of Brock's blows.

Stretching downward, Brock landed punches on the cop as he fell to the matt. The intensity of Brock's focus was redirected when the man's friend hollered, "Knock it off, punk!"

"Punk?" Brock repeated the insult.

The muscular off-duty police officer slid beneath the ropes. Taking a knee, he lightly slapped Brock's opponent and asked repeatedly, "You alright? You alright?"

Blinking into consciousness, reconnecting with his senses, he peered upward at Brock and nodded into awareness.

Brock shook his anger and snapped into his reality. "Whoa... shit, man... is he alright? I didn't mean to..."

"You lost your shit, bro. Know your limits. Your shit is only hot for a short time. We're all on the same team. We're sparring, working out some aggression. Not hurting each other for the sake of being mean-spirited. And if you can't tell the difference then you need to get the hell out of here." The off-duty cop barked at Brock. He displayed an uncharacteristic attempt at confidence, but Brock could sense the man's fear.

Brock's first instinct was to punch this stupid fogey in his face.

No one tells Brock Hills what to do.
Except Brianna.

He smiled.

"What the hell's so funny?" the man asked, pulling his friend to his feet.

"Nothing. Sorry. I understand, sir." Brock turned from the two men and walked to the edge of the ring, slid beneath the ropes, and vanished into the locker room.

The long hot shower calmed Brock's nerves. Stepping out of the steamy shower, he dressed, applied deodorant, dabbed cologne on his neck and genitals and left the gym.

The off-duty cops had left. The car they'd arrived in was gone from the parking spot across the street. In its place was a black van. Engine running with the headlights out, the vehicle appeared menacing. Brock couldn't verify why. Squinting to see, Brock watched the van and wondered if the cops had switched vehicles and were waiting for him to leave so they could kick his ass. Nonchalantly, he knelt down and pretended to tie his shoe while he secured his knife. He had a sheath for it that he kept around his ankle.

Did these assholes really want to continue giving him shit?

He didn't think they wanted a piece of him, but you never knew anymore. Plus, they were cops. They could get away with anything and they had the power of the police force behind them. In a town like this they could call up their buddies, have them rough Brock up and then leave him for dead in the middle of nowhere. Brock's word wouldn't hold any weight to the word of an officer. Rightfully, Brock thought. Maybe it wasn't too intelligent to be knocking out off-duties. He'd apologize to the man next time he popped in.

Life—including people—had become so aggressive in present times.

He nearly tripped over his own feet as he thought of the irony to his predicament. Minutes ago, he'd condemned society and people for over-aggression yet he'd aggressively beaten a weaker person moments later.

I'm such a dick, he thought.

The way he'd handled things—hitting that old man—wasn't cool. The owner of the boxing gym, Marty Shale would chew his ass out. Plus, the fact that he'd beaten on a cop wasn't going to score him any political points. Hopefully, he wouldn't be eighty-sixed from working out at this gym. He liked working out here.

"Screw it," he whispered into the icy night air then started walking along the cracked sidewalk, away from the gym. Christmas lights trailed along both sides of the street. The cold wind bit and chapped at his raw skin. Snow fell in steady layers. Luckily, he lived near—a few blocks away. When he got home, he'd grab his things, shower again—rid the residual stink—then meet up with Lance and Brianna at the Marriott. Thinking about Brianna going down on him and catching an unpleasant odor was unacceptable. He'd certainly take a few moments to shower. Cleanliness was godliness.

"He's too tough!" someone called from behind the metal door of the black van. The van door's metallic squeal was followed by mean-spirited cackles.

Brock's attention shot to the van. He smirked.

Do these assholes want some?

The laughter continued.

The inner turmoil he'd been groveling over was tossed aside. Brock marched across the street. Stopped about ten feet from the van.

Nobody laughed at Brock Hills.

After stepping off the curb, he halted at the sight in front of him. His anger morphed into anxiety. The van door was open. A man wearing a strange smiley-faced rubber mask tilted his head. Hard to see, but the mask looked like a smirking devil.

What the hell?

Brock watched three people— dressed in all black with stupid devil masks—stare at him. Tilting his head, he saw that the mask-faces were yellow with red streaks running downward from crescent horns that protruded from their foreheads.

"You guys cool?" Brock's nerves flailed and his display of machismo died.

The Smiley Devils remained silent. One of them retrieved a hatchet from the floor and smacked the flat end of the blade against his gloved hand. Then he ran his finger along the sharp edge. Brock could hear the fabric of the man's glove tear. The instrument was sharp as surgical equipment.

"What do you think you're gonna do with that, jack ass?" Brock antagonized.

More laughter erupted from the van. There were more. *Weird dudes.*

The driver contributed deep guttural and menacing laughter.

"I got better things to do, boy. Have a good one." Brock did have better things to do than look at three strange, masked, whack-jobs. The ax was disturbing, but not ultimately intimidating. If they were to brawl it would be three of them versus one of him. The odds wouldn't be in his favor. But they didn't know Brock's skillset.

Fuck this. Leave.

Stepping backward, Brock hopped onto the sidewalk, retrieved his headphones from his pocket, stuffed them into his ears, and cranked the volume. Electronic music settled his nerves after a hard workout. Pulling the hood of his sweatshirt over the top of his head he walked into a jog.

After walking a few yards his peripherals alerted movement. The van was following him. Now it drove parallel. Side door still open, the three masked figures—all holding sharp cutting tools—trained their eyes on him. And their antics were effective. Brock's nerves rattled. Still utilizing his peripherals, he surveyed his surroundings. There were various avenues to run and hide. Gut instinct, he'd need an escape route. Pulling out his cell phone—with a shaky hand—he pretended to change the song. Instead, he placed his thumb on the nine-button followed by consecutive one buttons. Things had gone too far. There was need for the police. Suddenly, he wished he hadn't punched the cop.

How long would it take them to get here? They weren't exactly quick these days. And Brock didn't blame them. Police work was a thankless job. People, especially college students, loved to lure the police with antagonism, force them to react violently, record their reactions on an iPhone, and then destroy their reputations on the nightly news. The boys in blue had their hands tied behind their backs. Sitting ducks. He shook his head, and this current thought. There would be time to ponder politics at a later time. He did not hit the send button.

He could handle these pussies.

Well, they had weapons.

Brock rounded the corner, kicked his legs into a sprint and listened intently as the van's tires crunched over thick snow while turning down the street.

"Run," one of them whispered. Steam drifted upward from his mouth.

Now he was pissed. Nobody told Brock Hills what to do.

"What did you say?" Brock faced the van.

The van screeched to a halt. Another of the masked men jumped out. This one was tall and muscular. His black clothing wrapped tightly around him. The axe in his right hand dropped and scraped against the frozen blacktop as he walked. Tilting his head slowly, he raised the axe. Holding the rectangular blade in front of his face, his index finger scraped along the sharp edge of the blade.

"What the hell do you want, dude?" Brock marched toward the masked man. Fists clenched tight as he walked. His nerves swam like sharks through the acid wash of his stomach.

"I wouldn't do that," the Smiley Devil called out. His voice was scruffy. *Maybe he was a smoker?* There was something about the tone of his voice and the manner in which his shoulders rolled that caused chills to run along Brock's spine. He seemed to grow. His posture was formed of confidence that Brock didn't recognize. The worst kind of confidence, given the context, Brock thought. Dominance.

Another Smiley Devil filed out of the van, followed by a third. They stood in perfect military-like formation. Two more jumped out. They held butcher knives. The blades were enormous, fourteen inches. The knives reminded Brock of the horror movies with Michael Myer's in them.

Halloween.

"On second thought, why don't you come here? Come on over and let me show you what I can do." The Smiley Devil tilted his head, *much like Michael Myers.*

"Take your mask off, dickhead." Brock forced laughter.

"Not yet."

"Not yet, why?"

"Because it's not your time yet."

"What the fuck is that supposed to mean?" Brock pried at this statement.

"It means you'll see us again," the overly confident Smiley Devil chuckled.

"I don't think so," Brock called out. He wondered what the possibilities were that this could be Jeff Torrance and his buddies fucking with him.

No, couldn't be. The masked asshole in the center was too big to be Jeff. And his voice clearly belonged to someone unfamiliar. There was a lot one could assume and familiarize by the size and proportion of a person. None of these freaks resembled anyone he knew. Sure, this could be a prank. In fact, he hoped it was a prank because—to be truthful—these assholes were starting to freak him out.

"Run. That's all you gotta do right now, tough guy. If you run we won't chase you. If I walk to you right now I promise they'll pull your body from the river sometime next week."

"What?" This statement struck a chord—scared the hell out of him, really. There'd been an abundance of drown victims near campus lately, enough that the rumor-mill was flooded. Foul play was common talk amongst the university student body. But that's all it was. Rumors. Still, the tone of this confrontation was beginning to feel doom-filled. He'd never admit, but these disturbed pricks were scaring him. And his damn ego wouldn't let go.

I'm being an idiot.

The sexual experience of a lifetime awaited him at the Marriott and he was fucking around with a bunch of assholes playing a Halloween prank near Christmas.

The tall one in the middle rested his hatchet in the palm of his hand. His right knee rose. He leaned forward and marched toward Brock. "If I get to you, you're dead. Serious."

He slapped the flat edge of the hatchet blade against his gloved palm.

Brock took a step backward.

The Smiley Devil stopped.

"What's your name?" Brock called out.

The Smiley Devil was silent, but after a moment answered, "I'm no one. I'm a servant of someone, someone bigger than us all. Call me the Smiley Devil."

The Smiley Devil on the right nudged his elbow into the tall one. The one with an average build—in the middle—tugged at the hatchet and said, "Stop."

"What?" the tall Devil with the Axe hollered. He didn't take his eyes off Brock. "Don't speak to me like that."

"I'll talk to you however I please. Now let go."

The tall Devil seemed to grovel this over. Clearly, he didn't respond well to orders.

"See you soon." the tall one said. "The fire burns for you." He turned to the van.

The remainder of the Smiley Devils about-faced and returned to the van.

Entering the vehicle, the tall Devil raised his hatchet, whacked the smaller one in the face—the one barking orders—with the flat side of the hatchet blade. The smaller one fell to his knees. When he lowered his head, the tall Devil swung his hatchet downward. A chunk of shoulder-meat spun to the street with a wet smack. The overly confident Smiley Devil had sliced off the edge of his buddy's shoulder. Brock could only imagine what this man would do to him. Brock felt bad for the screaming man that grabbed at his wound. Blood pulsated upward and between his gloved fingers. The axe must have sliced a vein or artery.

Now Brock ran. He was scared and he ran fast. These guys weren't fucking around. The tall muscular Smiley Devil stared at Brock. Slowly he raised his hand and waved patiently. The mask no longer looked silly, it was terrifying. And even though the man's face was covered, Brock could feel his smirk.

Lungs burning and legs chugging, Brock ran faster than he'd ever ran.

4

The Killer observed Brock running scared. For the first time since meeting Brock, he'd witnessed his fear and it was satisfying. The expression of fear on the face of a warrior minded person was something for The Killer to savor. The terror boiled his blood and coursed icily through his veins. The perfect drug.

"Should we follow him?" the tall Smiley Devil asked The Killer.

"We'll be patient."

"I really don't want to be patient. What if he runs to the police?"

"He won't."

"How do you know?

"Don't ask me again."

"But... "

The Killer raised his hatchet as if to swing at his fellow Smiley Devil.

"Forgive me."

The Killer looked to the wounded Smiley Devil and then another masked Devil and said, "Help your brother. We have much to plan."

"Sorry, brother."

He helped his brother into the van. Before sliding the door shut the wounded Devil picked up his torn flesh. It was tough to peel from the snow.

The gang of Devil's drove quickly into the night. As The Killer rested in the back of the van he thought about how pleasurable it would be to watch Brock's life drain from his perfect body. His dead face beneath the water was an image that pleased.

Baptized in death.

Beneath his rubber mask, The Killer's face was hot. Sweat ran down his forehead and along the contours of his cheeks. *Brock Hills would die well.* The Killer respected

Brock as he always respected his prey. And The Killer enjoyed a respectful sacrifice. When he was finished, he wouldn't dump the carcass into the river. He would remove his head and maintain it as a trophy. That was important. To remove the head was a sign of respect for one's enemy. *Without respect for one's enemy, one is not a warrior. And then one does not support a purpose.* The Killer renewed his belief.

As the van disappeared into the icy night, The Killer brought his index finger upward toward the body cam clipped to his shoulder. The camera resembled an ink pen. He flipped the record button off. The footage of this encounter would add suspense to his video.

Chapter 12

The Last Tango

1

Brianna arrived first. She'd demanded the boys not show up until the hotel room was prepared. And the room would need work. The online photos allowed her a glimpse into what she was working with. The current layout presented a commercialized tone. For the evening festivities, the atmosphere needed to be romanticized. Dedication would prevail. The white duvet would be sensational once the rose pedals were scattered across the fluffy appearance. The numerous mirrors on all sides of the room would reflect the warmth of candlelight and fill the room. This understanding was verbally solidified the last time they'd spoken as a group. Entering the lobby, a cold gust of winter wind forced pressure onto the revolving door. Cold melded with the heat, which enveloped her from inside. The warmth allowed for the tightly wrapped nerves swimming in her stomach to loosen. Her lips curled into a smug grin when she thought about the intense heat that was to come.

She'd stuffed her suitcase with candles, soaps, lotions, oils, rose pedals, lubrications, champagne, strawberries, whip cream, and a set of handcuffs she'd purchased. This night would be amazing. It would be right. It would be perfect. She would climax like she'd never imagined. And she'd reach these heightened pleasures with the men she loved. A rosy smile etched across her face. She was barely aware that the handsome Hotel check-in employee had been attempting to charm her.

"Can I help you to your room?" he asked.

"Sure." She invited the boy to charm her with seduction. Flirting with this boy enticed her excitement. She felt sexy and wanted. She wouldn't do anything with this boy, of course, but she appreciated his interest. She welcomed it. Being wanted was invigorating.

"Great." The boy turned to his fellow employee, a heavier woman that displayed her cynicism by shaking her head and rolling her eyes. She and Brianna locked into a stare. Brianna smiled, sharing the connection that all women share regarding sophomoric antics from immature men.

"You staying for the weekend?" the boy asked. His cheeks flushed red. Nervous now.

"I am." Brianna washed the boy's posture with squinted eyes. She could almost feel herself telepathically causing his erection.

They entered the elevator.

Brianna's cheeks tightened when a comedic thought struck. She would play a dirty trick on this boy. Make him feel special.

The elevator doors closed.

Brianna turned to the lobby boy. "You ever just get a hotel room with two of your best friends... and just stay in bed and fuck each other until your heads are filled with all kinds of crazy?" She grabbed the hotel boy by the back of his hair and pulled him close. She grabbed the hard bulge in his pants and had to fight laughter when he squealed. His face reddened. "Because that's what I'm doing here this weekend."

The elevator halted.

Brianna slid to the center of the claustrophobic car, away from the boy. He staggered and nearly fell to the carpeted floor.

"Can I walk you to your room?" he begged.

She leaned down, smiled, and told him, "You'll have your time, handsome boy, but not today." She leaned in close and planted her lips on his. If Brock or Lance could see her right now they would laugh until their stomachs split. The confidence erupting within her—for having tortured this poor boy—was enthralling. A euphoric sensation brewed within her sizzling insides. For a moment, she thought she might climax. She grabbed the hotel cart with her belongings and left the boy, shaky and hot, trying his best to hide the bulge in his pants.

Strutting down the carpeted hallway, she couldn't help but to laugh loud and hearty.

She found her room, placed the magnetic key to the pad and opened the door.

The room was fantastic.

The large window with polarized glass overlooked the river, which ran between two crests of eroding white snow. The town was so small from here. The people were scurrying ants.

Hell, wasn't that it? Weren't people just ants in a big ant farm? No way.

She couldn't believe that. There was more to life than mere feelings and sensations. She felt things for different people, spiritual things. She felt unique things for the two beautiful boys that were on their way here to love her for many hours. The thought of these boys removing her clothes and kissing her naked flesh lifted feelings and emotions that illuminated her soul. She had a soul, she knew that and she believed in a higher power. She had to believe in more than life.

What would God think about what was about to happened here tonight?

She didn't want to think about that brand of spirituality. Not right now, but then she thought: maybe we *should* think and talk about that. *Maybe after they'd concluded their initial romp?* Maybe then she could get the boys to talk about the topic of soul and God and what was right and what was wrong? It made sense. One of the points to this relationship was that they could be one hundred percent honest with each other about everything and anything.

A smile found her beautiful, make-up free face.

Next, she prepared the room. She set candles in the bathroom and lit them, making sure that there was enough light to see, but that the atmosphere was darkly erotic. She set candles on the countertop—vanilla scented—and then she placed them on the ledge of the marble tiled walkway that led into the shower. She was impressed with this shower. There wasn't a door. The space was open and vulnerable, big. She, Lance and Brock would be able to make love under the spray of warm soft water. The room was perfect although she didn't know if she was into the fireplace video that lapsed on the sixty-inch flat screen. *What the hell?* She'd let it play.

After the room was set, she stripped off her clothing, opened her suitcase and removed her lotions, oils, and scrubs. She showered, and—as she'd suspected—the water was soft. Not that hard-water that dried out one's skin. Soft water felt amazing as it coursed along the contours of her naked body. Perfect water-pressure. After showering, she towel-dried her hair, applied lotion and inspected every square inch and crevice of her body until she was certain that she was exceptional, sexy, and gorgeous. Then she pulled out her lingerie. A black strappy thong with a transparent bra and matching black high heels would do. She'd spent a fortune, but her appearance reflected the goddess Helena. Once she was dressed—well, scantily-clad—she posed. Leaning across the bed, she grabbed her phone and texted her suitors.

Lying on the soft comforter of the California King sized bed she sprawled out and waited for her boys.

2

Lance drove into the parking structure and then pulled into a spot near a thick cement pillar, inconspicuous. He hoped. Sure, he was being paranoid, but it didn't hurt to be safe. Also, Brianna still had a boyfriend. That was another negative to this arrangement. He liked Grady and thought of him as a friend. Here he was making love to his friend's girlfriend. He wished that this type of behavior were outside the realm of his character. Given his present lifestyle, it wasn't. There was cuckolding and then there was *this*—having a threesome behind a nice guy's back. He and Brock were doing unspeakable things to Brianna and in the process they were committing unforgivable acts toward Grady.

Best not to think about it.

Opening the car door, he pulled his iPhone from his pocket and texted Brianna that he'd arrived. He was greeted with a Smiley Devil emoji. Lance smirked before fully exiting the car. The screeching of tires on smooth cement startled him. Averting his gaze up from the faceplate of his phone he found himself face to face with the grill of a black van. He looked at the driver who wore some sort of a rubber mask. Holding his hands up and outward, Lance shouted, "I'm alright. Sorry, I wasn't watching."

The mechanical whiz of the van's driver side window lowering faintly drew his attention. A raspy voice called out, "But I've been watching you."

"What?"

"You heard me, but let me repeat myself: I've been watching you."

What the hell was this guy talking about? This was creeping him out.

Lance marched toward the driver's side, but the van backed up.

"I don't want any trouble." Lance pleaded. True, he didn't want any trouble. Brock was the martial arts-brutal-primitive type, not he. He was the gentle lover that could work things out with simple conversation. *Hell, we weren't primates anymore*, he thought.

"We know that. We don't want trouble either, but we wish to do some very awful things to you."

"What is this about?"

"Nothing, which is the greatest part. There is no reason, you were just randomly picked."

This made no god damned sense. Why and who and where did these assholes come from? Were they just a bunch of testosterone freaks looking to fight? He definitely didn't want to fight right now. He had much better things to do, like Brianna.

Lance's peripheral vision found the exit door to the left of the parking ramp. He would simply march to the door and sneak off into the hotel. These guys were probably stupid, but not stupid enough to want trouble from the police. There had to be video footage in this parking structure. These assholes in the van were probably aware.

Maybe that's why they're wearing masks?

He went ahead with his plan. Stepping off—left foot first—he crossed the lot. Fear soon became a reality. The van sped forward and blocked his escape. Now he was becoming upset.

"Get out of my way, please." Lance gritted his teeth.

"Sure, right away," the driver stated.

It was difficult to hear him clearly through that stupid looking mask.

The van had stopped beneath a hissing fluorescent light. Lance saw that the mask was some sort of Smiley Devil.

Weird, Brianna had just sent a Devil-emoji icon to let him know that she was here. He pulled out his phone again and looked at the emoji. Then he looked to the driver of the van.

Could this be Grady? Had Grady discovered them?

No way.

Well, maybe.

If he'd found out about the affair, he'd be entitled to mess with Lance.

Lance stepped back. The van backed up. Lance sprinted forward and fled through the parking lot exit. "Screw you, weirdo." he muttered under his breath.

He sprinted and jumped down three flights of stairs and eventually made it to the hotel lobby. Watching from a distance, Lance's eyes followed the black van as it slowly exited the parking structure. Another strange sight: the sliding door was open. Three more people dressed in all black and wearing those stupid masks were leaning out as if surveying the area for him. They held weapons too. From this distance he couldn't be sure, but it looked like one of them was holding a hatchet and the others were holding butchers knives.

Lance let out a quick breath, entered the hotel through the sliding glass doors and let this strange conflict flee his rapid thoughts.

He ran upstairs, walked down the hallway and allowed his lustful nerves to fray. When he arrived at the door he heard a voice call to him from behind. It startled him at first. A wave of fear struck. His heart pounded madly beneath his ribcage. But he was comforted when a male voice whispered, "Are you ready for me, dumb ass?"

It was Brock.

Thank God. Relief settled him.

He walked to his friend and they shook hands.

"I'm glad we're doing this. I look forward to our conversations this weekend too." Brock sounded mature for once in his life. *He really had entered the Twilight Zone.*

"Fruitful," Lance added.

"I'm not kidding. I think that we've tapped into something special here. This relationship is crazy, but it's special. It's something nobody can touch, except us."

"Save it for afterward," Lance halted the conversation. It was a conversation that he'd always wanted to have with Brock, but now that everything was happening, he found it annoying. *Funny, how that works.* You get what you want and it's not what you expected. That wouldn't be the case with the sex though.

Brock knocked on the door.

After a few moments, they heard light electronic music. Something like Enya, but not silly. *Maybe it was Enya?* Something Lance wouldn't listen to except in the heat of sexual bliss. Not that he ever had.

Soft footsteps rose in volume as Brianna strutted confidently to the door. Lance turned to Brock as the doorknob turned from the inside.

Both gulped.

The door opened.

For the first time, Lance thought that Brock was seriously nervous. Understandable, considering what was on the other side of the door.

She was stunning. Beautiful. Gorgeous. The lacy string of her under garments caused his blood to circulate to all appendages. Brianna had applied the perfect amount of make-up, just a hint of eyeliner to accentuate those emerald eyes. A subtle glossing of the lips and that was about all. Traces of expensive perfume permeated the air. And then she dragged both boys into the room. The door closed. The vanilla scented candles and the perfume intoxicated Lance and he wished—in that moment—that he and Brianna were alone. Again, he found himself wishing that something bad would happen to Brock.

Something major.

If only he weren't here.

If he were dead.

That's your best friend.

Stop thinking this.

Why do your thoughts become violent during moments of intimacy?

Lance reminded himself that this was an ideal situation. He also reminded himself that this was the only way he could love Brianna, outwardly and cohesively.

These thoughts were broken when Brianna grabbed the back of Lance's head. She yanked him in and then kissed him. Brock kissed her ears and then licked her neck, which drove Lance's jealousy to the point of madness.

Brianna pulled away. Lance took in the sight of her perfect beauty. It truly was fantastic. Her skin shimmered in the candlelight and her features were sharp. Her emerald eyes squinted. She was an exotic, erotic animal. The see-through lingerie permitted visual stimuli. Enough to become erect and lose patience. He had to taste her flesh.

"Both of you take your clothes off," she ordered.

"Yes... " Brock pulled his shirt off, but Brianna halted him.

"I didn't say talk. Don't say anything unless I ask you to. Just strip."

Lance removed his underwear. Standing next to Brock he felt insecure. Brianna acknowledged his expression by saying, "Don't you dare feel like you're less than Brock. His body and face are just as perfect as your mind and soul. There are no inhibitions and there are no jealousies here—just our fantasy, our pleasure, our intimacy. You can answer that you understand."

Lance wasn't going to argue. "I understand."

"Good. Drop to your knees, crawl over here, and kiss my inner thighs. Make circles with your wet tongue," she ordered Lance.

Then she looked to Brock and ordered, "You. Get over here and stuff my mouth."

Their pleasure was great. Their bodies twisted together intimately in every position. When they were finished they lay naked, lightly convulsing. Soon after their initial sex they crawled out of bed and showered. The enclosure was big enough that they fit perfectly. They were silent as the warm water ran over their glistening bodies. They shared smiles and soft laughter as they touched and stroked each other.

Lance loved Brianna. He knew that he should accept this experience for what it was. He couldn't. Hatred for his best friend polluted his fantasy. This hatred was uncontrollable. Couldn't shake it, but only hide it. After drying off they returned to the bed and cranked the heat until it was cozy. They cuddled, naked, between the threaded cotton sheets.

"This moment is perfect, my boys." Brianna looked from Lance to Brock. Humiliation possessed her and Lance could read it, easily. "I have love and friendship and lust. Having you both fulfills all my needs. I'm complete. How do you feel, Lance?"

She'd put him on the spot. This was a relationship of love and honesty. He'd agreed to that before they'd begun. Now, lying was his only option. His lies would taint this experiment and cause failure, but he couldn't risk the negativity of his truth. He spoke, "I agree one hundred percent. I get to witness my best friend enjoy you physically while I enjoy you mentally. I'm fulfilled. I really am." Lance smiled at Brianna. Gently, she kissed his cheek.

"I'm fulfilled too," Brock stated.

Lance hated his best friend so much. Seething, he watched the creases in Brock's forehead compress, a stern expression that reflected Brock's confusion settled. Brock struggled for words. And when Brock struggled for words it meant that he was about to lie. "But I enjoy you mentally as well."

"I didn't mean to insult you, Brock. I swear, I just said what I was feeling. I love this."

Brianna ran her fingers along Brock's arm and said, "He means it, Brock. He's your best friend and he's just saying what he feels."

"You're right, Lance. My bad."

Lance shook his head. "I would never insult you, Brock. The thing I appreciate most about this arrangement is that we are free. The three of us are free from lies, insecurities, and the impossible world around us." Lance almost laughed. The ridiculous nature of this shallow philosophical banter was too much. Brock was too much of a moron to understand emotion and mature love, physical or otherwise. And Lance enjoyed causing Brock's insecurity. The look on Brock's face, now, was worth every lie he'd spoken. This was the product of stroking Brock's limited intelligence. Brock was merely a test subject and the test subject believed Lance's lie. It felt good to serve his friend poison. Every few seconds, Lance turned to Brianna to see if she was listening. Believing Brock was intelligent and not just a freakishly fit and handsome boy with limited to no intellect.

"Wow, thanks Lance. I appreciate that. The thing that I enjoy about this relationship is that we get to display our friendship in a physical manner. I've never been this sexually liberated in my life. I've done just about everything with every girl, but I had to sell them on a lie.

With us, we can be whatever we want and do whatever we want without shame. You know?"

"That's what this relationship is about." Brianna capped off Brock's thought. She quickly appeared shameful.

Lance wished that he'd recorded this interaction so that he could laugh at the silliness of it all. Then, an answer illuminated his mind: he could record their actions. Next time they had an encounter he would secretly film it. He enjoyed being intellectually superior to Brock. But he hated admitting that he'd been dominated in the physical realm, with Brock. That part hurt. Honestly, he didn't know which part mattered more in life: being attractive and likeable or being smart and able to contribute to society. Who kept score and who cared?

"What's going through that big brain of yours right now?" Brock asked Lance.

Lance actualized that he'd been lost in thought. Physically, he'd been lying on a bed, naked, with his best friends, but they could see that his inner thoughts were a million miles away. Now he would have to explain. A random answer wouldn't suffice. "I was thinking about us, about this, about where the relationship is going and about where it ends."

When Brianna smiled, Lance weakened. Dread found his stomach and sent an icy sensation into his bowels. He felt physically ill at the thought of not having Brianna. "Does it ever have to end?"

"I don't know, does it?" Brianna's lip curled. She closed her eyes and snuggled close to Brock.

Brock contributed, "It doesn't. We've been best friends our entire lives. We know each other's darkest secrets and desires. We can keep this secret too."

"What does that mean though?" Lance challenged, thinking about how untruthful he was being. Lance was lying and if he was lying then certainly Brock was. Since Lance was considered the honest sect of the group then it was possible that Brianna was lying too. Like everything else in this life, this conversation about honesty was a lie.

"Well, for instance, Brianna is with Grady." Brock slowly ran his eyes over Brianna's shapely backside and touched her shoulder. His gentle touch rattled Lance's jealousy. "If she wants to stay with Grady and we want to continue this... then that should be our secret and we should continue. The same goes for later on in life. When we get married. If at the age of forty we still want this relationship to exist then we can continue."

Lance almost laughed at the stupidity of this comment. What an idiot. An asshole. Selfish. This sexual escapade would only last until Brock was sick of fucking Brianna. Lance didn't matter and Brock would later tell him that the only reason he introduced this threesome relationship was because he wanted Lance to know what it was like to have sex with Brianna. He'd spin and project his selfishness onto Lance. But Lance was far from stupid. And Brock knew how much Lance loved Brianna. That was the other part of Brock that Lance loathed. Brock was aware of Lance's disgust of Brock entering Brianna.

That fucking asshole! he wanted to scream, but couldn't.

Now he wondered if his friends could sense his hatred brewing behind his glossy eyes.

Were they watching him lose his sanity?

3

The only time they left the bed was to get drinks and go to the bathroom. Easing her bare feet onto the floor, Brianna shivered. In the past few hours she'd easily counted three orgasms. Sadly, she wished that at least one of those orgasms had been instigated by Lance. None had. She'd climaxed to thoughts and visions of Brock. She could no longer deny that she had madly, intensely, fallen for Brock. She knew that Lance was aware. *How long could she continue doing this?* The last time they'd made love she knew that she needed to have Brock all to herself. The sex was amazing, each orgasm new and different. She'd savored every moment of intimacy. Now, she hated that the pleasure she received from Lance was in vain. There was an unstoppable awareness eating away at her soul. She relished in the idea of breaking Lance's heart. Leading him into the abyss and crushing him was seduction. Each time Brock thrust into her she was not only pleasured by Brock's cock, but by the fact that she was cheating on Lance. In a way, Lance was the one that made sense. She should be in love with Lance. She was supposed to be in love with him. He was good. Smart. Handsome even. But he wasn't that *one thing* that Brock was: *unattainable*. She could never have Brock to herself even if she were to force the relationship, which she could. Every woman knew how to lure a boy into a relationship. But *those* relationships also included a trail of peripheral women and a lack of total commitment. Brock would never commit, not truly. If she were to force the relationship she might be able to get him to commit out of loyalty, but not love.

A girl could dream.

And how wrong was it that she enjoyed cheating? Just the thought caused her juices to flow. It was painful to hide this secret.

The thrill of being caught was insatiable. She decided to be honest with her boys. "I want to elevate the fantasy." She captured the boy's attention. "I want to cheat—with you two—while Grady is in the room." She whispered. A smirk curled her lip.

Brock erupted into guttural laughter.

Lance also was unable to contain his laughter. He giggled in wimpy bursts. Contagiously, all three joined in abrupt laughter.

"You like fucking Brock in front of me, don't you?" Lance seemed to toss this current train of thought and went for raw honesty.

Be true to this relationship, Brianna thought.

Brianna stammered. She knew that Lance was aware. Some things you just can't hide. "And you hate Brock because I'm in love with him?"

"And none of us can have what we want or need, but together we can have everything?" Lance led the conversation.

"Jesus." Brock contributed. He sounded stupid. "You guys really think that?"

"Brock, all you wanted to do was fuck me. You've wanted to since you hit puberty and you can't help yourself. You don't have deep meaningful feelings for me. You just want the sex. Your loyalty lies with Lance. Opening up the opportunity to get *me* in bed with Lance got *you* off."

Brianna's heart leapt as she watched Brock's eyes redden, gloss over, and spill tears. He nodded successively.

"Brock." Brianna ran her fingers across his chest.

"Yes," Brock whimpered.

"Fuck me in front of Lance while I tell you how much I hate him."

Brock turned to Lance.

Lance felt what Brianna was doing. He would experience ultimate sexual enlightenment if he allowed this belittling to occur. To accept ultimate humiliation would be ultimate bliss.

Brianna kissed Lance and then stated, "After I'm done fucking Brock while you watch and jerk off to how pathetic you are, we'll kick him out of the room and I'll make love to you like a real lover. I'll make love to you as if we were truly in love."

Lance couldn't contain his sobs. He crawled backward to the corner of the bed and watched Brock crawl onto the woman he loved and fuck her so hard that she screamed upon orgasm. Brianna had never experienced this level of pleasure. Lance knew it.

"I hate having Lance with us, he's so annoying," Brianna role-played.

Brock laughed, "Give the guy a break, he's my best friend. You want me, you gotta have him."

Brianna looked to Lance who stroked himself.

Brianna shook her head and laughed. "Lance, you're such a pathetic pig."

Lance couldn't resist. He stroked harder.

The fantasy unraveled.

4

"So, we give Grady a beer full of GHB and then wait until he passes out?" Brock asked.

"Safely." Brianna continued. "Well, as safely as drugging someone can be."

"And then we fuck each other... pretty much on top of him?" Lance solidified the plan.

"If that turns you on then let's do it," Brock stated.

"We're evil. It's this kind of behavior that makes me wonder if the devil exists." Lance smiled and shook his head uneasily.

They knew where the line was drawn and yet they'd grabbed each other's hands and crossed that line together, as one. They took the wrong road at the fork. Bit off *way* more than they could chew. Gone too far. They knew it. Brock was the most accepting of these ideas.

"The Christmas party at Jeff Torrance's house would be idealistic for this brand of debauchery." Lance extracted *sense* and *logic* from this senseless and illogical idea.

"Are you okay with this?" Brianna asked Lance.

"If you want it, we're doing it." Lance nodded.

Brock slid out of bed, looked to his partners and said, "I think somebody here deserves a little private time with you." Brock looked at Brianna.

Lance smiled in Brianna's direction. Brianna retorted with genuine adoration. She would live up to her word. Brock would leave now and let Lance live out his fantasy, the one where he and Brianna were in love.

5

The Killer sat at the hotel bar accompanied by another Smiley Devil. This meeting was different. Instead of masks they wore expensive three-piece suits. No one would recognize him with his hair slicked back. He wore glasses for effect. To the public—other patrons of the bar—these Smiley Devils appeared as two businessmen negotiating.

The Killer fought his urge to smile when Brock entered the dreary setting. The bar was lit with red LED backlighting beneath a clear plastic counter. The effect was to draw an attractive visual of the liquor. And it worked. Standing tall, Brock walked to the illuminated, red under-lit bar and ordered a clear-liquored cocktail that appeared unthinkably inviting in its crimson appearance.

Very soon, this man would be taken from existence. The Killer would truly smile while watching Brock's pupils dilate as the moment of death was captured by the faintest glimpse of his soul evacuating his body.

But what The Killer would perform afterward was the exciting part.

The fun would begin tomorrow.

Part 5: That Time of the Year

Chapter 14

A Night of Debauchery

1

Christmas was days away. The Killer's feet punched through the frozen surface of the snow. He was tired of the all the Christmas displays. The obnoxious twinkle lights. The drunken fools wearing Santa hats. The gifts. Wetness seeped in at the neck of his boots. Stopping in front of Brock and Lance's decrepit Victorian rental, he inspected the house. Aware enough, he invaded the home through the back door, by way of the garage. Peering in through the frosted square window, he acknowledged the wide space filled with overstuffed cardboard boxes and random clutter. Glancing upward, the Killer admired the darkness. Halting at the base of the cement stairs, he kicked the snow from his boots. Entering the house required no skill. He hiked upstairs and then strolled down the hallway to Brock's room. Here he would find the desired weapon to execute his plan. This serrated weapon was the accurate tool, necessary for sacrifice. Brock always touted that stupid fucking knife everywhere he went. Well, he wouldn't have too much time to miss it. Invading this foreign property, The Killer hydrated in the excitement of uninvited silence. These actions were obscene. Clearly, no one was home. This was a planned certainty. He'd witnessed both Brock and Lance entering the downtown hotel earlier in the evening. Then he'd watched Brock order a few drinks at the bar before returning to his room. Nothing about this criminal activity was unnerving and he was comforted by his belief that the Dark Lord walked with him. Guiding his dark intent.

The Killer wore all black to include a ski mask.

Heart racing and sincere, he prayed that Brock, Lance and Brianna enjoyed their final carnal activities. Each minute of their existence that remained should be savored. Soon, he would own their souls in Hell. Hopefully, each orgasm exceeded the prior. Involuntarily, his humanity couldn't resist the slight elevation of jealousy as it intruded his thoughts. *They'd better enjoy each other.* All joy would be stripped from them within the following twenty-four hours. Deranged and twisted pain was to follow this night. Torture. The Killer couldn't resist laughter at the promise of inflicted pain. Pondering the lives of those to be affected by this sacrifice stimulated his beautiful madness. The death and destruction of this loving friendship would birth black contentment. The Dark Lord would reward him for his actions in Hell. Sacrifice was a strengthening exercise. But this specific sacrificial crown was his masterpiece.

Entering Brock's bedroom, The Killer maneuvered around enormous piles of scattered clothes.

Wow, Brock was a slob.

This room had never been cleaned.

The pungent scent of cologne captured his nasal passages. The odor wafted upward from beneath piles of mold-ridden socks. Very foul smelling. Sweat and cologne erupted into a near-tangible cloud upon accidentally kicking another pile. Unable to hold back, The Killer coughed into gloved hands. Stumbling forward, he steadied himself on the dresser.

Reaching outward, his fingers gripped the lip of the wooden dresser. His gloved hand swept right then left until his dancing fingers detected the weapon. Brock's hunting knife. The hunting knife Brock displayed at parties as if it were a trophy, silly and bothersome to the intellectually enlightened mind.

Gripping the handle, his forearm muscles quivered. Squeezing the wooden grip, a stinger shot along his arm, beginning in his shoulder and concluding at his fingertips. This sensation was clearly the Dark Lord guiding him. He felt the presence. Tracing the shape of a circle on the laminated surface of the dresser, he then formed a five-pointed star in the middle with his index finger. A pentagram was the perfect symbol of worship to the Dark Lord. The Dark Lord demanded praise.

The Killer repeated this ritual until the wooden surface of the kitchen floor creaked. Then he halted before navigating his way out of the room. He crept down the hallway. Hurried down the stairs and then whisked out of the house. The mission was accomplished. Standing tall in the backyard, he glanced upward and stared at the home he'd violated. Spiritually, he'd grown. He didn't worry that he'd been seen. His faith was strong. The Dark Lord hadn't allowed visibility. This sacrifice was destiny. It was written. And the weapon was an important symbol of the darkness to follow.

He walked home. Rested well. Strength would be needed for the sacrifice.

2

Brock slept undisturbed for a long while and awoke just before noon. A thin beam of intense sunlight infiltrated the hotel curtains and heated his sealed eyelids. Once fully awake, oxygen pumped through his blood and surged energy into his new day. Twelve-hour slumbers allowed this welcome sensation. His heart thumped heavily when the heat radiating from Brianna's naked skin warmed him. The curve of her fit ass accelerated his blood flow. Then, all three bodies glowed with perspiration in the light of this new day.

Brock woke Brianna by gently rubbing her ass cheeks. She moaned into consciousness and giggled at the sight of Brock's smiling face and attentive erection. Once Lance awoke, they pried themselves from the bed and showered together. Barely any words were spoken beneath the warm soft-water spray. Last night they'd completed their bond, defined their unification. Tonight, they would execute Brianna's fantasy. Jeff Torrance's Christmas party began at eight o'clock sharp. A checklist needed to be completed. In order to pull off Brianna's fantasy they'd need to obtain GHB. Disturbingly, Brock knew where to acquire this cowardly chemical. Toby—bar manager at The Quarter— acted as a date rape distribution hub. For a small fee, he'd dribble an ounce into a designated cocktail. Brock hadn't the need for the stuff. Being the campus stud, he was up to speed on sexual prowess, the necessary avenue of persuasion. This current behavior resonated disturbingly to many parties. Hell, it was even more disturbing to inside parties. But that was the price for attaining unattainable sexual bliss. This brand of sexual assault would be digested into the category of *different*. The bartender didn't care. He openly broadcasted his services in gym locker rooms and after-bar parties. He'd assisted a number of his favorite bar patrons in obtaining their non-compliant sexual conquests. If a fellow playboy needed assistance luring a girl that wasn't quite sold—then for a modest fee—he'd slip a *little something* into the designated cocktail. This behavior was simply overlooked by the authorities, like J-walking. In addition, most of the violated women were afraid or embarrassed. Not much was reported and the process remained an unspoken secret sickness. A bottle containing the virus was full and one day soon the cork would pop or the glass would shatter. Not today. So far as Toby the barman knew, none of the affected had ever persuaded the authorities into investigating the matter or its source. And no one cared to sympathize with the receiving end of this deviance. Mostly, it was an age thing. Brock thought. And Brock didn't hate this bartender. He merely despised him.

He despised everyone.

He despised himself.

After a hearty continental breakfast, Brock, Lance, and Brianna separated.

Brianna cleaned up.

Lance and Brock debated and hashed out the details of Brianna's erotic plan. The emotional void that both men felt for Grady was intriguing on numerous psychological levels. One: the degradation. Two: the sociopathic behavior pattern. Three: the degree of perversion they were willing to adhere to for a simple orgasm.

Orgasms aren't simple. It's amazing how many complications are entered into the equation of deviated sex. Even natural, healthy orgasms are complicated.

Brock thought.

Brock entered the dingy bar, which smelled of stale beer, whiskey soaked carpet, and dish soap. The cheap dishwasher ran loudly from the kitchen. Brock stumbled when the bottom of his boot stuck to the floor. "Mop the floor, you fucking delinquent." He stepped toward the bar and called out, "Yo, Toby!"

"We're closed!" Toby hollered from the kitchen.

"It's Brock Hills!"

Toby's dark complexion held a hint of red and his face was swollen from the previous night's intoxicants, but he smiled. He stuck his head out from the swinging doors that separated the bar from the kitchen. His smile was wide, but his eyes were streaked red. They bulged. Obviously hung over, Toby shouted in a raspy voice, "Brock, what's up?"

"I need ... something. A favor. You alone?" Brock whispered.

"Look, if your sick of banging chicks and you're thinking about switch-hitting ... I ain't your guy."

"Fuck you, douche bag." Brock laughed.

"You want a Bloody Mary?"

"I won't turn one down." Ingesting liquor sounded refreshing at the moment.

Toby lifted a bottle of clear liquor from the bar, shook his head, and returned the bottle to its place on the top shelf. "Only the best, right?"

Brock shrugged, walked to the bar. "Right by me."

Toby dumped three sloppy shots of good vodka into two high balls and added a splash of tomato juice, a dash of hot sauce, plopped horseradish into the mix, and sprinkled celery salt on top. He handed one sopping glass to Brock.

He downed half of his drink in one swallow.

"Hair of the dog."

The Bloody Mary was a pulpy mess that Brock gagged on while chugging. The horseradish sauce burned his throat and sinuses. The vodka stung his nostrils, inside and out. Closing his eyes, he relaxed and let the hangover-drink course down his throat. Once the alcohol soaked into the lining of his stomach a warm buzz drifted upward. A comforting dizziness swarmed his head. "Good stuff," he lied.

"Right?"

"Right." Brock took another sip. This time it wasn't so bad.

"You got any GHB?" Brock choked on more horseradish sauce.

Toby laughed hard, spit up some of his drink. "How much would you like to see left at the end of the bar?" He stopped laughing. A stern expression found his swollen face. He had the look of a man that needed to shit.

Brock understood Toby's underlying message. It was stupid and ridiculous, but he understood. Toby spoke in drug dealer speak. Brock would explain how much he needed and then Toby would tell him how much cash he would need to set at the end of the bar. This way, the police couldn't bust Toby on the slight chance that Brock was recording their conversation. Toby was paranoid. He had reason to be. If the police learned that he'd distributed date rape enhancement drugs he'd wind up the *rape-ee* and not *rape-ist*.

What did that say about Brock? He wondered. Anonymously informing the police would be the morally correct solution, but he wouldn't. So what did that say about him? He decided not to dwell on all the faces of the females that had fallen victim. There were probably hundreds.

Brock couldn't even make eye contact with this sack of shit, which was strange given Brock wasn't exactly an innocent. "Enough for a full nights sleep?"

"You want me to administer the medication? Just tell me which bitch and drag her sweet ass to the bar." Toby made a strange noise that sounded like a wet fart, but came out as a sigh.

"Nah, just leave it at the end of the bar and I'll leave you a twenty-spot." Brock countered.

"Add five bucks for inflation," Toby negated.

"Sure." Brock dug into his pocket. "And don't say a fucking word."

"Have no fear, that's what I do. Or... don't do... rather," Toby winked.

Toby disappeared into the backroom, sifted through the pocket of his black leather coat and returned with a travel-sized mouthwash bottle full of clear liquid. He set the bottle at the edge of the bar and then downed the rest of his Bloody Mary. "You wanna rail a line of blow?"

"No, I'm good."

"I know you're good, but blow makes everything better," Toby persuaded.

"Ah, when you're right you're right," Brock smiled.

Toby removed a glass vile from his shirt pocket, twisted it open, and then laid out four thick lines of white powder. Rolling a dollar bill and placing it beneath his left nostril, Brock inhaled the first line. The bitter chalk crawled down the back of his throat and numbed the lining of his esophagus as it dripped. His attention perked. He nodded. Inhaled a second line up the same nostril. "Good stuff, my friend," he choked.

Toby took his turn. Inhaled heavily. Nodding, he rubbed trace powder onto his gums and then said, "Why thank you, sir. Have a good night. Maybe throw a Viagra down your throat if the coke gets too intense."

Drug dealers always knew what drugs to mix in order to compensate for the side effects of the drug they sold. These mixes were good on the outside, bad on the inside. They rotted the soul.

Brock pocketed the GHB and left the bar. "Later."

Toby grabbed a wet rag and wiped away remnants of the white powder from the bar.

3

For the party, Grady dressed casual and looked cool. His attire was more of a uniform. Jeans and a T-shirt. He never dressed appropriate for the icy Wisconsin weather. At first sight, most people thought Grady was an idiot because he didn't bundle up, but soon they realized the cold had no effect on him. He never complained. Even in freezing conditions he would wear a T-shirt and wouldn't rub his arms for warmth.

Running his wet hands through his hair, he styled the shaggy blond waves into something he agreed with. Squirted some decent cologne onto his neck and genitals and then headed out the door. He would meet Brianna at her dorm. From there they'd walk to the party.

The sidewalk was packed with freshmen and sophomore girls, bundled up in winter attire, laughing as they slid across the iced-over sidewalk. The snow fell heavy, making visibility difficult. These mostly attractive women tossed grins and smiles as they walked past Grady. Their seductive, drunken, inviting smiles explored him. He assumed this was a compliment. He hoped. Otherwise, it was an insult. Sometimes, he wondered if he was making an ass of himself by dating Brianna. Sure, she was gorgeous and had a great body. Her laid back attitude illuminated her attractiveness. Still, maybe she was playing Grady for a sucker. He was very aware that she possessed an abundance of deceit. Also, he could do better.

Whatever, she was still a great piece of ass and tonight's adventure would be fun.

Arriving at the athlete's dormitory, Grady climbed the steps, glanced over the directory and hit the numbers 0327 with the pad of his index finger. After an annoying moment, Brianna's voice echoed through the metal speaker, "Hey, babe." And then he was buzzed in.

He made his way to the elevator, pushed the "up" button and waited for the sliding doors to open. The low hum of the elevator car dropping to the lobby level rose in volume. At least three women giggled behind the aluminum doors. When they opened, a beautiful Latina girl with light caramel skin—not tall, but very fit—exited ahead of the other girls. She smiled at Grady and asked, "Are you that California boy Brianna goes with?"

Grady was smitten and this girl was aware. He didn't hide his smile. Quickly, he visualized what it would be like to go with her. Just hold hands and smile with her while they strolled across campus. Took shots at The Quarter. Made love on a rainy summer night. The images passed, as did the beautiful girl and her friends.

Maybe another time?

For now he was with Brianna. The relationship wouldn't last. That was for sure. In fact, as of late he wondered if he'd miss her. But then he remembered not to worry about it. The relationship would work out the way he'd planned.

4

Absorbing every fine detail, Brianna glanced at her reflection a second time. She wore tight, light colored blue jeans that hugged each curve of her body and complimented them with a powder blue flannel shirt. A silver heart shaped necklace dangled neatly, centered in her cleavage. Standing directly in front of the mirror, which hung at the far left of the bland dorm room, she smiled and accepted her appearance. Grady was in the elevator. Any moment he'd knock. She found it difficult to contain her excitement for tonight. Sure, the physical pleasure was enticing. But more than the sex, she was excited to make a cuckold of her boyfriend. Premeditated naughtiness was incredibly thrilling. Layered waves of emotion were at work. Some guilt, some thrill, some depressing, and some overwhelmingly attractive. All enticing. The only *real* guilt developed in the form of a question—question of her personal tolerance for evil. *Was she evil for doing this? A bad person, maybe?* She was about to drug her boyfriend, render him unconscious, and be ravaged by two boys while in his presence. These actions were degrading and criminal. And the raw thought made her feel steamy.

She giggled.

Grady knocked at the front door. She opened.

"Hey, babe." She smiled and kissed him quick.

"Wow, sweetie, you look amazing. As usual." Grady took a step back and digested Brianna's attire. "You always know exactly what to wear. Just these plain clothes and you look like a super model, minus the strung-out-crack-cocaine *thing*."

"Do you think supermodels are hot?" she asked, genuinely curious.

"Interesting question. I like the old school Victoria's Secret models. But those aren't the typical supermodels... I don't think."

"What do you think of when you think of a supermodel?"

"A gangly, skinny, heroine addict that's just been fucked by her uncle... standing around in her underwear looking like she hasn't eaten or taken a shit in three days." Grady stated, making intense eye contact.

Brianna leaned forward, covered her mouth and belted out laughter. "And they wear gaudy eye make-up."

"Don't forget the eye makeup."

She stood up straight. Pointed her index finger in Grady's face and then deepened her voice to sound like a strict adult and said, "I mustn't forget the eye makeup."

They shared laughter. Brianna wondered if maybe she could love Grady. She was about to do something so horrid to him, but yet her mind allowed her to think sweetly of him, in this moment. Not knowing what to do next, she pushed herself close to him. Kissed him.

"You wanna go a round?" Grady asked.

She did. She started to shake her head no, but the tingling sensation fluttering below her belt and between her legs influenced her actions. "Yes, please."

He pushed her hard against the cushioned chair and then unsnapped her jeans. Pushed his hand down her pants.

"I like that," she panted.

This wasn't lust. Well, it was, but there was sincerity to what they were doing.

Hearing the gusty, snow filtered wind whistling outside her window, she dreaded the short walk to the party. Only three blocks off campus, but it would chill her bones. The snow didn't bother her. The cold bothered her. But there was something else that troubled her as well. Maybe she didn't want to go through with her fantasy? But how could she retreat? These thoughts brought up images and visuals of her acting out her fantasy. And these thoughts continued turning her on.

Oh, these images.

She felt so conflicted.

Before long, Grady would be passed out in a chair while her two male friends degraded her in his presence. Her guilt was conquered by excitement. She was ready to commit to her fantasy.

I'll only be young once.

Brock and Lance arrived at the party thirty minutes prior to she and Grady.

"Grady, how goes it, buddy?" Brock smiled and slapped his hand on Grady's shoulder.

"Thirsty." Grady nodded toward the kitchen where a herd of drunken college boys had gathered. One of them distributed red solo cups. A short boy with shaggy brown hair, wearing a tight black shirt was pumping the keg.

When he was done, Brock shoved the boy out of the way and filled two cups full of beer. Grady didn't notice that Brock had taken *that cup* out from behind the toaster. Brianna could only assume that the date-rape drug was simmering at the bottom of *that cup*. When *that cup* was full, Grady grabbed it and slammed the liquid down his throat, eyes closed. After he was finished, he smiled, clanked glasses with Brock and then turned to Brianna and provided a lucid smile.

"Just what the doctor needed." Grady smiled and took in the sight of a cute blonde standing near the front door. Brianna couldn't deny that this girl had a beautiful ass. Her jeans accentuated the tight bump to her rump. She hated that she was annoyed by the fact that Grady was so blatant about checking her out. She was jealous. And her jealousy led her to kiss Grady. She grabbed his face and turned him toward her. She planted her lips on his while making eye contact with the cute blonde. She jammed her tongue between Grady's beer-soaked lips. When the blonde rolled her eyes and turned away, Brianna grabbed Grady's hand and pulled him upstairs.

5

Brock stood at the back of the kitchen near the sink. He and Brianna shared a seductive glance while she yanked Grady upstairs. It'd been half an hour since he'd unknowingly drunk the GHB polluted beer. In ten minutes he'd be a breathing fuck-doll—window dressing for the twisted erotic-theater production that'd be performed in his unconscious presence.

"We'll wait fifteen minutes." Brock leaned forward and whispered into Lance's ear.

Lance waited for Brock to straighten himself out before holding the faceplate of his iPhone parallel to his face,

"She just texted me. Grady's out like a light. We need to go up there in ten." Lance smiled.

"Sounds good." Brock shook his head and laughed. "Poor bastard."

Lance enjoyed smirking, arrogantly, like Brock. He now understood the sensation behind Brock's favorite expression. The prideful release of energy that coupled with arrogance was now understandable. It was thrilling. Others responded. "I'm starting to like this shit."

"Shit?" Brock was proud to see his partner—his brother—come around.

"Yeah, you know, playing Grady for a cuckold." Lance's laughter was involuntary.

"I've created a monster." Brock tussled Lance's hair.

Lance maintained his composure. "What?"

"What's wrong?" Brock keeled the expression.

"Why would you say that like that? This is Brianna's fantasy, I'm just enjoying it."

"I know, man. You don't think I think it's hilarious to bang Grady's chick while his dumb ass is passed out in a chair?"

"Sorry, I thought you were implying that I was turning into an asshole."

"You did that a long time ago."

Lance resumed laughter. "Let's make this dude a chump."

"Let's have a drink first."

"Cool."

Brock and Lance walked toward the kitchen. A brunette wearing a baseball tee with deep cleavage—probably store-torn—took interest in the boys. She looked familiar. With sexy, fluttering fingers she grabbed Brock's hair, tilted his head back, placed the lip of a tequila bottle to his lips and poured the smooth burn down his throat. The liquor slid straight to his head. He felt dizzy. His inhibitions ceased and when the brunette kissed him with full lips, he kissed her back. Her tongue was salty and sweet and worth reciprocating. But it was simply a kiss before indulging in Brianna's fantasy.

6

The darkness of this night was upon them. The Dark Lord clearly enhanced and energized this frozen evening. The cold burned painfully yet pleasant. The Smiley Devil's wore no masks. The Dark Lord would shield them. They'd arrived to this party early. Some had driven many miles, some not. Their presence was everywhere. Now that God was dying and almost dead in the minds of all humans, the Dark Lord was able to destruct. Once the humans believed they were ants in an ant-farm then God would allow them to be treated as such. His love held condition. And he tested his children.

The Smiley Devil's mingled. To the sad, pathetic non-believers that worshipped their non-existent super-intelligence, the Devils were smiling, tan faces in the crowd. These university students were blind to the evil lurking amongst their party, their existence. To these fools, the Smiley Devils were ordinary. Background noise. But beneath their smiles was boiling rage. Starved for murderous sustenance. They wouldn't don their masks until Brock Hills and his boyfriend Lance were alone in the warehouse. Only then would they reveal the dark powers permitted to them by the Dark Lord, under the guidance of their ferocious leader. And *He* would do awful things to these three. Their actions would include more than drowning.

In the end, their deaths would appear as accidents, suicides, or the work of someone innocent. Thoughts of a displayable aftermath would develop later. That was the closing. For now they would concentrate on pursuing awful-greatness. With weapons, sharp objects. The Killer demanded serrated pain. The Killer would need to be careful. The wrong move would spoil the plan. The Dark Lord would punish him if things went wrong. Their evil would need to be heightened. No detail would be left stray. This was a certainty.

Now, he executed the first move toward ending their lives.

College coeds possessed no clue as to the depravity of the presence they mingled amongst. Death was in attendance.

7

Adrenaline sizzled through Brianna's blood as she took the last step leading to the third story bedroom. She cringed. The room held the faint and disgusting odor of sweaty socks and stale beer, commonly known as the college-male-smell. She quickly adjusted to this scent. Her nasal passages eased. A hint of beer fart lingered, but Brianna refused to ponder on these sensory discrepancies now. She focused on the event about to unfold. The most intense physical pleasure of her life would take form soon.

Grady's fall from consciousness was too easy. After pulling him upstairs—where Jeff Torrance had specifically ordered everyone *not* to go—the job had become simple. They'd begun to kiss when he dropped into unconsciousness. She'd worried that they'd given him too much GHB. She worried that he'd overdosed. But then she watched as his chest rose and fell. Her concerns diminished. The dosage had been accurate. She briefly questioned her morality. Then forgot about it. These ideas were easily conquered by thoughts of sweaty intimacy. Remembering that she'd be young only once was identified as proper redundancy. She held merely a small portion of life to explore these lustful acts. They were for the young. *Fuck it.* She laughed at the thought of Jeff

Torrance's face if he were to discover the depravity of what was about to happen in his room. He'd been upset by their exploration of the house at the prior party. She, Brock and Lance had convinced him that they'd never meander past the first floor of his house, ever again.

He was wrong on that front.

Setting Grady in a chair near the bed, Brianna remembered speaking with him while he sipped on the sedative infested beer. She hoped that the residual GHB hadn't penetrated her system when she'd kissed him. She wiped her lips with the back of her forearm and took a sip of water. Prior to unconsciousness, Grady had talked up a storm. But then his eyes drooped. His speech slurred. Within a few minutes he stumbled. His remaining beer fell and splashed onto Jeff's pillow, which Brianna found amusing. Couldn't help but to laugh. Laughter was involuntary. In this moment, the misery of others was joyful. She enjoyed the thrill of being naughty. Everything that was bad was funny or thrilling and felt right. She experienced *the now*. Shoving Grady to the side of the bed, he moaned loudly. She worried that the drug would wear off early. To ensure that Grady was comatose, she slapped him.

Nothing.

She slapped him again.

He farted.

Good.

He was out cold.

She finished posing him in the chair when her lover's footsteps clunked up the creaky wooden stairs. The noise grew louder as they continued down the hallway. Images of naked flesh melded with heightened sensations and anticipation while nerves fluttered in succession. Her heart beat rapidly. She was ecstatic. Wet. She shook. No patience, she wanted to be violated, do awful things. Any feelings of guilt had shed.

The door creaked.

"Did somebody ask for two studs?" Brock smirked like an idiot.

Moronic statement, but Brianna smiled anyway. She removed her shirt then pulled her jeans off and said, "Now, bend me over the bed so that I can stare at my boyfriend while you two wreck me."

Brock grinned.

Brianna knew that the pleasures she would soon experience would haunt her forever. "As you wish, dear."

Lance pushed past Brock and shoved Brianna toward the bed. She nearly fell on top of Grady.

"Whoa, where did you come from?" Brianna smiled. She liked being shoved.

"I didn't tell you to talk," Lance barked. He looked ashamed of himself, but when she laughed he slapped her. She turned to Brock who was lost. Clearly, he was conflicted.

Would Brock tell his friend to stop?

Or would he allow this abuse.

Was abuse pleasure?

Brianna hoped he would allow this abuse.

He did.

She nearly screamed when Lance slammed into her.

"What kind of a dirty bitch cheats on her boyfriend with two scumbags?"

Brianna remained silent until Lance smacked the back of her head with his palm. She twisted her head to look at him.

Lance shoved her face into Grady's chest and then pumped into her, hard.

"Yes!" she screamed, pleasured, while struggling to breathe. Finally, after inhaling cheap cologne, sweat, and beer—as it wafted outward from Grady's pores—she was able to breathe. Grady hardly budged when Brianna's face slid across his perspiring chest.

"You're a dirty bitch?" Lance reiterated.

"Yes," she agreed. She was starting to feel degraded, but she enjoyed every measurement of her present situation.

"Say that you're a dirty bitch. Then tell Brock to walk around to the other side of the bed and stuff your filthy mouth."

She wondered how pathetic she looked while her head thumped forward into Grady's ribs.

She didn't care.

She enjoyed her fantasy of Lance. She quaked with pleasure by what he was doing. She thoroughly enjoyed being violated in the presence of her boyfriend.

The lousy cuckold.

If he only knew how wet she was.

"Brock, walk around to the other side of the bed and stuff my filthy whore's mouth." Brock did as ordered. He stuffed her mouth. Held his member steady. Then thrust forward. Practically screaming, Brianna nearly fainted. In part, she was so turned that her heart rate had increased upward of healthy. On the verge of orgasm, she couldn't contain this level of physical pleasure. In part, she nearly fainted for lack of oxygen.

Brock laughed when Brianna gagged while he slid rapidly between her lips. Brianna spun. She wanted to focus on Lance's reaction to Brock's laughter. Immediately, she knew that Lance was unequivocally uninhibited. He'd *let go* and *gone with.*

Brock was about to blow. He pulled out of her mouth, placed the head of his member over Grady's face—above his cheekbone—and ejaculated.

Brianna choked and choked and laughed and choked and laughed and choked more as the heavy load struck Grady's forehead and then spilled down the side of his face.

8

The Killer was aware that he'd be subjected to this degree of degradation. He was prepared. His discipline was of the highest caliber. Being ejaculated on was a small price to pay for what he'd soon receive. In a few hours these people would experience a world of searing pain. These thoughts allowed him the patience to deal with this sexual abuse. The way Grady saw it, semen running down the side of his face bought Brock an extra hour of Hell on earth. In this moment, Grady—*The Killer*—decided that he would skin Brock Hill's face off while forcing him look in the mirror. The image of Brock's muscle covered skull chattering while capillaries and arteries spurted blood in every direction allowed for The Killer to remain patient. He was glad that he'd been able to swap out the beer laced with GHB.

The clueless lovers exhausted their orgy when Brianna convulsed into grandiose orgasm.

Grady pretended to snore and then rolled over and farted, an additional act to add credibility to his performance. *Wait until they felt the experience he'd soon provide them.*

Then he lay silent and listened.

"You two leave. I'll stay here until he wakes up," Brianna instructed.

Grady had to bite his tongue. He wanted to laugh at Brianna's two dead-as-fuck-loser friends.

Their lives would end before the first light of tomorrow morning.

"You sure?"

"Positive."

Oh good, Grady thought. He'd lay with his girlfriend and enjoy her. Enjoy her the way he enjoyed women, so many women.

He listened to Lance and Brock zip up. Soon after, they exited the room. Blaring music and drunken college students revving on intoxication past natural limitations drifted into the room. Then the door closed and it was only The Killer and Brianna.

9

"Let's bolt." Brock grabbed a half empty bottle of whiskey from the knoll post as he hit the last stair on his way to the first floor.

"I'm worn out, man. I could use a nap," Lance added.

"What was up with you back there? I've never seen you take charge like that. You sinister bastard," Brock laughed.

I fucking hate this guy, Lance thought. He looked at Brock in an entirely different light. He couldn't give a shit about Brock anymore. There was nothing left. If Brock were to slip on the ice and snap his neck, Lance would laugh.

Brock didn't give a shit about anything, why should he?

"Felt good to boss that stupid bitch around." Lance smiled.

Involuntarily, Brock coughed whiskey all over a girl that had passed out on a cushioned chair in the living room. She didn't move as the whiskey streamed down her neck and stained the rim of her blue sweater. This caused Brock to giggle like a small child. "Where the fuck did *this guy* come from?" Brock clapped Lance's shoulder and pulled him toward the door. "That was fucking great."

"You don't care that I'm talking about our friend like she's some kind of a whore?" Lance antagonized. His laughter simmered to a chuckle.

Lance buttoned his coat and stepped outside and onto the porch. The wind chilled his overheated body. Snow sifted heavily onto the town.

"It's fucking cold, huh?" a voice called out from behind Lance. He turned in search of the foreign call. He didn't recognize the boy or the girl standing behind him. They were both attractive, in their mid-twenties—young, but a bit old to be college students.

"Damn skippy," Brock contributed.

"Which way ya'll headed?" the girl asked. She was cute. Yet, there was something different happening with her eyes. Her pupils were dilated. She was clearly high on some form of amphetamine. Meth was current and popular.

"Home. You?" Brock asked. He glanced at the girl without concern for her male friend—*probably her boyfriend.*

"Maybe your place. What do you think?" She placed her hands on her hips and curled her lips seductively.

"Is she your girlfriend?" Brock asked the boy.

"Hell no. She's my cousin." the boy said. "Take her home and give her a spin. All I ask is a couple of beers while you do your business."

"Cool." Brock extended his arm to the girl. "What's your name?"

"You can call me Smiley." She grinned and then shared an awkward smile with her cousin. Lance didn't like the way these two strangers interacted, offsetting. The innocent comfort was lost.

"I live on Seventh Street. Need somebody to bullshit with?" the boy asked Lance.

Lance watched Smiley tug Brock into a short jog. Then he looked to the boy and said, "Yeah" The metal pipe tucked under the boy's long sleeve slid downward into his grip. He swung. The apparatus cracked Lance upside the head. Skin tore jaggedly. The blow ended his consciousness.

10

Brock watched the metal pipe tear Lance's face open. Blood painted the falling snow red, off the sidewalk. Thick blood spatter spread forward while Lance dropped to the ground.

In one well-rehearsed action, Smiley stuck a syringe into Brock's neck, but was unable to thumb the plunger.

"Bitch!" Brock turned and punched the Smiley bitch in the face. Blood erupted from her nose.

"You hit like a girl." She giggled, raising her fists like a boxer.

Brock thought about fighting this cunt, but then remembered that Lance needed help. He ran toward the boy, jumped in the air, and crescent kicked his boot into this psycho's solid chest.

The boy stumbled back, shoved Brock's foot into the ground and punched him in the ribs.

Brock cringed. White-hot pain shot upward through his body.

Another fist crashed into his face. The girl slammed her elbow into the corner of his eye. His skin tore neatly and blood pulsated in thick torrents. He was certain that these two meant to inflict great pain.

Finally, Brock caught a glimpse of Smiley's face and side-kicked her in the jaw. She stumbled back, slipped on the ice, but regained her balance. She settled. And Brock rammed his fists successively into her chest, ribs, and face.

"You're dead," the boy shouted. Brock dropped the girl and ran toward the boy. Brock deflected the boy's fist while he attempted to punch. Leveraging his weight with his hip, Brock tossed the boy up and over his shoulder. The boy was heavy, but he flew and twisted through the air. Finally, landed on his back. A heavy cloud of steam escaped his mouth. He was winded. Brock didn't halt. He slammed his fist square into the boy's face. He repeated this process even though his knuckles were battered, bruised, skinned, and maybe broken. Then the girl jumped on his back. She placed him in a chokehold. Brock reached backward, grabbed her wrists, and tugged forward. This action enabled him to pull his head free from her arms. Like slipping out of a noose. Still holding her arms, he flung her forward over his back. He used all of his strength to slam her into the icy sidewalk. Watching her lay there, he felt confidence rise within him. The air shucked out from her lungs. Instinct dictated. Brock slid to the right. He watched the boy miss and slam the metal pipe into the snow-covered cement. A hollow clank rang in his ears. With the back of his fist he hammered Smiley in the face. Then he kicked her in the stomach. Afterward, he leaned forward and stomped on the boy's face.

Confusion struck. Brock's vision went hazy.

He threw a sloppy punch at Smiley's cousin.

His vision spun. His stomach weakened. Vomit heated his throat. Acid bubbled upward.

He attempted to kick, but slipped and fell. His sight found the syringe that had been plunged into his neck. There was no liquid and the plunger was deflated.

He didn't know how long he'd been laying there but laughter echoed along the lining of his eardrums. The cackles were mean spirited, damning, twisted and emulated madness. He was scared. The evil laughter frightened him more than the physical beating.

Fists and feet punched and kicked every area of his body. No flesh was spared from this brutality. The black sky pushed his vision into the blankness of night. He tried to focus on the stars, but the punches and kicks denied focus.

Another large needle punched through the skin of his neck. The last sensation he felt was bitter cold. He was defeated. Doom crept in like poison.

Chapter 15

A Cold Place to Die

1

The cold was bitter. Not freezing. And Brock frantically wiggled his arms. Disregarding the hard edge of pain in his wrists that were bound to something metal. He felt blood run from the jagged tears in his wrists and hands. Rolling onto his back, he attempted to scream. Muffled gags of soft anger were the extent of his attempt. Torn cloth had been stuffed into his mouth and gagging was all he could muster. Tilting his head amplified the pain, which lingered in the many cuts and bruises along his neck and face. Fresh, painful lumps jutted out from the back of his head and throbbed terribly. Dried blood acted as an adhesive on his eyelids. Forcing his eyes open, blood cracked like dried superglue. Exerting his threshold for pain, he blinked into clarity. The image before him eluded terror. An icy sensation lined the acid wash of his stomach.

Harsh LED light penetrated his pupils. Sanity fled. He couldn't tell if the images in front of him were real or mirages. Six large figures dressed in black wore ridiculous rubber Devil masks.

A thought struck.

That black van outside the boxing gym.

"Wakey, wakey." Brock recognized the familiar, laidback voice.

A moment passed before an image paired with the voice, the familiar, throaty tone.

Brock's eyes widened. Attempting to swallow, his throat locked. No saliva remained in his mouth. Spittle and foam escaped his lips.

Grady was here.

Lowering himself, Grady removed Brock's gag.

"What the hell are you doing?" Brock struggled.

Trying his best to appear inconspicuous, Brock's eyes darted in all directions. Surveying his surroundings. Straining to see through his damaged eyes was difficult. Sight finally permitted clarity. The walls were tall, maybe seventy feet. This building was a warehouse the size of a football field. Another thought struck; there was a gaggle of warehouses tucked off of a desolate road near interstate 40. They were holding him outside town along the dirt road that led toward a scattered gaggle of dairy farms. Law enforcement rarely took interest in these parts. No reason to, so far as they knew. But Brock knew this area—all the good drug infested underground rave parties were held in these warehouses. On one of those nights he'd dropped a tab of LSD and chased it with ecstasy. *Candy-flip.* That experience took place in this specific warehouse. He remembered dancing his ass off to some local DJ that was untalented. To him the music had sounded like pots and pans being thrown at cement floors.

"You, sir, I'm doing *you*... you big stud. You are going to die. Think of it this way: only the good die young." Grady found Brock's predicament to be hilarious. "I can tell by the way you're checking the place out that you maybe-sort-of-know where you are, but still can't quite place yourself." Grady stopped pacing. Oddly, his demeanor was still approachable. The smile on his face set everyone at ease.

Guess not this time.

What the hell possessed this guy to lead such an evil existence?

That's right, he and Lance were fucking his girlfriend— but how did he find out—oh, maybe because they'd had sex on top of him? Jizzed on his face.

"Look... " Brock started.

"Brock, shut up. I don't care about Brianna. You'll find that out soon." Grady turned to his rubber-masked friends and smiled. "I sought you out about three months ago. It doesn't take long to find the leaders of any college campus. These likeminded friends of mine are the ones responsible for the drowning victims you've heard about. You know... all the white athletic types that've washed up in nearby riverbeds. We like victims to be a challenge. You should be flattered. Plus, you know a couple of these Smiley Devils."

A large body lifted his hand and waved condescendingly. Brock knew that this was Toby, the bartender at The Quarter. He must have told Grady about the GHB.

"Those were accidents. Drunk ass-wads walking home, stumbling... falling into the river." Brock became defensive out of fright. After taking a deep breath he realized that he was only trying to convince himself because he was terrified that Grady was telling the truth.

"Drunk ass-wads walking home and stumbling into... " Grady repeated and then motioned his arm outward, displaying the Smiley Devils. "Us. They stumbled into us. The most enjoyment we receive is reading articles about town councilmen blaming alcohol and out of control youth. Sure, those elements fall into the equation, but they don't pull the metaphorical trigger. People like Ricky Mack and Toby and certain waitresses at diners set the stage. Pick the prey so to say. And then this happens."

"You're full of shit." Brock needed this conversation to continue. Just a few minutes so that he could figure a way out of this mess. He needed to pump Grady's ego. Keep him talking. If Grady stopped speaking he might start killing. Brock was certain that Grady was telling the truth. Still, riling him up might throw him off. Change his mind. Get him to make a mistake. Enable an escape route. Maybe, maybe not, but Brock had to try something. *And where the Hell was Brianna and Lance?*

"We're good about making these deaths look like accidents. Just go online and Google 'Smiley Devils.' You'll find that these strange deaths occur around college campuses. We operate all across the country. But you, Brock, you are different. You're my greatest challenge. The Dark Lord cast golden fire around you. You're special."

"What the fuck does that mean?" Brock asked. "You dress up in black robes and worship the devil. That shit's stupid." Brock watched Grady's sly grin morph into a stern, angry expression. He couldn't let Grady smell his fear. Grady needed to know that he wasn't going to play the *scared-beg-for-your-life role.* The role Grady expected of him.

"I'm going to fight you to the death. And after I kill you... I'm going to skin you, char you, and eat your flesh. Then I will torment you in Hell. I've also set you up to take the blame for this massacre. I'm going to drag your name through the mud so that even in death you are tormented."

This satanic crap was getting the best of Brock. He could tell that Grady believed every word of it. The way he spoke was reminiscent of a legitimate evangelical pastor. The ones he saw on TV that truly believe in what they are preaching. For now, he needed to keep the banter going. "I have to fight all of you assholes?"

"Nope, just me. If you win you're free to go." He glanced at the whack jobs in the rubber masks. "My friends won't touch you. In fact, if you win they'll give you the keys to my car. You can go back to town and inform the police about what I've done. You'll be a hero by the end of it all. Imagine the headline: local college student breaks up satanic cult in rural Wisconsin. That's what the people want to hear."

"Why?" Brock was naturally curious now.

"Satanic panic. People want to believe that we're out there, in their small communities... that we've penetrated the safety net of suburban college towns. People need to know that evil exists. It cancels out their boredom. Creates paranoia. People are desperate to know that the devil exists and that regular people are out there, sacrificing humans." He stopped and smiled. "*Satanic Panic*. I like that." He shook his head. "If you win the fight, you'll be the testimonial that these ideas exists."

This freak was out of his mind. Oddly, he was convincing. Small town folks enjoyed campfire tales of evil serial killers, unsolved mysteries, and Satanists performing evil deeds in the dark woods. Brock opened his mouth to say something. A familiar voice distracted him from behind a stack of wooden pallets wedged against the back wall.

"Where's Brianna? What did you do with her?" Lance hollered through a broken mouth. He gargled on his own blood.

Brock tilted his head then turned until his eyesight found Lance.

Tied to a chair, Lance had been brutalized. The chair had been knocked over. His bound feet were visible from above the stack of wooden pallets. Brock leaned forward until he could see Lance. His face was bloody. His lip was swollen to the size of a fat caterpillar.

"Brianna isn't here. She's not safe either. I can't wait to get her for you. But the plan is simple. If Brock kills me with his fists then he'll have to pass another test. Then, if he passes that test he'll learn about what we've done with Brianna and where to find her. I'd like to think that he won't get that far, but he's good. Tough. You know what I mean?"

"Fuck you. Where is she?" Lance yelled. "If you let her go..."

Brock felt Lance's blazing eyes from behind. The sensation was nearly tangible.

"You'll what?" Grady asked.

There was a powerful silence.

The sound of twisting rubber masks annoyed Brock.

The Smiley Devil's were averting their gazes.

"I'll kill Brock if you let her go," Lance spoke in monotone.

Grady stopped pacing. His eyes widened. He smiled. "Say that again."

Brock and Lance made eye contact. Brock knew that his friend was simply trying to pull off an escape tactic. He'd never kill his oldest and dearest friend. *Would he?*

"I'll do it, I'll kill my best friend if you let her go."

Grady laughed. So did the freaks in the rubber masks. "So if I untie you and give you a knife you'll just kill Brock?"

"Yes."

"Lance, let me take care of this. You don't know what you're talking about." Brock was annoyed.

"Grady," Lance called out. "I want to kill him. Please let me kill him."

"Are you fucking serious?"

"Yes, I'm fucking serious. I can't stand him. All I care about is Brianna."

"Let me chat with my associates," Grady announced as he made his way over to the group of Smiley masks that circled around him.

Brock looked at Lance. He remembered his friend as a child, riding bikes together in the woods behind their homes. He remembered Lance falling off his bike and then helping him up. Laughing at his misery. And then it struck him: Lance hated him. Lance was in love with Brianna. Lance was jealous of the fact that Brianna loved Brock. Most importantly, if Lance hated him—as much as he imagined that he did—in this moment, then he would be glad to kill him. Killing Brock would give Lance an out for both their dreadful friendship and out of this twisted situation. Gripping the side of his chair he pulled at the duct tape that bound him. There was a small pocket of wiggle room. As nonchalantly as he could he exploited this space.

"I think that I have an answer for you, Lance."

"Please. I want to kill my best friend. If you give me Brianna's location then I'll do it."

"You will?"

"I swear."

Grady walked toward a stack of wooden pallets tucked into the corner of the warehouse. The rest of Grady's Smiley Devil friends laughed behind their rubber masks. And when Grady retrieved the wood axe from behind the stack of pallets the Smiley Devils burst into laughter.

"If you chop his legs off, then his arms, and then his head, and in that order... I will let you walk out of here. Additionally, I will give you Brianna. And I assure you that you'll never hear from us again."

"What assurance do I have?"

Brock wished that he could muster a burst of strength. All he could think about was ripping through his binds, grabbing Lance by his scrawny neck, and twisting until it cracked and he died. But what if his friend was merely trying to get loose, get the axe, and then help. *Could Lance be on his side?* Simply try and get a weapon to save them both. It made sense. *Lance wouldn't kill his best friend.* He'd been loyal for so many years. Sure, there was the "being in love with Brianna" thing, but that had been going on since they were kids playing kick-the-can in the neighborhood. Chasing each other through the streets of their small town.

A small tear in the duct tape gave him hope. Still he had to remain secretive. Reaching around his back without wincing was hard, but the blood caked to his face masked many expressions. With quick fingers he tugged at the tape.

There was no way his best friend would kill him?

In this moment, hope died.

2

Grady begged to know what Lance was thinking. Literally, his life depended on this answer. A simple thumbs-up would mean that Lance lived. Thumbs down meant his soul would depart and descend into the fiery pits of Hell where it would await its master.

Seconds prior, Grady alerted the Smiley Devils to shoot Lance if he attempted retaliation. The Smiley Devils *would* shoot him. That was a certainty. They would shoot the axe out of Lance's hand, and then shoot his legs, repeatedly, until they were shredded flesh and bone particle. After that, they would watch him flail and flop and bleed and scream. They'd laugh while committing heinous, awful evil things—evil things that revved the heartbeat of those who enjoyed the greatness of atrocity.

What would it hurt to find this answer?

Grady went to Lance. Untied his hands, and then freed his feet.

"If you try anything stupid... "

"What can I do? There are six of you. Seven if I include you." He relaxed. Stood tall. Glanced at each masked face. "Hell, what are the odds that you would take me into your group?"

Grady laughed, unable to believe Lance's approach, his strategy. Nervous ticks were unremarkable and visibly nonexistent. He found this odd. Normally, when a desperate victim begged for their life using this methodology they possessed specific ticks. Flustering of the face, spastic cheek muscles, even involuntary twitching of the eyes. Lance looked stoic. Hard. Silently excited. He would do well at the card table.

Maybe Lance would make a fine addition?

Then again, Lance was the pussy of the pack. Brianna had bigger balls than this guy, but not now. Now, Lance flirted on the opposite side of decency. Possibly seducing greatness. Hell, Grady didn't know if his actions were an attempt to escape or not. Maybe Lance *did* hate his best friend. He certainly filed enough reason to hate his supposed friend, to be jealous of him, and to benefit from the removal of his physical existence from earth.

"Here." Grady handed Lance the wood axe. Then he stepped back, far enough away that Lance's anticipated swing wouldn't reach his flesh.

Grady looked to the Smiley Devils and nodded. Then he raised his hand and motioned for his gang to lower their guns and knives and hatchets.

Lance stepped toward his friend of many years, *all his years.* Well, Grady didn't know if Brock and Lance were true friends—brothers—in the diabolical present. Their sexual devices and deviances had compartmentalized their loyalty to one another and created an excellent pathway for the Dark Lord to strike and seize their souls. On a more logical playing field, too much bad blood had boiled the softness from their friendship. It was a sinking ship that would not hold water. A leaky bucket at best.

Funny what sex will do.

"You understand that this is for Brianna?"

"Fuck you. You're really gonna do this?"

"I don't have a choice. I love her more than anything."

"You're a pussy-whipped fuck who doesn't know his dick from that wood axe."

"When I'm done with you I'll have Brianna all to myself. I won't have to worry about her falling in love with you anymore."

"She fell in love with me the day we met seventeen years ago! You stupid, lovesick, fucking asshole!" Brock was screaming and crying.

Tears streamed down his face and melded with the snot spewing from both nostrils. It was a sick and saddening sight. Pathetic really. Grady found it repulsive. The gambling compartment of Grady's brain assumed that Lance would attempt to free his friend. This banter was a distraction strategized to exploit an ambush.

Right?

But this performance was good.

"I loved you like a brother!" Brock screamed.

Lance stepped closer. Grady watched his knuckles turn white when they gripped the wooden handle of the axe.

"Please, Lance. You know my mom. You know the people that love me. What will they do?"

"They'll secretly hate themselves for the joy they feel for not having you in their lives." Lance raised the axe above his right shoulder.

"No," Brock whimpered.

Grady couldn't hold it in any longer. He laughed out loud and joyfully.

Lance stopped raising the axe. He turned to Grady. "Why are you laughing?"

"I'm really glad you asked," Grady responded.

Grady walked toward Lance and Brock, but kept his distance, just in case Lance decided to get brave and swing the axe at him.

"Can I be completely honest with you?" Grady pried.

"Fuck you! You're only doing this because I fucked the woman you love." Brock spit at Grady.

Grady laughed harder.

"No, Lance is going to kill you because you fucked the woman he loves. Honestly, I don't care in the slightest that you two are fucking her. I launched a couple nuts her way, and I have to admit that she's good. Those legs go on for days, don't they?" Grady shook his head and smiled. "The reason you're both here is that I worship a higher power. I was drawn to you. You were a chosen challenge."

"Stop it with that stupid Satanist bullshit. You don't really—" Brock stuttered. His voice quivered as though he'd temporarily forgotten that he was bound to a chair and about to be sliced in half.

Grady's laughter faded. He continued speaking, "I worship Lucifer. Satanists don't believe in God or the devil. They're atheists to tell you the truth. I believe in God and in Jesus and I certainly believe in the Devil. When I finally arrive in the fiery pits of Hell I will be awarded slaves to worship me. Now, despite how grotesque and pathetic Brock looks, he will make the ultimate slave in Hell. I don't want weak souls worshiping me. I only want fine, polished souls. Their torment is more robust. That is why I'm doing this to Brock. This is my belief."

The intensity in Lance's glare was telling of his sincerity. Grady believed him.

"So, if I kill him then he'll have to worship me in... in the afterlife?" Lance's eyes turned to the left as he pondered the gravity of this notion.

Grady watched Lance's head droop and his eyes shift from side to side. He was familiar with this expression.

Lance was clearly considering the idea that Grady would accept him. And he was right.

"Please, can I join you? The idea of Brock worshipping me while he burns in Hell is a very comforting thought." He was almost whispering.

"Your initiation will be to execute your friend with no remorse."

A muffled voice called out to Grady, "You might want to do that sooner than later."

Grady hadn't noticed that Brock had escaped his binds.

Brock's fist slammed into Grady's jaw, spinning his head and knocking him to the ground. Brock followed the punch with a focused kick to the groin. Grady curled and watched as his disciples enveloped Brock.

Brock screamed, "Come on!" While his disciples circled in.

Brock crescent kicked the Smiley Devil that rushed center. The Masked Devil sailed into a stack of wooden pallets. When his head hit the top pallet his mask lifted. It was Ricky Mack.

"Why?" Brock whispered, but Ricky heard him.

"Because the world is already on fire and it's burning me. Grady taught us to enjoy the flame."

Impressive. Brock might fight his way out of this, Grady thought.

Why is the Dark Lord punishing me?

Have I not been evil enough?

He's very gifted with violence.

All the more reason for him to worship me in hell.

Grady turned his head to the right and watched Lance spin toward the Smiley Devil's when they engaged him.

"No!" Grady held a flat palm out and shouted to his disciples, "He's joining us."

The Smiley Devil's parted from Lance and rushed Brock who was handling two Smiley Devils. Three more

Smiley Devils threw punches into Brock's kidney's and ribs.

Grady continued to watch Brock—exhausted—insufferably bludgeon his followers. He looked like a modern comic book hero fighting his way through a gang of mobsters. Invincible.

3

Arteries pumped rich blood through Brock's heart. His blood pumped and pulsed quick and heavy beneath his ribcage and revved his surrounding organs. Adrenaline continued to pump. Instinct allowed for the throwing of furious punches and kicks. Blood shot through his veins. The brutalizing that he continued to absorb should have rendered him dead. For each punch or kick delivered, Brock absorbed three. No time to think, Brock combined martial arts technique with the quick hands of boxing he'd recently acquired. If the fight took to the ground he'd be toast, and he knew it. He was an excellent wrestler in high school. But now he was tired. Fighting five to six people was exhausting, especially when one of them was a football hero. He no longer knew how many people he was fighting. All he saw were random faces and feet and hands and tossed bodies and blood. He stopped thinking and reacted: punch, punch, grab, flip, toss, stomp.

Kick my way out of this sick, twisted satanic mess.

In the back of his mind—oddly—he thought that if he were to survive this night that he'd straighten his life's path. Morally. Maybe even go to church. Say hello to the imaginary man resting on the clouds. Give up meaningless pussy—because to be honest that *is* what got him into this disaster.

The middle knuckle of his right hand shifted and clicked when his fist rammed into the mouth of one of these stupid fucking masks. The rubber tore and when

Brock pulled his hand free he took the mask with him. The face behind the mask was familiar. She was the waitress at the diner that he, Lance and Brianna had met at to discuss their erotic plans. He'd seen the next Smiley Devil too. He'd been watching him at a bar. Presently, Brock's recall was poor, but the connection sparked a clear image in his mind. He'd bumped shoulders and shots with this guy at The Quarter. Sharp reality struck. These people kept tabs on him. They'd followed him, gained access to his life and now they were striking like hunters of men. This dizzying thought heightened his rage. Paranoia overwhelmed. Adrenaline surged through his blood like electricity through conduit, which led to a hard kick that began with his foot flat on the floor. The foot then swung upward. Toes curled, his right foot hammered through the Devil's under-chin. Front teeth and three inches of this *Smiley Fuck's* tongue snapped free, flung and then glopped onto the floor. No time to think, Brock sensed the next Devil jump him from behind. Brock rammed a side kick into his chest. The sole of his boot absorbed the audible break of the Smiley Devil's sternum.

Wait.

There was something different about this chest.

The unmistakable softness of female breasts was present. Slamming an open hand downward, he ripped the mask free and saw that she was attractive, even in her anger. Her blonde hair and icy blue eyes were hypnotizing.

"You bitch," he screamed. The image of fucking her doggy style flashed across his mind. This woman had seduced him to gain access to his life. He remembered taking her home from a bar a few months prior. These sick bastards must have followed him for months.

Years?

Her pretty face was un-prettied by the stomp Brock laid into the middle of her face. He stomped twice. The second time he felt the bridge of her nose collapse and blood exploded upward. She couldn't scream, only gargle. Sheer adrenaline permitted Brock the strength to devastate the bone structure of her face. Blood sopped upward and absorbed into the material of his cheap boot. Behind the girl he saw Grady. In this moment, Brock thought he would accept death if he could have thirty minutes alone with Grady. A one-on-one fight would suffice. Then he could die with dignity.

A fist flew past Brock's face. He dodged it, grabbed the clenched hand, twisted it, and then yanked it downward onto the bony portion of his left shoulder. The arm snapped. The masked devil screamed. Brock ripped the Devil's mask off, grabbed him by the head, and twisted until his spine splintered and severed the spinal cord before snapping. The body didn't fall. It dropped downward and hard.

Quickly, Brock surveyed his surroundings.

Where's Lance?

4

Lance watched—amazed—as his best friend was brutalized. These Devils didn't care that he was once a child. Innocent. Had parents that loved him. In this moment, Brock was Christ-like. Lance was Judas. But Judas loved his friend. Lance no longer loved Brock. He didn't know that he ever did. Being drawn to a person because they were stronger struck many of the same triggers as love, but was something different than love. Now, Lance was proud and unable to deny his understanding of the truth. Vindictive, he meant to kill his friend. And when faced with intense adversity Lance cared only for self-preservation. He would run or fight, whichever insured his survival. As for justification—given how tough Brock was—he didn't feel bad about leaving him. He knew that Brock *could* manage, he just wouldn't.

Brock fought with tenacity. Watching the impossible fight within him was spiritual. A higher power sheltered this night. The notion was unshakable and nearly tangible.

If Brock survived, Lance would convince him that by leaving he was buying time. Finding help. Sadly, Lance explaining his ineffectualness would come easy. Explaining to Grady that wanting him killed was a ploy—part of the master plan—and not outside the realm of possibility, *if Brock lived.* But Lance was certain that Brock would fall.

Lost while attempting to focus, Lance adjusted his current understanding of logic. He would have to explain why he didn't sever Brock's binds. This would be hard. Brock wasn't *that* stupid. Lance's intention was clear. Brock continued to fight through these demonic assholes. Arguably, he was winning. Inevitably, Lance would need an explanation. That or Brock would kill him too. A new thought involved selling Brock on the idea that he was planning to cut through his binds, earlier, when he got close enough.

How was he to know that Brock was capable of escaping on his own?

Brock breaking his binds was impressive. Dismantling these tormented and disturbed individuals was impossible, but he executed well. And these psychotic assholes were giving him their best. Brock was a wounded animal. Keeping him bound hadn't worked. God or Satan had placed a hand on this massacre.

A hollow snap happened to be another splintered spine. The neck belonged to the blonde woman. The post-mortem groan echoing through the warehouse chilled his blood. The tone and pitch were that of a wounded canine.

Back to work, Lance thought. He glanced across the warehouse at Grady who watched the fury unravel. A sly grin never left his expression. After a brief moment, he caught Lance's glance. He turned, faced him, and smiled.

"Still want to join us?" Grady hollered.

Lance spun from Brock to Grady.

Grady gleamed.

Quick odds struck Lance. Numbers explained that Grady was going to win.

Bet on him.

Two Smiley Devil's remained. Brock had deactivated the lives of the other three. Lance and Grady knew that Brock would finish triumphantly. The next assessment was Grady.

How well could he fight?

Brock possessed inhuman strength. But Brock was exhausted. He could barely breathe.

Grady would champion the battle.

Finally, the answer was decided. Lance would kill Brock, accept Grady's offer. They would leave this nightmarish hell intact. Together. From there, Lance would devise Grady's demise.

Lance couldn't conceptualize his life within the occult. Joining was a survival option and he would stay only long enough to dispose of Grady and rescue Brianna.

How had he attained this level of depravity?

Only a few months ago he was an average college student with a crush on a girl. That crush led downward into perversion and then twisted until he found himself in the pit of Hell. Never in the bowels of his most creative ideas would he have believed that he'd join a cult of psychotic-mask-wearing Satanists. The idea sounded like a terrible B horror film. Who knew, maybe if Lance survived he'd write a book based on this evil night.

Enough pondering. Lance needed to act.

Grady or Brock?

What an asshole.

Lance ran toward Brock. Raised his axe.

Brock twisted the life from the fourth Smiley Devil. With bleeding eyes, he shakily tilted his face upward.

Made eye contact. Lance witnessed a lifetime of disappointment in his eyes. In this disappointment Lance saw hatred. The disappointment wasn't displaying the fact that his friend intended to kill him. Hurt radiated from the betrayal. And hatred stemmed from Brock's inability to harm his friend. Even after everything Lance had done, Brock still loved him too much to harm him.

Childhood memories of playing tag at the park melded with the remembrance of teenage angst. Drinking their first beer. Smoking their first cigarette. And then thoughts of Brianna took over: the pounding sensation in his chest when she was near, her distinct smell. She was his only love.

The axe swung downward. Brock kicked the metal blade and it slid then crashed. Intended to break and split Brock's head, the axe, instead, slammed into the foot of a dying Smiley Devil. The agonizing howl released from the Devil demanded Lance's curiosity.

Brock jumped forward, grabbed the final Smiley Devil at the base of his skull and slammed his face downward. Broken skull echoed loudly. And then there was only Brock, Lance and Grady. They stood amongst a sea of gore and chaos. The amount of blood sprayed, splashed and spread across the warehouse was maddening. Silence was unnerving. Brock, gasping for his breath, dominated the room. Lance found no words. Involuntarily, his mouth opened. "Let's get out of here." Lance held his open hand to Brock.

Brock's dripping face quivered with contained insanity. His entire body quaked.

"You know God damn well that you meant to kill me."

"I didn't," Lance lied. He was aware that he sounded like a preteen making excuses for being out past curfew.

"Is this a *brothers-gotta-fight* kind of moment?" Grady stepped forward and asked. He walked toward Brock and Lance. There was no shake to his posture. No quiver to his walk. He was confident. It was clear that Grady held experience in this category of depravity. "You both know that Lance wanted to kill Brock. Sure, you're his best friend, but Brianna is in love with Brock and that is very hard for Lance to accept."

Did that even matter anymore?

Metal crashed into the cement.

Lance couldn't believe what he'd done. His action was difficult to understand because he wasn't very aware that he'd committed it. Brock's eyes never left Lance's while this betrayal took place. Disappointment, anger and defeat remained in his gaze as he fell.

Lance looked at the blood dripping from his axe. He'd slammed the wood axe through his best friend's neck. Brock's head nodded, fell to the floor and then rolled a few feet, stopping at Grady's foot. Lance's eyes travelled up Grady's legs until he saw the smiling face in front of him.

"You did it," Grady stared at the rolling head and then kicked it as if it were a discarded apple core. "Here I thought that you two were attempting a rope-a-dope."

"I told you I wanted him dead. I did what I said. Now, you said you'd tell me where Brianna is."

"You're right. And I'm a man of my word." Grady slowly shook his head. "Do you remember what else you said?"

"I said that I wanted to join you." Lance dropped the axe. The metal blade landed with a loud clank and stuttered in a spreading pool of Brock's blood.

"You don't know what the group is." Grady placed his index finger below the tip of his own nose. "Let me ask you—did you feel good just now?"

Lance smiled. Unable to hide the truth, he'd never felt this confident. He didn't care that he'd lobbed off his best friend's head. He felt no emotion. No guilt. No shame. No grief. Maybe this was insanity. "Killing the person that meant most to me felt great. I feel nothing right now except horny. Hell, I might kill Brianna."

"That's the spirit."

"Right?"

The two men embraced.

"Beer?" Grady offered nonchalantly as if they'd just finished an oil job or completed a good run.

Brock's body convulsed.

"Sure," Lance answered.

With a slight tap from Grady's foot, Brock's head rolled and settled, face upward. His eyes involuntarily shifted to the right.

"Cool," Grady remarked.

Grady walked to the warehouse entrance, opened the door, exited, and popped the trunk of his car. The blustery winter wind howled. Snow shifted sideways. A blizzard had begun.

Grady returned. His hair had accumulated flakes of snow that immediately melted, dampening his hair. Slick with wetness, Grady walked to Lance, handed him a beer and then cracked his own. They clanked cans and slammed their beer.

The beer was sweet and cold and was the greatest drink. It went down smooth and icy, the first consumption to his new existence.

"After this beer, you'll tell me where Brianna is?"

"I said I would."

"Cool. " Lance finished his beer. "And... ah... what's going to happen with... " Lance pointed to the dead bodies strewn across the warehouse.

"I'm going to call someone that is in my little group, have them come over with a giant drum of acid, a good amount of bleach, some gasoline, and some sort of flame. They're going to dissolve all the human flesh except for Brock's heart, which I will eat, and then they'll set the warehouse on fire. No one is ever going to know what happened here."

"Do I need to do anything?" Lance asked.

"Do you think that the Dark Lord wants you to join his Army? If you do then there is an abundance of exceptional hatred that will consume your life in the most successful ways. The Tribulation breathes down our neck, Lance."

"What does that mean?"

"That means that you'll *do* what you want *when* you want and no one will ever *tell* you not to. This world will be ours," Grady explained. "Is that something you would be interested in?"

Lance fell to his knees. He was enlightened with soul and spirit.

"There are two things in this world that I want. One: Brianna. Two: to worship with you and destroy flesh in the name of the Dark Lord." He couldn't believe these words were spewing from his lips. But he'd also lied. He only desired to kill Brianna. Thoughts of keeping her corpse for personal pleasure held appeal, but owning her was more important.

Grady extended his hand to Lance, and Lance took the hand. They stood together.

"For now, go and be with Brianna."

"There are no hard feelings?"

Lance looked to Brock's convulsing body and severed head and smiled. For the first time, Lance felt masculine. Standing over the corpse of the friend he'd conquered, Lance allowed the final edge of this masculinity to settle. Now, he could journey through life with the knowledge of *real power*. No obstacle would stop him. If he *wanted*, he would *take*. Simple.

The jangling of keys snapped Lance's attention.

"When will I see you next?"

"I found you once. I'll find you again, and very soon. When I find you... you must be ready. We do things like meet in the Arizona desert and sacrifice weak humans."

Lance smiled, grabbed the keys and asked, "What car?"

"Take mine. It's the blue Ford out front. It's registered and in good condition. Just leave it in the parking lot of my apartment. Brianna is at my house, the one across the street from Jeff Torrance's house. She's tied to a chair in the back bedroom." Grady opened his arms. "Don't be upset with me."

"I'm not." Lance exited the warehouse. He stopped and raised a finger. "By the way, was Jeff in on this?"

Grady looked across the warehouse and across the strewn bodies in Devil masks. He walked to the left, knelt and then pulled the mask upward and off of Jeff Torrance's dead face.

Lance smiled.

Grady pulled out his cell phone, smiled mischievously, and tapped a number into the phone.

"Enjoy."

Daniel P. Coughlin

Part 6:
Season of Sacrifice

Chapter 16

Beginning Again at the End

1

L ance drove slowly down the slush-ridden highway, accelerating only his anxiety. Tempted, his desire was to hammer his foot on the gas pedal and leave his problems behind. Driving slow left him feeling vulnerable. The plump snow fell in diagonal droves that accumulated thickly on the windshield. The sheets of slush caked onto the windshield faster than the cheap wiper could dismiss.

Visibility quickly diminished.

Whenever a layer of ice was wiped clear from the windshield a fresh sheet would replace it. Straining to see, he watched the yellow divider lines disappear beneath the car. Focused, his eyes never left these reference points. Probably, they were the only reason he'd maintained his place on the road. Every few minutes he would clear his head with the thought that he'd soon be with Brianna. All troubles would be dismissed. Then he would kill her and do whatever he desired with her physical body. Maybe he would take her back to the warehouse and torture her, rape her and then kill her while Grady watched. Maybe then he would kill Grady and stage the warehouse to make it look like Grady had done everything, *which he kind of did.*

Enticement grew into excitement. Excitement died when the sensory explosion of red and blue police lights spun into the blustery night, driving Lance to the soft edge of madness.

"Oh no, God, no, no, no."

2

Lance opened the creaky door and stepped into the frozen night.

When the police officer saw the body he immediately slipped on the ice creating vulnerability. Lance almost smiled. This was the end game for Grady the entire time. Grady was setting him up. He expected the officer to arrest him, and then somehow the police would be drawn to the warehouse where Grady would somehow blame the entire massacre on him.

Well done. Touché.

The officer continued to grab at his shoulder. For a cop with a stern expression he suddenly looked frail. His arm twitched when he went for his gun. Briefly, the officer's gaze traversed to his left shoulder. He steadied his shaking arm.

Lance's only thought was escape, but he also knew that something was wrong with the cop.

There was no way he was having a heart attack.

Maybe there was weight to this higher power bullshit?

In over his head was an understatement, but he never in his life thought that he would enjoy this level of depravity. Given the crimes he'd recently committed, his life would be over if discovered. Prison was off the table. He'd eat a bullet before he'd finish his life in a cage, fighting day in and day out for survival. A very delicate situation was at hand.

Giving up wasn't an option. He'd just killed. He knew that he could do it again. Maybe this officer had a family, maybe he didn't. Lance didn't care.

Survival of the fittest.

The officer would have to kill him. That or he would die on this desolate road from a heart attack. This guy did not look good. He was straining to stand up and he was clenching his chest.

Someone is going to die.

Placing his hands outward as if to surrender, Lance turned to the police officer. The officer was falling now, grinding his teeth. The man was pained. The icy wind and snow pummeling his face didn't help. He quaked. Something other than the cold caused his quiver. This was deeper than merely a shiver. Fear painted the officer's face.

Lance watched on, amazed by the unraveling of this situation.

What were the chances?

Bad nerves?

Let's play this out.

Lance stepped forward.

The officer gasped. His knees buckled and he cried out.

Lance stepped forward again.

"Freeze, right there. Get on your... knees!" He was grabbing at his chest and his shoulder again. Nearly collapsing, he grunted and then straightened out. His expression was that of terror. His pistol nearly fell from his hands.

An anomaly of confidence riveted through Lance. He marched toward the officer. *Now or never.* He didn't care. And that was a first.

Kill or be killed.

Fear morphed into adrenaline, morphed into courage, morphed into perverted confidence.

"I said stop!" Sad desperation stole the officer's authoritative tone. He was no longer demanding. His head sunk on his neck creating a thick fold of skin—*a triple chin.* His eyes widened. Clearly, he was suffocating. With a clawed hand he ripped at his chest. The police issue pistol fell into a pile of slush.

"You don't look so good." Lance stared into the dying man's face.

"Atttaaa..." His lips contorted into a silly, drooping manner. "Heart... howt—atttaaack."

Lance watched the officer's body convulse as his life died out like a dancing flame. This had to be the work of the Dark Lord. "What the fuck?" Lance blurted out. Devils and the like were such silly notions. But maybe it was time to believe. He couldn't deny that a presence was with him. There was no way this was a coincidence. A higher power had its hand on this entire situation. Normally he would believe that these notions were simple brain chemistry at work, connecting dots, but this was something more. He could sense spiritual warfare on another plain as though it was visible.

The officer was dead and Lance couldn't believe that Grady had planned this night. He'd observed potential victims. Selected he, Brianna and Brock. Devised a plan and *literally* executed. For the second or third time—in his life—

Lance acknowledged that something bigger than him was at work. And Grady was the captain steering this ship. And he was good. He was organized. He was sick. He was demonic.

Grady was at the warehouse disposing of the deceased. Probably setting fires, burning evidence. Setting his stage. And Lance assumed that Grady was aware that the local police didn't check on these empty warehouses often. And if they were to investigate they wouldn't possess investigation kits comparable to those on television. There would be no black lights or high-end electronic data collecting equipment. Crime Scene investigative shows were nonsense. Entertaining, but utter nonsense. Grady would not be prosecuted for these heinous crimes. Shit, Lance was quite certain that he wouldn't be implemented. The man was experienced. He knew, all too well, what he was doing. He'd clearly done this before.

Lance glanced at the pathetic officer lying dead on the cold road collecting snow. His face was frozen into a sick expression that displayed humiliation in his demise. Snow filled his motionless eye sockets.

The manner with which this man had expired was pathetic, strange as hell. Oddly, Lance believed that Hell played a part in this man's death. That or he wasn't cut out for this line of work. *He looked cut out for it.* And that was good. The local newspaper would read, "Hard-edged veteran police officer dies of heart attack while issuing a traffic ticket."

"Stop! Fuck! Stop! I was normal three months ago," Lance thought out loud.

How had these bizarre ideas infested his logic?

By way of sexual deviance and the exploration of darkness. He, Brock, Brianna and Grady had permitted evil into their hearts. That was the reasonable explanation. Still, this idea drained his sanity.

"Stop crying, you pussy!" he shouted at himself while the winter wind howled.

Fast, wet, icy snow pelted Lance's face. The sting reset his thoughts on what would need to happen. The time to end this scenario was at hand. The need to explore what would happen next chewed at his curiosity. Lance stepped over the dead officer. He would need to dispose of the body. This man's constituents would soon search for him.

"Enjoy the afterlife!" Lance attempted to grasp the idea that God was currently judging this man. The intensity of this idea was altering his entire outlook. Because of *this night* he *believed*. The gravity of what this meant was impossible to absorb. He'd been seduced and manipulated by evil. God and the Devil were real.

But was this bad? Wouldn't he enjoy the fruits of his spiritual labor for the Dark Lord? The idea brought a sense of catharsis. His grin widened.

Leaning downward into the snow, Lance relieved the officer of his weapon. With his free hand, Lance curiously pried the officer's lips open. Stringy blood stretched into the wind from between his purple lips.

A drifting thought struck.

He turned to the rear of the car.

Squinting, fighting the wet snow from distorting his vision he looked to the taillight.

Lance shook his head.

Grady was something else.

Anger and rage filled Lance. He was fucked. His life was fucked if he didn't act now.

But guess what? Grady wouldn't see him coming.

Grady had expected Lance to be arrested out here on the highway. He'd probably called the police himself.

3

Lance tugged Brock's survival knife from his lover's torn throat. That stupid fucking knife that Brock carried around with him. Sticking it into all the furniture. Leaving it stuck in any countertop or desktop or tabletop he could find. Always with the knife, Brock was, and what a brilliant detail for Grady to acknowledge. Blood was everywhere. Crimson gore covered every square inch of the trunk to include Brianna's lifeless corpse. With his index finger and thumb he pulled the blood caked hair away from her face. Lust still strummed his heart. When this was over he'd conclude with physical release. Being dead, she'd never control the depth of his animalistic desire. He would desecrate her flesh.

"No!" he screamed long and hard into the howling wind. And he felt humiliated. Spinning around in circles, nearly slipping on the ice, he tilted his head to the moon dangling in the starless night. Grady's fallen angel was delighting in his misery. Intensity and gravity had shaped and formed his new perspective. His new life would begin right now.

Crying, he leaned forward and kissed Brianna's forehead. Remembering the precious moments in which he'd made love to her. Alone in the hotel room was the only intimacy his recollection could stumble on. Memories of childhood flooded in. Chasing each other through backyards while playing kick-the-can. Watching scary movies in her parent's basement. Dances they attended together while in high school that were so important at the time. All these images and thoughts and feelings crashed into a culmination of unstructured sensations.

Then grief was purged. He stopped crying. With the back of his hand he wiped away the tears. Face icy, he glanced upward to the sky—the Gods—and laughed. He no longer felt. Sensations and emotions were like dead nerves. Numbness. Twisted excitement took over.

Then his glance fell to the gutless officer.

What weakness?

The reaction of a take-no-bullshit-testosterone-driven-cop in the face of real danger was to have a heart attack and die. This was divine intervention. No other explanation. Then, a cackle escaped the officer's mouth. Lance believed this to be his death throe. Gas escaped his collapsing lungs. His eyelids remained open. Fresh snow melted and buried his face. His soul had left his body.

The passing time hindered Lance's reaction. Closing his eyes, he allowed his wandering thoughts to pass.

There was no denying his primitive instincts anymore.

He enjoyed death.

And, this particular situation had become interesting.

Certainty as to whether he was responsible for killing the officer was foggy. No, he hadn't shot the man. No, he hadn't even threatened him. Still, he felt responsible. Clearly, there was a connection. Sensations of weakness followed.

Accept the situation.

Go with it.

Worship the Dark Lord.

It would be much more fun than worshipping the latter.

Sure, he'd miss Brianna. But he'd experienced everything with her. Their journey was clearly over. Now that she was dead, Lance realized that he hated her. The guilt had passed. A tingling sensation now filled his stomach and he hoped that she'd suffered. Grady had organized her demise. Therefore, Lance was certain that it was gruesome. Grady spared nothing. *Look at what he'd done to Brock.* Grated him like cheese.

Absorbing the scene before him, Lance realized that he enjoyed evil. Taking the officer's gun, he thought about the consequences of his actions. Prison for sure.

No way.

Holding the gun tight, he placed it between his lips and then wrapped his finger around the cold metal trigger. If it came between getting arrested and eating a bullet then he knew his option.

Ending his life would be easy. He knew he could do it.

How enjoyable to feel this free? This light.

Time was up. He lugged the heavy officer over his shoulder, carried him back to the police cruiser, set him inside, placed his foot on the gas pedal, cranked the steering wheel and then pulled the shifter into drive. He closed the door, quick as possible.

The cruiser maneuvered well in the snow. Swerving then straightening and gaining speed the cruiser plunged into the ditch, spun out, and then slammed into a frozen maple tree. The officer was thrown from the windshield. Lance lost sight of him. The trajectory of his body was impressive.

That would explain the missing gun.

After the cruiser bounced from the maple tree it rolled upside down and slid down the slick embankment. Lance suspected that the scenario he'd created would appear accidental.

No villain except for the weather conditions was to blame. Or so the authorities would concede.

Now, what would he do about Grady?

Lance shed the skin of his former life and smiled, reborn, as he walked back to Grady's car. His anger over the death of his fallen lover was replaced by his insatiable hunger for murder. The ordinary drone of his existence— moving through life an imp—was over. Killing Grady would be a rewarding challenge. The greatest challenge he'd ever commit.

4

Nearing the warehouse, Lance killed the headlights. Guided only by instinct, he shifted into neutral and allowed the car to glide across the gravel parking lot. The front tires halted when they struck a snow-covered stack of wooden pallets. The vehicle stopped, smooth. A couple hundred yards from the warehouse—even in the howling blizzard—he heard the Smiley Devil, Grady, stirring inside the damning structure. Exiting the car, he crept along the aluminum wall, stopping often to place his ear to the freezing metal with hope of an update on the position of his prey. The howling wind was brash, but permitted estimation of Grady's location.

He thought of his best friend, *the warrior who died a pathetic death.*

Brock had been tough in life. Physically, he could dominate and defeat Grady one-on-one. But he'd fallen. He hadn't accurately predicted Grady's chess-like maneuverability or his manipulative skillset. Grady had defeated Brock on a deeper level of play, below the dermis of physicality. Grady was smart, logical yet spiritual. The Satanic elements were truly frightening, and thoroughly alluring. They'd resonated. Stuck to Lance's psyche. Never would he be the same.

The sensation of fear melded with panic did not cite Lance. Newfound excitement and confidence thrilled him. He crept to the door, wrapped his hand around the knob, took three deep breaths and flung the metal rectangle open. He raised the stolen pistol outward.

Startled, Grady's smile was only inches from Lance's face. The barrel of Lance's pistol was eye level.

Grady glared at him. Confidence never left his expression.

Sympathy sought Lance. *Maybe he wanted this life. Maybe Grady would be true to his word. And maybe this was Lance's true calling.*

"It took you long enough," Grady whispered. He glanced past the pistol and aligned his focus with Lance's eyes. That bright white California smile never left his face. "How do you like what I've done with your princess?"

Lance was torn. Didn't know if honesty was best in this scenario. "I—" Lance stumbled.

"You don't know if you should kill me or follow me. But the truth is that you're glad to see that whore dead and that muscle bound degenerate shredded to pieces. It excites you to know that a profound existence awaits you. All you'll have to do is give up *everything.* But remember:

everything is what has weighted you. The weight of your existence has disabled you. Follow me. It's what we both want."

Lance attempted to squeeze his index finger. He stopped short of depressing the trigger. An unexplained, unearthly force hindered his compliance.

Mental block?

Influence.

Persuasion.

Grady's sick, sharp, twisted yet beautiful mind was at work. And it was working well.

"You're not going to end me, Lance. You're going to join me and you're going to enjoy your life."

"You set me up."

"I freed you from all that you know. Societal structure, the disease that pollutes the human mind shall shed from you. You will taste sensation, the true essence of life."

"Say that again."

"Listen. You can shoot me." Grady opened his arms giving Lance a free, wide target.

Lance didn't take the shot. He couldn't. A million thoughts punched through his mind. He wanted to taste the sweetness of this life that Grady spoke of.

"I'm listening, but I want answers," Lance managed.

"If you would have given in to the cop then you would have gone to prison for all of these murders. That's for certain. But you chose to end the officer's life. It felt good and you know it."

"The cop had a heart attack," Lance included. "And how did you know about the cop?"

"The cop died from the arsenic I fed him an hour before I told him to kill you. I wanted to test you. That police officer paved the way for me to get away with those drowning's. He was a brother in a large organization, Lance. The test was for you to kill him. The poison was my insurance."

Lance cocked the dead officer's pistol. This time Grady flinched. In this moment, Lance witnessed a miniscule amount of human weakness. He wondered if Grady had displayed this weakness deliberately. *Detail-oriented* was an understatement when speaking of Grady. His specific calculations were infallible. Grady was a master of persuasion, control, and manipulation.

Maybe he should pull the trigger. Get this over with.

But he wanted—needed—to hear about the details involved in this lifestyle that Grady offered. Something pleasurable, spiritual, and thrilling was illuminating his discarded soul. He felt that purpose might accept him if he followed. Never had he felt so close to the supernatural. So close to believing. The desire and want to explore hedonistic pleasures overwhelmed him. To shed stress and the guilt associated with animalistic acts seemed logical. These current feelings were the discovery of a higher power.

Funny. The devil—in fact—does seduce.

Lance had always wanted to believe in a higher existence, but his logical make-up hadn't permitted adherence to these ideas. A new avenue of thought struck. No longer was the notion of a divine entity irrational and without merit. There was no disputing the feelings and sensations that he currently felt. Factual evidence could not dismiss. For too long, Lance's scientific mind would not contemplate any such evidence that would support a God or a Devil. Therefore, these ideas couldn't exist. Now, it was good to believe. Deeply, he inhaled and felt that his lungs had opened and his head was clear. Clarity of mind and body came with true spirituality. He was unable to deny the illumination of his soul. And he acknowledged that it was dark.

Grady stepped forward and began, "You want something from me. You want to join me. You want me to show you dark things. You'll enjoy killing."

"I'd probably enjoy killing you."

"There's no question that you would. If you enjoy killing then you would definitely enjoy killing me. If you do kill me I suggest that you do it slowly. Savor it. Wear my skin."

"If I join you... " Lance began.

"I'll show you the exceptional benefit of true sacrifice. I'll show you how to enjoy the pleasures that this world has to offer, both worldly and spiritually. If you were born to be evil then you must accept your destiny. Am I right?"

Lance felt a tickle in his stomach. The same tickle he'd experienced when he'd first met Brianna.

Could this be the designation of life's pursuit?

Could this be the answer to all of life's questions?

"I want to join you." Lance stood straight. Lifting his head and extending his spine he felt an inch taller and more powerful. Bigger. He tilted his head downward at his new world. The blood-soaked building was a work of divine-murderous art. Reborn, he was a religious man.

"Let's go." Grady smiled, walked to his new comrade and embraced him.

5

Grady discovered the partner that he'd searched many years for. He felt the nourishing connection quench his desire. He'd begged the Master for this companion. In Lance, Grady found true camaraderie. The Dark Lord had sent him a pure disciple. Through the sacrifice of Brianna and Brock he'd been shown the completeness of a loyal and dark hearted disciple.

His life's plans had changed in a matter of seconds. He'd been delivered. He was thankful. The Dark Lord spoke and the Dark Lord was pleased.

Near tears, Grady held his new friend.

"You can never be Lance again. You know that?"

Lance parted from Grady. "That's been made very clear."

"Then let's leave right now. We'll go to California. We'll go to the Arizona desert."

"What's in the desert?"

"The greatness of evil."

"What does it feel like?"

"Heaven."

"Then how do you know if we are evil or if we are good? If good is evil then how do we define the sensations we enjoy?"

"That *is* the answer to *all* we seek. The moral scale extracted from judgment. When you act upon things you're drawn to—do you feel good?"

"I feel guilty for disobeying the learned morality that has been implemented upon me."

"You're ignoring the soul... that element of existence that feels good. And is good. We have much to explore, you and I."

"What about this mess?" Lance asked.

"You can help me stage it to look like Brock committed this atrocity. Or, you can watch... or, you can do whatever the hell you'd like. The Dark Lord has led me to you. I know that you are my ally."

Paralysis struck Lance. He trembled with the spirit of his new lord.

What was happening? This was not normal human behavior. This was not the manner in which his DNA was coded. Or so he thought. Two months ago, he was a logical, sense-driven human being with a functional moral compass. Now, he was capable of perversion at the highest level. Murderous deeds had been engaged in. Disturbing sexual activities, a taboo relationship, the witnessing of ritualistic satanic sacrifice had been enjoyed. In one passing moment he'd extracted interest in the woman he'd loved his entire life in order to feel the divine power of his new God.

Truly American.

And then he laughed.

"What's funny?" Grady asked.

"Everything. You have to remember who I was two months ago."

Grady stood, dropped the masked corpse that he'd dragged toward a giant vat of hydrochloric acid, placed his index finger to Lance's chin and said, "I always move through the perspective aspects too quickly. You went from the average American college student to a satanic stud and now the reality of how great this is going to be has sunk into your grey matter?"

"Yes."

"Then that's it." Grady smiled.

"What's it?" Lance responded, expecting conventional wisdom from a psychopath.

"You've abandoned all hope. You've stripped yourself of false goodness. Turned on the one's you love. Acknowledged how good the brutal truth feels. You've hit rock bottom and realized that in doing so you've climbed the highest mountain." Grady reciprocated.

"What's next?"

The pain Lance felt was intense, searing even.

6

Grady enjoyed this part. Although he desired a partner, he knew that his Dark Lord was simply testing him. He shed his desire to rely on another human being. Ending life was what the Dark Lord demanded. He'd convinced a strong person to abandon all morals, maturity, and hope. He'd stripped the man of all goodness and then shot him in the face. Lance was no more. He was a headless corpse convulsing on the floor like discarded trash—a slave in Hell awaiting his master. Soon.

And now he would shed the blame of all this death on this pathetic being and destroy his once decent reputation.

This was true sacrifice.

He would be rewarded.

Epilogue

A Video

G rady whistled, pulled the rolling chair away from his desk and took a seat. The 40 inch flat screen monitor hummed to life. The spinning white circle rotated, center of the screen.

Grady twirled in his chair while waiting for the images of his final cut masterpiece to fill the monitor. Finally, the halted image—slightly pixelated—sharpened within the display monitor. The paused image of Brianna's beautiful face smiled at him. The angle was slightly crooked—*Dutch*. The camera's operator was hidden near a gaggle of poplar trees. Students from the University scattered like ants on this fall afternoon. Then the image zoomed forward into three young, beautiful adults scampering across campus. Brock, Lance and Brianna smiled and skipped. The boys lightly punched each other as boys often do. A formation of fresh female students in trendy stretch pants or sweats stopped to adore Brock as he returned an arrogant smile. The camera shook. The frame tightened on Brock's beautiful face, specifically his smile. From behind the camera a voice whispered, "That's our sacrifice." Grady titled the camera upward below Ricky Mack's fat chinned grinning face. "He will be a challenge. A worthy challenge."

"Put your life on it?" Grady asked.

"I wouldn't betray you… or *Him*." Grady lowered his voice and titled his head.

"If I get the girl I'll get to the boy," Grady informed.

The image cut to black.

The next angle was taken from a laundry pile in Brianna's dorm room. Clearly she didn't know she was being filmed as Grady had bent her over the couch, naked and pummeled into her in the most animalistic manner. He climaxed on her ass. She smiled, turned to kiss him and then went to the bathroom. Once she was out of the room, Grady moved toward the camera. Looking over his shoulder every other step, making sure she was still gone, his face filled the frame. "Step one and done."

Fade to black.

The sound of far-off shouting was heard and melded with music. Blurry images were taken at a crowded bar— The Quarter—and Brianna was introducing Brock and Lance to Grady. The images were very shaky and grainy. The body-cam that Grady wore was tucked into the chest pocket of his hoodie. The freeness of Brock's body language and dialogue mirrored his drunkenness.

Fade to black.

A wide angled frame was taken from the house across the street from Jeff Torrance's house. The image was very bright, daylight. The images cut to Jeff Torrance staging the camera while it recorded. The camera filmed his house across the street. The snow-filled glass window was in focus, revealing Jeff's reflection. He was perfecting the angle on the upstairs bedroom of his house. "All this snow sucks."

"Don't worry," Grady returned.

Fade to black.

The following images were again dark. The image of Grady leaving Jeff's party from the front door was overly grainy. The camera operator zoomed in on the upstairs bedroom where Brianna, Lance and Brock engaged in a kiss. "Whoa, didn't see that coming. Kinky." Jeff Torrance giggled.

Fade to black.

The next shot was blindingly bright and filmed from the kitchen of The Quarter. The camera had been hidden behind a stack of off-white colored plates. Brock and Toby were conversing, conducting a transaction for date rape drugs. Grady turned the camera to his own face and stated, "This is my masterpiece. This is a gift from *Him*." He flipped the camera angle on Brock as he left the bar out of focus.

Moaning and grunting sounds rose in volume. The camera breathed into focus, but bobbed up and down as the image was shot hand-held from Grady's body cam. This image was of Brianna being ravaged by Brock and Lance in the presence of Grady. Then Brock's Penis came into frame and he ejaculated onto Grady's face. Once Brock and Grady left the room, Grady's middle finger erected into the frame. Brianna laughed as she cleaned off in the vanity mirror. She didn't even notice that Grady had awoken and plunged a syringe into her neck. His thumb was large in the close-up shot as it plunged downward, sending the sedative into Brianna's blood stream. Jeff Torrance's laughter infiltrated the video. Then there were two boys lifting Brianna and taking her down a flight of stairs. The camera continued to record as they left the house, went to the dingy garage and threw her into the trunk of a car.

Fade to black.

In the next image, Brianna was swarmed by six naked Smiley Devil's doing awful things to her. When they finally backed off of her it was apparent that she was bound to a chair, which was bolted to the cement floor. There were strawberry-like pinch marks covering her breasts and stomach. Her face was bruised and bleeding. The camera waved as it was brought close. A red-hot poker singed her skin and branded a Pentagram onto her chest. She screamed through her gag.

Grady pulled the gag from her mouth. She was silent.

"Come on, you have to have questions. Comments?" Grady pleaded.

Struggling for breath, she stated through swollen lips, "I never believed in God before right now. Not really, anyway." She looked up at the camera. Her appearance was unfazed by the recent abuse. "So, I'm praying for forgiveness."

"You can't just say you believe in God and go to Heaven. You're going to be burning very soon. Just think about the gravity of that statement. In less than ten minutes your soul will have fled your body. Your skin will burn and you'll be tormented," Grady debated.

Shaking her head she looked up at the camera. A Smiley Devil punched her in the mouth while laughing, mean-spiritedly. Still, she spoke, "I see what you've done. I've witnessed simple, but cruel actions destroy multiple lives. The passage of Satan has been made clear. I wholeheartedly believe in the Devil. I cannot deny his existence. He's real and that is terrifying. But if I believe in the Devil then I know that the God of love and mercy is real too. There's no denying this any longer. So, I'm begging for forgiveness because I don't want to go to where you're going. And I can feel redemption coming—"

Her final words were cut short. The sound of blood erupting in her throat gargled viciously. The camera displayed Brock's hunting knife plunge into her neck and slowly carve—jaggedly—across her throat. The knife remained in place as blood spouted around the metal blade. Her lifeless body slumped in her restraints.

The image of her pupils dilating filled the camera frame. A twinkle of light in one pupil caused pixilation.

The image was black.

The End

About Your Author

After graduating high school in Watertown, Wisconsin, Daniel P. Coughlin joined the United States Marine Corps and served four and half years as an infantry Machinegunner in an Amphibious Raider Unit (Fox 2/4).

After being Honorably discharged, Daniel attended and graduated from California State University at Long Beach where he studied screenwriting under the mentorship of acclaimed writer Brian Alan Lane (Star Trek Next Generation, Remington Steele, Moon Lighting) and also interned as a script analyst for his favorite director, Wes Craven (A Nightmare on Elm Street).

Daniel is the screenwriter of three commercially successful films Lake Dead, which was selected as one of After Dark Film's 8 Films to Die For, Farmhouse, starring A-List film and television star Steven Weber (Wings, Desperation, Single White Female) and Ditch day Massacre (starring Bill Oberst Jr.).

Daniel is the author of six novels and an anthology of short fiction.

He's sold numerous short stories to such publications as 18 Wheels of Horror, Hell Comes to Hollywood 2, Strange Tales of Horror, Macabre Cadaver Magazine, and Dark Gothic Resurrected Magazine.

Daniel was hailed by Macabre Cadaver Magazine as, "A Promising New Voice in Old School Horror."

Daniel is a proud member of the Horror Writer's Association (Los Angeles chapter). He holds a professional certificate in Technical Writing from Cal State Dominguez Hills and a Master's Degree in Creative Writing from Full Sail University. Check out his works at

www.danielpcoughlin.com.

Other HellBound Books Titles
Available at: www.hellboundbookspublishing.com

The Other Side of the Mirror

Carl Duggan has worked as a Detective in the City for a long time. The kind of 'long' where you've seen everything, and seen it twice. With that in mind, it comes as no surprise to him when a pregnant nineteen year-old girl washes up on the banks of the Styx. But something about this one is different, and before Carl gets any answers, two more bodies join the pile; a corrupt Judge and a big-shot lawyer. Carl's gut tells him there's a connection, the little things, the tiny details that others would ignore.

The bodies keep on coming when a second case rears its head; three young men with nothing in common except their sexuality, each murdered in their own home. Gaining little assistance from his fellow officers, Carl goes it alone into the darker regions of the City. Along the way he makes acquaintances and enemies of the City's more colourful residents, including the beautiful sister of the first dead girl, a Catholic hit man dubbed "His Holiness", and a shady casino owner named Dice.

The closer he gets to the truth the more Carl's life is put in danger, forcing him to move further and further away from the rule of law. Never once does he suspect that the two cases are so intimately linked, or that the truth could be so close to home.

The Matchless

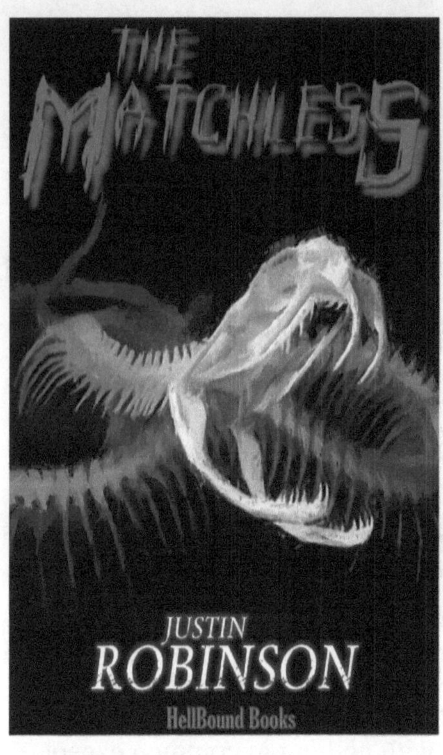

There are certain special individuals who can harness their genius and madness to gain powers beyond the imagination of normal people.

These are the Matchless.

Nadia Eskandarian learns she can harvest physical manifestations of power that the Matchless leave in their wake, and use them to perform miracles.

But there are others out there with the same abilities, and they're all fighting for the same finite and dangerous resources.

And the Matchless don't want to be harvested.

The Dead Room

A week before Christmas, terrorists detonate dozens of dirty bombs throughout Britain and release a man-made contagion, leading Nicola Allen to begin a frantic hunt for her husband and daughter while a nation burns.

Fleeing from a horrendous event she refuses to speak of and desperate to find shelter in a dying country, Nicola's sister-in-law Cate takes cover in a partly destroyed hospital.

Terrorised by visions of mutilated bodies and the screams of phantom children, Cate joins with a group of survivors, all of whom are under attack by ruthless scavengers and looters.

If Nicola is to have any chance of finding her family and if Cate is to escape from the siege, they must reunite and then descend into the belly of the ruined hospital where the horrific truth of what truly connects the two women is waiting for them.

Waiting for them down in the dead room.

Deadly Nightshade

Thirteen years ago: summer's end. A final night of vacation at New Mexico's Gila Cliff Dwellings. A picnic under the moonlight for high school sweethearts meets a deadly end...

Things will never be quite the same again.

After eloping, newlywed Virginia Campbell's bright future grows dim. Eerie night visions begin to haunt her. Are they real or imagined? Her husband's sudden aloofness raises suspicions of an affair. Unable to sleep, doubts torment her—doubts about her marriage, her unborn child, her sanity. Then, there is blood. She awakens to blood-soaked sheets.

Is it too late to save her unborn child? Her only hope is her charming doctor for whom she is falling. Can he save her from this living nightmare?

Ten-year-old Kyle also suffers from insomnia and eerie night visions. Something, or someone, sinister has brought them together... waiting for the moment to strike.

Three years later: Mother's Day.

The nightmare is not over.

A surprise visitor greets Virginia with a gift one morning. What begins as a day of celebration is twisted into a violent, bloody confrontation as festering wounds reopen.

Shopping List 3

By popular demand, the third volume in our bestselling anthology series, twenty-one spine-chilling, terrifyingly creepy tales of terror by a bunch of the best independent horror authors writing today!

Featuring horror stories – and shopping lists – from: Richard Raven, Dhinoj Dings, Jeremy Thompson, Jeremy Wagner, Nick Manzolillo, Steve Stark, Jeff C. Stevenson, Kevin McHugh, James Watts, D.W. Jones, Nick Swain, Mark Thomas, Brian McGowan, Jason Gehlert, Mark Deloy, Richard Barber, Sergio Palumbo, Megan E. Morales, Alizure Indigo, JN Cameron, and David Simon

Schlock! Horror!

An anthology of short stories based upon/inspired by

and in loving homage to all of those great gorefest movies and books of the 1980's (not necessarily base in that era, although some do ride that wave of nostalgia!), the golden age when horror well and truly came kicking, screaming and spraying blood, gore & body parts out from the shadows... This exemplary 80's themed/inspired tales of terror has been adjudicated and compiled by one Mr Bret McCormick, himself a writer, producer and director of many a schlock classic, including *Bio-Tech Warrior*, *Time Tracers*, *The Abomination*, *Ozone: The Attack of the Redneck Mutants* and the inimitable *Repligator*.

Featuring stories from: Todd Sullivan, Timothy C Hobbs, Mark Thomas, Andrew Post, James B. Pepe, Thomas Vaughn, Edward Karpp, Jaap Boekestein, Lisa Alfano, L. C. Holt, John Adam Gosham, Brandon Cracraft, M. Earl Smith, Sarah Cannavo, James Gardner, Bret McCormick, and James H. Longmore.

A HellBound Books LLC Publication

http://www.hellboundbookspublishing.com

Printed in the United States of America